As if she'd marry for less than love!

"Give me a date. I like to plan ahead." Godfrey's fingers gripped Valancy's shoulders. "I know it's too soon after that idiot jilted you, but you have to think about it."

"Have to?" Now she was furious. How dared he do this cold-blooded thing, proposing just because he wanted to found his dynasty, and she was so suitable for the purpose?

He said harshly, "Yes, you must. I'm being fair. I know he was the one you planned to spend your life with. But you and I work well together—we laugh at the same jokes—we strike occasional sparks off one another physically.... I deserve an answer, Valancy. Or are you too frightened to even consider it?"

Books by Essie Summers

Season of Forgetfulness

Essie Summers

Harlequin Books

TORONTO • NEW YORK • LONDON
AMSTERDAM • PARIS • SYDNEY • HAMBURG
STOCKHOLM • ATHENS • TOKYO • MILAN

Original hardcover edition published in 1983
by Mills & Boon Limited

ISBN 0-373-02645-5

Harlequin Romance first edition September 1984

Dedicated to my daughter-in-law
Patricia
also a cat-lover
and to those two ideal study-cats,
James and Susie
Who purr when I start typing
and who protest when I stop.

CHAPTER ONE

THERE was nothing else to do but give in her notice. Valancy loved this job, but it wouldn't be possible to go on working side by side with Justin, her ex-fiancé. The whole staff would be wondering, watching, gossiping. She could just imagine the whispering and the surmises. It would make her stiff and unnatural with him. The ordinary, joking give-and-take of the office atmosphere would suffer. It could, even, upset Justin's marriage. Greer herself could know doubts.

That girl was a brick, to take on nursing Justin's mother. That stroke had left her so dependent upon others, and there was no other son or daughter to relieve Justin and Greer in this duty they were tackling. Justin hadn't been able to do anything else but ask for a transfer back to the Christchurch branch from Wellington.

He and Greer, when his mother had made that miraculous return from long unconsciousness, had come to see Valancy. She'd known when they'd rung her what it was they would have to ask of her: Permission to come back. So she'd made it easy for them. She had said, quickly, 'I'm sure they'd give you a transfer. And it's not as if you've bought a house up there, is it? You're just renting a flat, aren't you? I know it won't be easy, but your mother's house is so large, you'd still have some privacy of your own. Only she can't live alone, that's for sure.'

They had gazed at her, astounded. Greer had found her voice first. 'And you won't mind ... working with Justin again? It could be awkward. We wondered——' her voice had trailed off.

Words Valancy hadn't meant to say had come from her lips. 'In any case, it won't be long. Look, naturally I've said nothing at work yet, but I've been thinking ever since—I've been thinking for some time I must get

7

out of the rut I'm in. One job during the whole of my
working life is a bit stodgy. I'm rather tired of proofing
dry-as-dust textbooks and doing all that research and
verifying. I'd rather work for a firm more varied in its
publishing ... a bit of fiction, or autobiographies ...
but all these technical terms and statistics and reports
... they've been getting me down. Ask for your
transfer, Justin, and we'll take it from there. I shouldn't
be with Andersons much longer. Do it right away, in
case Hughsie makes a quicker recovery than you think,
and needs to come home.'

They'd been almost embarrassing in their gratitude,
but Valancy had the knowledge that she had done the
right thing, even if, inwardly, she bitterly resented the
fact that this had once more turned her life upside-
down. At the time, when Justin had broken it to her
that he couldn't marry her, she had felt so sorry for his
sincere distress, she had pretended in a magnificent
flight of imagination that she was really relieved, that
she'd fallen out of love with him but hadn't summoned
up the courage to break it off.

But to keep this up was different. To work side by
side with the man you had been engaged to, more than
that, had dearly loved, wasn't to be borne.

There had been a note from Justin yesterday. The
sight of his writing, even, had given her a pang. It was
to say the Head Office was releasing him sooner than
expected. So now she must give in her notice and get it
over. Mother and Dad, though they'd loved having one
of their family still home, had looked at the whole thing
from her angle, and felt it would do her good to spread
her wings and take off. So she must tell her boss right
now.

Mr Anderson was marvellous. His regret at losing her
was so genuine, but their long association made him
admit she was doing the right thing. 'We'll give you the
most splended references, Valancy. In fact I'll start
making some enquiries of my own among other New
Zealand firms. Most are in the North Island, though
there is one in Dunedin, of course, nearer home for
you.'

'It doesn't matter how far away—in fact the further the better. I'm inclined to be homesick, and it's too easy if you're within a day's journey of Christchurch to hop in the car and come up for the weekend, and, as you know, Justin was always . . .' she stopped.

He patted her hand. 'He was always the boy next door.' He cleared his throat. 'Devilish situation. And you were the one who had to make the best of it. I admired you frightfully—I felt damned responsible. I was the one who recommended him for the job in Wellington. I thought he'd get promotion that way, and could return to a higher position here. If he hadn't gone he might never have met this other girl and you'd——'

Valancy managed a grin. 'Don't be embarrassed. I'll finish it for you—I'd have been married to Justin by now. Mr Anderson, I think it was just as well. This might have happened *after* we were married. I think Justin just drifted into our engagement. I'd always been around. He had to come up against the real thing to recognise that. I'd rather a clean break than a slow disillusionment, you know.'

Mr Anderson said nothing. Valancy said, 'And I couldn't hate Greer. I tried. But she's a really super girl and a fine nurse, I believe, which is what Mrs Hughes needs now. You'd almost think it was meant to be.'

Mr Anderson snorted. 'Valancy, don't be too magnanimous . . . don't do violence to your natural feelings, trying too hard to be philosophical.' He paused, then said, 'I don't usually tell anyone this, it's too long ago, but I'd a broken engagement myself. That was why I left England and came to New Zealand. I was a highly-strung young fellow in those days.' He grinned. 'Never think it now, would you? I thought my life was completely blighted. It wasn't, just a bit frost-blackened round the edges. I used to write a bit of poetry, had a few things published in magazines— fortunately under a pseudonym. If my wife had read 'em, she'd have thought me the victim of a hopeless passion, and herself second-best, for sure.

'I thank God whenever I think of it, which isn't often, that the first one did fancy someone else and left me cold, because my life with Theresa has been more than I could have hoped for. I wrote a poem or two later. I've felt like quoting one verse to you ever since Justin broke your engagement, but I didn't have the nerve. But I will now. I found it out for myself and I think you will too, if you seek fresh pastures, as I did.'

He looked down at his desk and said, without looking at her,

' *"Sweet is the season of forgetfulness,*
  Succeeding thus the passion and the pain,
  The healing time, the quiet time of pausing
  Till, in God's wisdom, you will love again." '

He cleared his throat. 'Take the rest of the day off, Valancy. Go home and tell your people you've given me an indefinite notice, and when you've found yourself another job, or we've found it for you, you can leave. And, Valancy, for a redhead, you've been a little too acquiescent ... too accommodating. Throw your weight round a bit more. Odd thing to say, I know, but ...'

Valancy rose, bent over his desk, dropped a kiss on top of his head and said unsteadily, 'Thank you ... I appreciate the verse. I'm glad you had the courage to tell me what you did, to share that long-ago sad time of yours. I hope some day I can use *my* sad time to help someone else. See you tomorrow, Mr Anderson.'

As she put her hand on the door-knob, she looked back and said, 'And would you write that verse out for me? It could help me live through the next little while.' And she was gone.

She had a terrible sense of loss. Not just because of Justin and the dreams they'd woven of their future, but at the thought of severing the ties with Andersons. Firms of that integrity were few and far between. Only rarely were there upsets among the staff or disruptions. It all boiled down to the calibre of the owner and management. A happy ship from the captain down was the saying, Valancy thought. She got her little car out of the staff car-park, had to concentrate on the traffic, and was glad to find herself in the quieter streets of St Martin's, just below the Port Hills.

Mother would be on her own today. She'd be glad Valancy had taken the first step. She turned into the drive, rounded the bend, and saw beside the front door that ancient, perfectly-kept Fiat that meant Great-aunt Cecilia had driven down from beyond Springfield, among the foothills of the Southern Alps. She was a grand old sport, but Valancy could have done without her right now. She'd probably say to come up to her and Uncle Robert, and help them with a bit of shepherding. A sort of compensatory holiday for a broken heart! Never mind, Valancy, in you go.

She was guided by the sound of voices in the living-room and paused as she heard Aunt Cecilia's decided tones. 'Of course she must leave that firm. She's been through enough. She mustn't be thought to be wearing the willow for that fellow. Horrible situation! When I got your letter I said to Robert I must come down. I wanted to be here for the Wool Market meeting, anyway, but I was terrified the lot of you, including Valancy, would be all stiff-lipped and stoical, and decide to carry it off as if it didn't perturb you in the slightest.

'I thought if she stayed here she'd be fool enough to go in to sit with Mrs Hughes to let Justin and his wife have a night off. It's possible to be *too* forgiving. We might have been told to turn the other cheek, but it was never said to let the enemy go on slapping it *ad infinitum*. She needs a new job, new people, new surroundings entirely. And I've found the very thing for her! It's tailor-made. *If* we can get her to apply for it.'

Aunt Cecilia paused for breath and into the silence a voice, Valancy's, said, 'What job is this, Aunt? I've just given in my notice, so I'm all for it.'

Both mother and aunt jumped. Valancy managed a chuckle. 'You could have said worse, so don't look so guilty! What job?'

A bland smile overspread Aunt Cecilia's face and out of a huge black leather bag she drew a newspaper cutting. 'This was in my paper at the motel this morning. Look!'

'Motel, Aunt? But you always stay here, there's loads of room. How come?'

'I thought your mother might be caught up preparing to get Mrs Hughes home, and I'd make extra. But your mother tells me she's not coming home till Justin and that girl come down.'

Valancy said calmly, 'Justin and Greer, Aunt. Don't speak of her as if she was a snake-in-the-grass ... she's a thoroughly nice girl. These things are always happening. I'm only clearing out because I can't face the boggling eyes and the whisperings. And I love Hughsie. I couldn't resist going in frequently to see how she is, and that wouldn't be good for Justin and Greer. So I'm off to pastures new. What advert did you see in the *Press*?' Then she said hastily, 'But it's no good to me if it's in Christchurch, or even in Canterbury. In fact I'd prefer the North Island. The farther away the better.'

'Well, it's the South Island, but the Far South,' said her aunt, 'Beyond Dunedin, on the coast, which ought to take your fancy, with your love of the sea. It's on a sort of delta formed by two branches of the Motuara River, like that part of the Rangitata at the mouth that they call Rangitata Island. And it has quite a few farms on it.'

'Yes ... with the main road going over two bridges, the north branch and the south?'

'Well, they don't call this Motuara Island ... they call it Inchcarmichael, same as a similar formation of the Clutha is Inchclutha, because of that province being largely settled by the Scots. But the Carmichael part is after the pioneer family there, the whole Inch is one estate.'

'Wait a moment ... I'm not a qualified landgirl!' protested Valancy. 'What bee have you got in your bonnet now, Aunt Cecilia? Where could I fit into this? Is it a big sheep station? Do they want someone to keep the books? But that's not in my line, I——'

'Listen to this!' Aunt Cecilia's voice was triumphant. 'It could have been written with you in mind. "Author needs an efficient secretary, expert in typing and shorthand, not afraid of a somewhat isolated existence, excellent private quarters provided, with meals at homestead. Good salary to the right person. Some experience of farming life an advantage but not essential. Apply to Mrs Helen Armishaw, Inchcarmichael Station, Rural Delivery 5, Badenoch, South Otago." '

Aunt Cecilia stared hard at Valancy. 'What could be more ideal for you? All those holidays up at Rimu Bush with us, helping with everything on the farm; you're a natural for a country existence ... you've even worked for a publisher. You'd be a godsend to this man.'

'*Man?*' Valancy boggled. 'It says: "Helen Armishaw." I've never heard of her, much less read one of her books. So——'

Something flickered in the keen blue eyes in front of her, so that for a fleeting moment Valancy wondered what her great-aunt was up to. Then it was explained. 'You'll think me an interfering old warhorse, but I rang this place, and got this Helen Armishaw. The author is her great-nephew. I said I wanted to know a bit more about it, that I'd a young relation who could be interested. I said no more than that, so I got a shock when I found out it was Godfrey Carmichael, author of those powerful pioneering-based novels. They show signs of developing into sagas.'

Valancy looked blanker than ever. 'I've never heard of him either.'

Aunt Cecilia was shocked. 'Well, you'd better read some pretty damned quick if you're going to work for him. Never do to admit that.'

'Aunt! You're going too quick for me!' protested Valancy. 'There may be umpteen people after this job.'

'Not with your qualifications and eminent suitability. Not a lot of people with publishing experience, and especially one with a certain amount of rural expertise, or not minding isolation; and the Catlins district can be isolated.'

Valancy knew this was true. She took the clipping. 'He could want a male secretary. That's probably his idea, putting in the advantage of farming experience. He mightn't consider a woman.'

'Well, of course these days, you aren't allowed to discriminate in advertising. Perhaps just as well in this case, because it would have discouraged you. But if that man has any gumption at all, and he sounds as if he has by his books, he'll jump at you.'

Valancy's heart lifted. That was possible. Oh, to be away from here, to start a new life! She thought of something. 'I wonder why it says to apply to Helen Armishaw. I find that odd.'

'No mystery. He's in Canada at the moment, checking out a chunk of early history there. His novels have a basis of fact. The family he's writing of emigrated to Canada from the Highlands first, then to New Zealand. As he has a bit of a blackguard in it, he had to make sure his fictional character doesn't come too close to the bone in reality. Authors have to be aware of the horrible chances of coincidence. He'll be away for three weeks yet and is desperate for secretarial aid for when he gets back. In fact he's got the early chapters so well revised, he's left a huge pile of manuscript ready for re-typing. They want the application in letter form. Right—get cracking!'

Her mother protested, 'She's going to have some lunch first. Over here, Valancy. We've had a bacon-and-egg pie with salad, and there's a good wedge left over.'

Valancy enjoyed it, but was bustled off immediately she downed the last mouthful, by her managing but lovable great-aunt.

She'd said, 'That must have been quite a conversation you had, long distance. Better let me pay you for it.'

Aunt Cecilia looked scornful. 'I don't waste time twittering about the weather on toll-calls. You don't, anyway, when you're talking to strangers. Don't be absurd.' Again Valancy had a sneaking feeling the old warhorse was being too bland. But that was silly. It was just self-satisfaction at pulling a possible job for her out of the hat.

There was a sun-porch Valancy and her father

shared, as a sort of study when they had letters to type. Aunt Cecilia sat down, said, 'No need to wait for the testimonials you'll get, you can state you're still working, but are desirous of taking a position in the country and that you've had holiday experience all your life on your uncle's high-country sheep station in Canterbury. Another thing—don't sign it Valancy Adam-Smith. Just use your initial.'

Valancy blinked. 'Why? What's that got to do with anything?'

'Well, I always think they'd have been better to have given you a good plain sensible name like Jane or Mary or Anne. Sounds more like a secretary ... now don't look at me as if I'm daft, of course I know they didn't think about what you'd do for a crust, but Valancy sounds such a frilly sort of name, more like a film star.'

Valancy burst out laughing. 'Aunt, you're crazy! But good fun. That's just an association in ideas.'

Aunt Cecilia looked puzzled. 'What do you mean?'

'Well, the frill round a bedspread is called a valance! But all right. I'd like this job, and if V. Adam-Smith sounds more businesslike, so be it.' Now buzz off, my dear aunt, and stop breathing down my neck. I'll rough something out.'

'And bring it through to the living-room when you've pencilled it out ... before you type it. You'll probably play down your qualifications, and that's a stupid thing to do when applying for a job.'

Heavens, the old dear *was* keen on her getting it. Perhaps she thought some complimentary copies might come her way from the author! However, both she and Valancy's mother approved the composition, and Valancy returned to the desk to type it. Aunt Cecilia came in before she was finished. 'Now, address it and I'll post it in town. I've got to go to the Main Post Office in any case.'

As Valancy drew the envelope out of the machine, her aunt said, 'Love, I've got a parcel in the boot of my car for your mother. Take my keys and get it out for her, will you? Ten to one I'll forget it if it's not done now.'

Valancy went out. Her aunt picked up the immaculately-typed letter, looked down on the signature, V. Adam-Smith, and a little smile touched the corners of her mouth. She picked up a typing eraser and quite deliberately erased the hyphen. Then she folded it with great precision, slipped it into the airmail envelope, stuck it down, put the stamp on, and rose.

'Oh, thanks, Aunt,' said Valancy, blissfully unaware. 'You *are* sold on this job for me, aren't you?'

Her aunt looked at her in a way Valancy had never seen her look before. She said drily, 'I've no desire to see you waste as many years as I did, attached to the idea that I'd lost my true love. Certainly mine was by death ... but I'd no right to hug that grief so long. I nearly lost Robert over that. He'd waited a long time hoping I'd come out of my trance. It wasn't till my grandmother told me, quite untruthfully, that he was going off to Australia, instead of staying on in New Zealand, that I came to my senses. He—Robert—was the better man, anyway. If the experiences of our own youth can't help the younger ones of this generation, they've been wasted.'

Valancy chuckled, something she'd not felt like doing since she'd known Justin was coming home, next door, then she gave Aunt Cecilia a hug and said, 'Anybody ever tell you you're a perfect darling? Fancy you even admitting your grandmother lied! I can't see *you* doing just that, though. You're a tell-the-truth-and-shame-the-devil sort of character, aren't you? You just told me to get on and get out, you didn't plot and devise.'

Just as well she didn't see the interesting old face as Aunt Cecilia marched out of the room ahead of her. Well, rubbing out a hyphen wasn't to be compared with telling a downright lie! Nevertheless, she only hoped Valancy never got to know how she and Helen Armishaw had schemed. If things worked out as they hoped, surely they could summon up enough acting ability to pretend they'd not met since their long-ago schooldays and hadn't had the faintest idea of each other's married names!

Valancy was amazed to get a night-letter telegram delivered at her home with the mail, three days later, simply addressed: 'V. A. Smith.' It said:

'ON RECEIPT OF YOUR APPLICATION WITH OBVIOUSLY ACCEPTABLE QUALIFICATIONS FOR THE POSITION I TELEPHONED MY NEPHEW IN CANADA AND WISH TO ADVISE YOU THE JOB IS YOURS STOP YOU MENTIONED YOU HAD OWN CAR SO WOULD LIKE YOU TO START AS SOON AS POSSIBLE STOP ROAD IS SIGNPOSTED FROM BADENOCH STOP PLEASE WIRE DAY OF ARRIVAL NOTHING MORE NEEDED

ARMISHAW'

Close on the heels of this came the news that Mrs Hughes was leaving hospital, so Greer was coming down ahead of Justin to receive her. Mr Anderson released Valancy immediately and she sent her own telegram. They seemed casual folk, had accepted her quickly. She'd reply in kind.

'LEAVING HERE EARLY NEXT SATURDAY ARRIVING APPROX FIVE IN EVENING

SMITH'

Nobody in the family ever used the hyphenated name in a telegram. Well, what were best done were best done quickly ... or whatever that quotation was ... it applied not only to murky deeds in *Macbeth*, but to situations like this.

She loaded up the Mini on the Friday night and set off. The goodbyes had been brief, even nonchalant. Mother and Dad had guessed at the feeling of desolation that had assailed her that last night, she was sure, and had been determined not to do anything that might cause her to brim over. She'd been far too long at home.

She had never wanted a flat of her own ... mainly because all her dreams for the future had been with Justin, and it was so handy having him just through the garden hedge, and all her plans had been centred round that ideal house in the same suburb. What a good thing Dad hadn't got further than the foundations when it seemed as if Justin might be permanently in Wellington, and providential he'd found a prospective buyer who felt it couldn't be improved upon. She blinked rapidly . . . Valancy, this is to be a clean cut. Don't look back in anguish! You're on the highway, spinning along to a new life. In seven hours or so you'll have left the Canterbury Plains behind, crossed the Border of the Waitaki River into mountainous Otago, gone through Dunedin to Balclutha and turned towards the coast and Inchcarmichael. It's a glorious morning in mid-spring, with all the lovely October flowers out, daffodils and narcissi lingering here and there, and hawthorn hedges breaking into white and coral clots of blossom, fruit trees showing pink-and-white, and the glorious gold of kowhai on trees bordering the road.

When at Clarkville beyond Dunedin, six hours later, she passed on the west, the turn-off to Central Otago, she was, at last, on a roadway she didn't know, and a sense of adventure quickened her pulses. Here was all unknown territory, here was her new life. She even ceased to dread meeting Godfrey Carmichael, stopped wishing she'd been able to interview her prospective employer before meeting him.

Her dreads, she knew, had been coloured by some of the testy textbook authors she had met in the years at Andersons . . . who flew into rages over misprints, never seemed to understand that publishers' offices were prone to gremlins, always thought their own works should have precedence . . . she'd even wondered if an author writing fiction—well, fiction based on fact— might be even more temperamental . . . but now, oddly, her spirits rose. Inchcarmichael, here I come!

She went across the enormous bridge that crossed the Clutha River, fifth fastest in the world, into the town of Balclutha and beyond, then turned east to the coast. The tarseal became shingle, with ridges and corrugations that bounced the little light car . . . like a road to nowhere. A road that would stop at the sea. Before the sea, in fact, because she'd have to cross a bridge on the Inch itself. Strange to be on a river delta that was all one estate, with two houses on it, plus men's quarters.

The sun still was high in the sky, but then sunset and
twilight would linger here, because the farther south
you went, the longer the evening.

The farms looked prosperous, the pastures lush, as
well they might be. South Otago had a fair rainfall.
Valancy saw willows winding about on her right ... the
Motuara must lie over there. She pulled into a wider
strip of verge and took out her make-up kit. First
impressions counted. That was why she'd worn this
severely-cut suit; it toned down her vivid colouring a
little. It was oatmeal, with brown corded pipings and a
demure-looking cream blouse under it, with a simple
Peter Pan collar added to the effect. Her make-up was
discreet, not blatant, her nails tinted a frosty-pearl and
almost unnoticeable. She subdued her coppery fringe,
combed the sides back over her ears.

A signpost said Motuara East Bridge, so she was
nearly there. The river had huge stopbanks, indicative
of flood-risk, then she was going down a steep gradient
to the bridge, sturdy rather than beautiful, and the
banks were high and ferny. She knew so little about
here. It was largely a forgotten coast, off the main
tourist area.

She left the hollow-sounding bridge planking, and
was on the Inch. Coming over she'd seen where the two
streams divided, and realised how apt the Maori name
was, meaning 'Island in the path of the canoe.' Any
canoe, coming down the narrowed gash there, would be
head on for the centre point, and would have the choice
of either *maui* or *katau*. Sometimes the current would
determine that choice ... the left one looked the
stronger, so *maui* might have been the one more used
for water-traffic.

The road verges became more silty and the landscape
gentled as the horizons closed in. The trees seemed
taller, there weren't so many sweepingly broad
paddocks, and it gave the impression of a small world
of its own. Then, surprisingly, because she'd seen only
sheep and cattle this far, were acres of market-garden
produce and glittering spreads of glasshouses. Now a
modern house, ranch-style, low-set, with cedarwood

paint and white sills, a pillared patio and a bright garden. So close to the road too. Not the homestead she had expected.

She slowed up. It had some Gaelic-sounding name on the gate and underneath, L. Birchfield.

Half a mile on she knew as she saw the carved thistle-head on one gatepost, the acorn and oak leaves on the other, that this indeed was the homestead of Inchcarmichael. She'd looked up the name Carmichael in the big reference book at Andersons and found they belonged to the Stewart clan, whose plant badge was the oak and the thistle. The trees of the avenue almost met overhead, magnificent limes. Her heart lifted . . . to live in a place of trees, wide paddocks, and within sound, if not sight of the sea, would be an ideal existence.

She turned a bend and the sight that met her eyes caused her foot to release the accelerator momentarily . . . oh, no, what Philistine had done this? Who had cut down the giant trees that must have clothed that stark, square homestead with leafy beauty, and surrounded it with birdsong? Only huge, ugly stumps remained. And what magnificent and varied trees they must have been. Even the debris hadn't been cleared but lay, in huge mounds, ready, she supposed, for the burning. It struck dread to her heart. What manner of man was this Godfrey Carmichael to lay such loveliness waste?

Sometimes a tree had to be felled, if it was robbing a house of light, or wrapping its roots round drains, but this was desolation, vandalism. A shrubbery at one side looked as if the growth of many uncaring years was being stripped away, and a huge ploughed strip might mean preparation for a flower garden, but the trees, by themselves, would have softened the stark outlines of this ugly duckling of a residence.

All Valancy's dreams of one of the gracious spreading homesteads of yesteryear, with gables or cunning dormers, and creeper-clad porticoes, disappeared in an instant. She'd seen a few examples of this type of pioneer architecture round Canterbury, uncompromisingly square, too tall for its width, but there, to protect them from the fierce hot winds that swept over the plains, great shelter-belts of pines and blue-gums had redeemed the harshness. This was painted a dingy cream and had a red corrugated iron roof.

She gave herself a shake. 'You aren't buying the place, Valancy. You're only going there as a secretary. You're far too sensitive to beauty of surroundings—comes of having a builder for a father. You're there to do a job and it doesn't have to last for ever. Now, on you go, up to that centre door and ring!'

She mounted the steps and pulled at an old-fashioned jangly bell. It stuck and kept on jangling. Valancy felt her face going red. They'd know it wasn't her fault, but it made one feel, and look, impatient. She heard someone positively running, a thump, another thump, and the bell subsided. Then someone began to wrestle with the handle. Wrestle was the word. She ought to have gone to the back door, which was customary in the country.

A young voice called out, 'Would you mind pushing from the other side? Push really hard.'

Valancy pushed, but it didn't budge a fraction of an inch. She stepped back, charged it, it stuck on the doorstep, then gave, and she shot through, past whoever it was but who skipped nimbly backwards, and positively hurtled through into the hall by several feet, fetching up against an arch hung with curtains. She hastily disentangled herself from the swirling folds, and turned to behold a slim imp of a child with hair as bright as hers.

Two startled brown eyes met her blue ones. 'Oh . . . sorry . . . you see, I'd thought you'd be the new secretary and have big hefty shoulders.'

Valancy boggled. 'Big hefty shoulders? Why?'

A grin dawned. 'Men do have them . . . mostly.'

Valancy's brow creased. 'But I *am* the new secretary. Why——'

The ten-year-old looked more surprised than ever. 'You can't be! *Your* name can't be Adam!'

Valancy grinned now. 'I think you've got things

mixed, love. My name is Valancy Adam-Smith—
hyphenated. I mean the Adam-Smith is. Mrs Armishaw
couldn't have told you that.'

There was a giggle, then a sobering up as the child
clapped rueful hands over her mouth. 'That's torn it! He
certainly didn't want another woman secretary. Nossir!'

Valancy knew an instant dismay, then pulled herself
together. 'But my aunt rang Mrs Armishaw before I
even applied. I think *she'll* know. You're mixed up. But
not to worry, it's easy to do. I'd better——'

Ginger-top darted down the bare hall, opened a door,
called out, 'Aunt Helen . . . it *is* the secretary, but he's
not a man, he's a girl!'

Valancy advanced, prepared to chuckle with Mrs
Armishaw over the youngster's mistake, and was
relieved to see a white-haired gracious-looking lady
emerge, but she wasn't saying, 'Don't be silly, dear, of
course it's a girl. I knew that,' she was wearing an
equally bewildered look, and said uncertainly, 'Oh,
dear, are you really the secretary, or do you mean
Adam Smith couldn't come and you're his substitute?
Oh, yes, that'll be it.'

Valancy stopped dead and said in a firm clear voice,
'My name is Valancy Adam-Smith, with a hyphen.
Adam-Smith is my surname. It's been a surname in my
family for hundreds of years, long before any of them
came to New Zealand. But you *must* know . . . I mean
must have known from the start that it was a girl who
was applying. My great-aunt saw the advertisement, cut
it out and brought it to me, but before even that, she
rang you to get a few more particulars, and told you her
niece could be interested.'

Flakes of pink she hoped weren't signs of anger
appeared on the beautiful old cheeks. 'She didn't, I'm
afraid. She said a young relation of hers might be
interested. She asked where this property was, who the
author was, and said this relation of hers had all the
qualities required; had stayed on her own sheep station
for months at a time and could handle sheep like an
old-timer, but didn't know much about cattle. So
naturally I thought you must be a man.'

Valancy felt as if the stuffing had been knocked out of her. She remembered now. Aunt Cecilia *had* used exactly that phraseology when she'd repeated it to Valancy. Trust Aunt! She always had the notion that her hearers knew exactly what she was getting at, even when she interjected some totally irrelevant topic into existing conversation . . . so it was to be supposed that on a long-distance call she'd be terse and not elaborate at all!

She spread her hands out in a despairing gesture. The older woman came forward, took those hands in a warm, helpful gesture and said, 'My dear, you've given up your job in Christchurch to take this on . . . dear Godfrey will just have to put up with a female secretary. I do hope you can prove to be so good that he completely reverses his opinion of women in the position.'

The redheaded imp, whose eyes were positively sparkling with excitement, said with great relish, 'That'll take some doing . . . his last one was a real trimmer!'

Mrs Armishaw said, 'Rachel, if your mother could hear you she'd sit on you! So I suppose I should too . . . though to be quite candid, she certainly was a trimmer,' and she giggled as helplessly as any teenager.

Valancy repressed a mad desire to join in, but said with despair, 'If only I'd taken no notice of Aunt Cecilia and put my full name instead of V. Adam-Smith, all would have been well, but she had the quaint idea that Valancy sounds a frilly name and secretaries ought to be Jane or Anne or something. Quite stupid really, because I daresay Mr Carmichael would never have heard of bed-frills being called valances.'

'I hadn't heard that myself,' said Rachel, to which Mrs Armishaw replied squashingly, 'The dictionary's full of words *you* haven't heard of, Rachel.'

'I know, and Mum says she's surprised some of them *are* in the dictionary, but it's awfully good fun going through it to find them.'

Mrs Armishaw sighed. 'Now, don't sidetrack me— you're always doing it. Valancy, bring your things in,

and we'll help. I'm sure everything will be just splendid
when we get it sorted out. Godfrey's left a stack of
typing for you, so I'm sure when he gets back to find it
all done, he won't care what sex you are. Besides, it's
my fault. My eyesight can't be as good as it was, if I can
overlook the hyphen in somebody's name. But I just
thought: Adam Smith, how lovely for me.'

Valancy blinked. She felt she was going to do a lot of
puzzled blinking following Helen Armishaw's conversation, to say nothing of Rachel's. 'Why lovely?'

A look of tender pleasure crossed the face in front of
her. 'My husband's name was Adam. I thought I'd get a
great deal of pleasure in using the name again.'

Valancy felt a warmth towards her. 'Perhaps you
could talk about him to me, sometimes.'

'I'd like that. But you must tell me if I overdo it. That
can be one of the biggest losses, not being able to use a
person's name every day.' She glanced towards Rachel.
'This child's a great outlet for me. She mops up tales of
what she calls the olden days.'

'You lucky thing, Rachel,' said Valancy. 'Some
youngsters are cut off from earlier generations and their
lives are poorer. I had a gem of a grandmother who was
a born story-teller. Now ... I've got a lot of stuff. I
brought my own typewriter in case I didn't like Mr
Carmichael's, and some reference books, and quite a lot
of my own favourite books for re-reading. I can't live
without them. And winter and summer clothing,
because Dad said it can be cold here, even in
midsummer.'

Rachel said, 'Very wise. Because though Invercargill
is farther on, the Catlins district is really the farthest
south, the bottom of the South Island slants west, so
the winds from the South Pole hit us first.'

Mrs Armishaw said severely, 'Don't be so off-
putting! I'm quite sure Valancy will love it here and my
great-nephew will come to think it a happy mistake.'
Valancy had serious doubts.

CHAPTER TWO

RETURNING, laden with things, they went through the kitchen, turned right on to a sunny, glassed-in verandah, and out a door at the far end, turning left along another verandah that ran the length of what appeared to be a small cottage, one-storeyed, set at right angles to the back of the house. This made the garden in front of it almost a courtyard, because the far angle was trellised and festooned with creepers.

It was a complete contrast to the ugliness in front. Here no vandal hand had been permitted to destroy. It was so sheltered that already the summer flowers were budding, bees sounded busily, and azaleas in every colour blazed among the smaller plants, pansies, primulas, alyssum.

Their burdens were too heavy to stop to admire, and they passed some French windows, standing wide open to the still, cool air. Mrs Armishaw waved at the room. 'That's Godfrey's study, two small cottage rooms knocked into one ... you'll see it later. That's where you'll work. The rest of the cottage is all yours.'

Valancy stopped out of sheer amazement. 'You don't mean it ... a wee house of my own? How lovely!'

Mrs Armishaw said shrewdly, 'Well, don't expect modern lines ... there are inconvenient steps up and down and the bathroom has plumbing that gurgles like a dragon, and the bath isn't built-in yet ... it stands on old-fashioned iron legs, horrible to dust under ... and the bedroom ceiling slopes a bit low, but at least you'll be able to get away from us and from your atmosphere of work. Everyone needs some privacy. This is your sitting-room.'

It had a black-leaded register grate, with quaint old tiles surrounding it and a fire set ready for a match. It would throw out a wonderful heat, Valancy knew. There were two shabby but comfortable-looking armchairs with winged sides and high backs, a ditto rocking chair with a crocheted antimacassar on the back, a beaded hassock, rather too many small tables for most tastes, but Valancy loved them. Always somewhere to put your book down, a magazine, your knitting.

She approved a drop-leaf table she could use for meals if entertaining, and a davenport where she would write her letters home. They took the cases through to the bedroom, Rachel pointing out details as they went.

It was blue and white, but not cold-looking because it faced north-west so would get the sun all day. It had a honeycomb white quilt with a fringed border, but a huge eiderdown rolled at the foot of the bed was covered in gay chintz, rose, cream, lilac, and green. A small passage led to the kitchen which had, praise be, a table-size electric stove as well as the kitchen range, which Valancy knew nothing about whatever. Beyond it a scullery held a combination refrigerator/deep-freeze and an obviously new bench unit all laminex and stainless steel.

'We can give you all your meals with us if you wish, but if you prefer it, you can draw supplies from our storeroom and see to your own breakfast and lunch, or, if we should be having midday dinner, your own tea. Dinners, of course, always with us. Dinners take time to prepare and Godfrey works his secretaries hard, so that's the best way.'

'Sounds lovely to me. But tell me, how much help do you have in the house?'

'Rachel's much older sister is a landgirl here but gives me two full days inside. She does all the vacuuming, most of the ironing and washing, and Godfrey gets window-cleaners out regularly.'

'Do you do all the meals?'

'I like cooking and housekeeping. I'm not ready yet to retire to my holiday home at Lake Wanaka. I'm very happy doing it, and it helped Godfrey realise his dream.'

'His dream?' queried Valancy.

'Of buying back and living in the house his pioneer ancestors built. They worked the property till the rabbits drove them off, ruined. But now Inchcarmichael has come back into its own. Now I must put the last touches to the dinner. I hear the men coming,' Mrs Armishaw added. 'You've half an hour to settle in. I left the kettle filled, and some cookies under that throw-over. I'm sure you'll want a cup of tea. Rachel, come with me. You can talk Valancy's head off later, and fill her in with all she should know and probably a bit she shouldn't.'

'Yes, Aunt Helen,' said Rachel with surprising meekness.

Mrs Armishaw turned back. 'You don't mind me calling you Valancy, do you? I like it—so euphonious.'

Valancy felt that what ever the formidable Godfrey was like, she had allies in Mrs Armishaw and Rachel.

There were two men, Rod Forsyth, in his mid-twenties, and Bill Watson, nearer fifty, who seemed to have been on the place for years. They quite openly chuckled that Adam Smith had turned out to be a girl. 'I hope I'm round when the boss finds out,' said Rod. 'His face will be a picture! Never mind, personally, I'm all for it. He'll mellow. After all, no one could have the ill luck to be landed with two like Carlotta.'

Bill Watson smiled at Valancy. 'Not to worry, lass. Apart from your hair, you're nothing like that one. I'm not a great believer in first impressions, but I can tell that. For one thing, she had nothing like your experience. She was a typist, nothing more, and carried away by the fact that one of Godfrey's books was to be filmed. Thought he was on the road to being a millionaire, and set her cap at him.'

Valancy felt more and more dismayed. 'My great-aunt was shocked I'd not read one of his books. Evidently she loves them. But if it was a film I ought to have known something about it. What was it called? And was it filmed here?'

Bill shook his head. 'It didn't come off. Godfrey backed off.'

'Backed off? Isn't it usually the film company does that? Finds out costs are too dear or something.'

'The script writers wanted to change it too much—radically, he dug his toes in and finally withdrew the option. Even wanting money as badly as he did, to restore this place, he wouldn't come at that.'

The dismay lifted a little. Anyone with enough strength of will, moral guts if you liked, to do that, must have integrity. Also, one hoped, a sense of justice, and wouldn't take it out of her for not being a man. But of course it could just add up to pigheadedness.

Rod said, 'So he's burning the midnight oil trying to catch up on what he's faced with. He'll do it too, he's so thorough in his research. That's why he's away now. And he'll come back brimming over with umpteen new ideas too, I'll be bound. Have all his typing done for him by the time he returns, and he'll not care tuppence that you're female, not male.'

Valancy determined she would do just that, beginning at first light tomorrow. She was a little surprised when, an hour after the meal, Bill Watson tapped at her sitting-room door.

'I won't stay long, I can see you're busy settling in.' He indicated the cartons of books she was emptying.

'I'm not worrying about getting my recreational reading on the shelves,' she told him. 'I'm just sorting out my reference books. At the office we all had extra meanings and jottings in the margins of the books we used most.'

He nodded approval. 'I don't recall ever seeming to interfere in anything before, like this, it's not in my nature, but I'm hoping you'll take it well . . . because I'd like this to work this time. The boss needs someone like you to help him. That Carlotta, she fair put the cat among the pigeons—very vain, very much with an eye to the main chance. Trying to make an impression on everything in trousers. Very conscious of herself, if you know what I mean. It irritated Godfrey, I could see that. I guess it sort of interrupted his train of thought. He lives with his stories. Make allowance for Godfrey's natural annoyance at discovering you aren't a man after all, and be on your guard. I . . . heck, I don't know how to put this . . . you could get mad. Well, what I mean is, play down your charms. Keep to business.'

To his great relief she didn't take umbrage. She felt the opposite, as if a warmth flowed out to him, guessing it had cost him something to come. She put out her hand and grasped his. 'Thanks, Bill Watson. I appreciate that. I take it you're quite fond of your boss. That I like—I was fond of mine. Point taken.'

He said, turning to the door, 'It's a hell of a task he's taken on here. He needs someone at his right hand to grease the wheels, not to disturb things. Goodnight, Miss Adam-Smith . . . all right, then, Valancy.'

Helen Armishaw came through later, to tell her what she was expected to do, and show her the study. The desk allotted to her was large, the light came through on the left, and the window it shone through looked right through two sloping hills, and it seemed as if the land beyond must drop right down, for only the tips of some distant pines were visible and the afterglow had stained the sou'west sky with amber and rose.

She needn't have brought her typewriter; this was electric and as good as they come. A manual one stood on the author's own desk.

'That's usually up aloft. He uses it to compose on . . . which is a good thing, as his thoughts fly so fast it makes his writing hard for him to read again when he's revising, ready for final typing. He likes solitude for the first spinning of the story, but he's been weeks without help so he brought that machine down here. Now on this side table are five chapters of the book he wants typing. He's left instructions on top, weighted down, and if you're in any doubt about the presentation, carbon copies of former books are in that seven-drawer file over there.

'He hoped I'd get someone quickly, and said if so, and the chap were speedy, then there are the notes of some trips to be copied up. You'll find typed copies of similar ones in those folders there—I'm afraid those are in longhand. He jots continually as he travels or as things happen. Important details in those to be underlined in red, as indicated. I don't suppose you'll even get that far, but if you do, this concertina file of newspaper clippings needs classifying. Some are on aspects of farming, some to be divided into areas, first into provinces, then into specific features he might be writing about. Dear me, hope I've got it right.'

Valancy looked at her with respect. 'I think you're wonderful. In fact spot on.'

Helen Armishaw's lips twitched. 'I'm glad you didn't say "wonderful for your age". Most people spoil a compliment with that. Godfrey never does, bless him, even if he's careful to see I don't overdo. But to him I'm still a person in my own right, not just an elderly relative. And he knows that for me it's a dream come true too . . . Inchcarmichael coming back into our family. I knew I couldn't achieve it, That sort of money was beyond me, and anyway, my husband was a teacher and we moved around. I little dreamed when Godfrey was born that he would become the masculine counterpart of all I ever wanted to be. I'll tell you some day, but right now you must be tired and wanting to settle.'

Valancy found herself patting her hand. 'I'll look forward to hearing about it, and your Adam. I'm going to turn in soon, though, because I want to be up early to get on with the job. I believe I've got to make myself indispensable. Oh, you said he did his rough manuscripts up aloft. Do you mean in one of the rooms in the big house?'

'No, I should have shown you. That's not a glass-fronted cupboard over there, it's a tiny staircase. It was put in when the big house was first built and the verandahs weren't glassed in, to give access when the weather is bad. The room it leads up to is a funny shaped one, tucked into the angle of the back of the house, and gives a view of the sea. Feel free to go up there. Only never go into the room it leads into . . . on the upper storey of the big house. Godfrey's made that out of bounds to anyone but him, because it leads into his sleeping quarters. And, by the way, my dear, lose no sleep over the fact he wanted a male secretary. The fault was entirely mine.'

It was a good thing for Valancy's peace of mind that she didn't see Helen Armishaw stop on the verandah when she left the study, put her hand over her mouth to stifle a giggle and say to herself, 'Well, not *entirely* . . . oh, what fun!'

Valancy set her alarm and had done an hour's typing before she made her breakfast. Never mind if Sunday was one of her days off, she was going to use it to good advantage and hoped the pile of typescript she would achieve would impress the woman-hating Mr Carmichael.

However, by the end of that hour she was definitely mellowing. She liked his style. He was also practical. He had left a resumé of the preceding chapters, and a list of his characters and their ages and colouring and relationships to the others, beside her typewriter. Another good thing was that she herself was an exceptionally fast reader. If it meant she had to stay up half the night, she was going to read those preceding chapters in full. The story gripped her so much, she just had to know all that had led up to this: the emigration of the heroine's family to New Zealand, to what they'd hoped would be better conditions, and were, in the realm of freedom, but not in ease of living. She was glad Andersons had published so many factual pioneer histories, she wasn't covering completely new ground. For a man not over fond of her sex, he wrote well when he was writing from the women's viewpoints, and understandingly. Now was he just observant or . . . or did he know women very well?

Rachel came to ask her to go out exploring with her. 'Aunt Helen says you aren't expected to work Sundays, and I'd love it. I'm keeping her company at nights just now, but when my chores are finished I'm free.'

'I'd love it too, Rachel, but if Mr Carmichael's been without a secretary for so long, I need to get as much done as possible for him. I noticed he's got a lot of notes piled up upstairs for another novel, so I guess he wants this one off his plate quite quickly.'

'You're probably right,' said the child gloomily.

'Anyway, as it's the combined parish church service today, which is too far for us, we're staying home. We only go when it's at Badenoch. Dad said if time was hanging on my hands I could go over home and finish my project for school. It's not to be in till Thursday, but he's a demon for being ahead. I'd rather he was happy-go-lucky.'

'Then you'd always be in a flap,' Valancy pointed out. 'Thank your lucky stars your father isn't a putter-off. I'm the same, so scram. I'll explore with you when I've earned time off. Mr Carmichael has to be considered first.'

'Aren't you going to call him Godfrey? Everyone does, even me.'

'I will if he asks me to. I always called my former boss Mr Anderson, never David.'

'How old was he?' Rachel grinned shrewdly.

Valancy grinned back. 'Too old to be asked his age! But then I don't know how old Mr Carmichael is.'

'Thirty-three.'

'And you don't call him uncle?'

'He's not my uncle. Dad works for him. We run the market garden part. But I'm so much younger than the others, I like being over here. *They* boss me round and Godfrey and Aunt Helen don't. She's not my real aunt, just a mannerly one.'

'You mean a courtesy aunt.'

'Yep. Thought it sounded funny. I say, did you know your door locks? The one that leads into your sitting-room? There's a key in the other side. I love rooms that lock. All old houses have locks on every door. Modern ones don't, only handles. You get no privacy, especially with older sisters and brothers.'

'I daresay your father would put a tiny bolt on your side for you. As long as you didn't abuse the privilege and lock people out if you're in a bad mood.'

'Never thought of a bolt. I should have when I saw Godfrey putting a bolt on his bedroom door. The one that leads into the room aloft. I said why, when there was a key, and he said because keys were two-way, bolts only one. I wonder what he did it for.'

Valancy was certain Rachel knew why. She thought
herself it would have been to keep Carlotta out. Well,
he'd never need to lock a door against her ... she'd
show him one woman was only interested in being his
secretary!

'I've no idea, Rachel, and it doesn't matter. I love
talking to you, but I can't type and talk and I dare not
make mistakes, so——'

'So scram,' said Rachel cheerfully. ' 'Bye ... see you
at one. I forgot to tell you. We always have midday
dinner on Sundays. I say, wouldn't you rather write
stories yourself than type other people's?'

'Go!' ordered Valancy, pointing to the door.

In three days she realised how much more interesting
this was than the work at Andersons. She felt
completely caught up in the spell of this story ... it had
everything ... adventure, challenge, passion, integrity
and a subtle something that made you long to keep
typing, to come to the end of it.

She'd read all the preceding chapters in her own time
and never once fallen asleep over them. Now she was
reading his very first book, published six years ago. The
personal details on the back of the cover intrigued her.
When he'd written it he was a shepherd on a high
country run, Dragonshill, in South Canterbury, son of
an accountant, who hadn't wanted the big cities, but
had returned to the pastoral activities of his pioneering
forebears ... those ancestors hadn't prospered as had
some, but had been ruined by the introduction of
rabbits.

She was impressed when an excerpt from a review on
the back of his second novel said it had—despite the
difference in the setting—a touch of the calibre of *The
Forsyte Saga*. She agreed. She wondered when and how
he had bought this property back again. But she
wouldn't ask. Aunt Helen fairly doted on her great-
nephew, you could tell, and was only too eager to chat
about him, but Valancy felt it was not the thing to
gossip about one's employer. She'd form her own
estimate.

None of the books carried a photograph of the author, so her image of him had to be wholly a mental one. Perhaps that was good. It would be of the inner man, that way. Despite the very real apprehension she knew whenever she anticipated their first meeting and he had to face the unpalatable fact that he had another woman secretary, she felt herself being disarmed as she built up that picture of him. It was like a skeleton unclothed with flesh, as if she were analysing his mind, quite divorced from any animal magnetism or charm he might possess.

She gave herself a mental shake. Just because you like what he writes, the characters he builds, don't mesmerise yourself into thinking him other than a curmudgeon she told herself. Keep what's probably his true image in front of you ... a harsh man, impatient, rather ruthless ... as witness those trees sacrificed for money. Aunt Helen had said once, shaking her head over the ugliness ... 'but one must understand the money was desperately needed.' Odd, in a man who wouldn't compromise about his book being made into a film. Well, she was prepared; be he ever so saturnine and scowling, she was ready for him. Coolly efficient, entirely uninterested in him personally.

She laughed to herself. He could be a meek little man, with a depressed-looking walrus moustache ... or bumptious ... or merely cross-grained. It was plain stupid to fit any of his well-drawn and very masculinely attractive heroes to himself. He might be writing of all he ever longed to be.

Mrs Armishaw protested at her hours, at her refusal to go into Badenoch with Rod to a dance, to go shopping when Bill Watson went in for stores. 'You're driving yourself mercilessly, dear Valancy.'

'I want as much done as possible for his return, Mrs Armishaw. Especially as it's awkward working for an author who's absent. Every writer makes some mistakes, and though I've typed a lot, there are several pages that will have to be retyped, if what I think needs checking—by him—is found to be in error. But I admit there's less of this than I'd thought I might find. And his filing system I can't fault. This Carlotta may not have suited him, but I couldn't fault that.'

Mrs Armishaw burst out laughing. 'It was hopeless when she left. He had to completely reorganise. And once when he had to spend time in the shearing shed, and she couldn't get on, she put the time in rearranging his bookcases. Thought they'd look nice in the shelves, with books all the same size on every one! Some she even sorted to colour! Poor Godfrey! The very earliest days, pre-colonisation, whaling, etc., were all mixed up with farming in the eighteen-eighties and World War One. That's only one example. He got me to help him after the final showdown when he sent her packing. It took us a week, and it was a nightmare. Have you really got as far as that, love?'

Valancy sparkled. She knew she'd worked hard and fast, and this praise was sweet. She thought it hardly likely that Godfrey Carmichael would enthuse like this.

Then she said ruefully, 'The only thing is that I'm afraid Mr Carmichael will think I've let the cats get into very bad habits. I simply can't keep James and Sue out. I like to work with the French windows open, and all the scents of that courtyard garden coming in, but the cats think it's an open invitation. James takes the seat at his desk, even, no matter how I hunt him off on to the window-seat at the far side. And Susie ... the little ginger minx ... even curls up on the desk—mine! But perhaps they know they'll have to vacate when Mr Carmichael comes home.'

Mrs Armishaw burst out laughing. 'He's as soft as butter with them. I've known him reluctant to disturb James, and get himself one of those dining-chairs out of your sitting-room. He vows they're slave-drivers, the perfect cats for an author ... they only get happily settled when he starts typing. They purr like mad then.'

'That adds up,' said Valancy. 'They even make protesting little squeaks when I stop typing to check something. I thought I was imagining it. They must like the rhythm of the keys.'

She told herself she must have a horrible nature. She'd built up the curmudgeon image in her mind ...

the saturnine hooknosed being with a permanent scowl on his brow ... and he was too softhearted to push that huge grey-and-black striped animal, James, off his chair! She herself didn't want to soften towards him. She was going to show him she had about as much time for men as he had for women. ... Mrs Armishaw was still oohing and aahing over what she had done.

Valancy nodded. 'By the day after tomorrow I should be able to start typing up his notes of various trips, though there was something I should consult you about. Up in the sanctum, in the jottings he has ready for his next book, there could be things he wants checked. I didn't like to start reading it, some authors are very sensitive over their first rough draft, but I did notice he had a jotter beside the notes, with questions on it like: "Is Cape Kidnappers in Hawkes' Bay the only mainland nesting-place in the world for gannets?" and "Find out the price of butter-fat then as on page fifty-five", and 'When were headers first used in South Otago?' If I had your permission to go through what he's done so far, I might find other things to verify. I've attended to the ones specified.'

'Go right ahead,' said Aunt Helen firmly. 'Nothing but good could come out of that. I give full permission. If he's not pleased I don't mind being on the carpet for *that*.'

Her emphasis caught Valancy's attention. 'What do you mean? Oh ... you think you'll be brought to book for not making sure of my sex? It wasn't your fault. It was due to my not using my full name. In fact I'll lay it at my Aunt Cecilia's door.'

Aunt Helen said quickly, 'Don't mention your aunt.'

'Why not?'

'Well, it could give him a thing about aunts. *Me* not making sure, *your* aunt not even letting you write for a job yourself—you know.'

'I don't know. It's absurd to study a man's warped opinions like that. Aunts are women. I daresay if an uncle had made the mistake he'd have thought nothing of it. If he feels he can't take another female secretary, he can jolly well advertise again, and I just wish him well of trying to word it so that he gets applications from males yet doesn't get accused of discrimination. Oh, what a mad, mad world!'

The older woman chuckled. 'You'll be very good for Godfrey. You can stick up for yourself. And for me too.'

'I should think so,' said Valancy wrathfully. Then she giggled. 'This passion of mine to rush at the work probably reveals a horrible nature—a real flaw. I want to show him no male secretary could have achieved anything like as much as this. *And* if there's time I'm going to paint that summerhouse roof. Rachel said Godfrey was going to do it and that the paint's been sitting there for weeks. Then I could tack the trellis back on. I can't till the windowsills are painted the same colour as the roof, and it looks awful with those rose branches trailing on the ground. Outside and inside help he wanted, and outside and inside help he's going to get!'

Aunt Helen went away happily sure Godfrey wouldn't want to get rid of this one. She was more likely to fight with him than to try to lure him. Though of course, Cecilia and she were hoping they'd fall for each other. But oh dear, how she wished he was back and the explanations over.

However, next day a cable from Canada announced that he was delayed. It would be next week, but not till the Sunday. Valancy typed and researched and filed, rushing madly and happily on. She finished up every single thing in the study, and began brushing down and sandpapering the peeling summerhouse roof.

She said to Rachel wrathfully, 'The men turned down my offer to help tail the lambs, stupid things, so at least I can show Mr Carmichael I'm capable of sprucing up the place. And Rachel, if I start up the motor-mower, would you mow the lawns? Mrs Armishaw is going to trim the edges.'

Fate decreed she was not to start the painting yet. That day's mail brought in the proofs of his next book, a large volume. Valancy's heart sank. She could pick up printer's errors, but all authors liked to proof-read their own work in the final count. Some mistakes only an author could pick up.

She looked at the deadline for return and said to Helen Armishaw, 'If I go through these thoroughly twice, at least I'd pick up the obvious stuff and could send his publishers a cable to say we could get them to London, after his return, three days later than specified. I'm a quick reader. How is he? Would that be okay?'

It was the best they could do. It was very clean copy, but she was dismayed to find at least two mistakes that could be attributed solely to the author. She didn't relish having to point them out; he'd resent her doing that. If he'd been here and found them himself he'd not have lost face. Well, she'd have to tell him to save him time. Added to everything he'd probably be suffering from jet-lag, and that would improve nobody's temper.

She had a headache herself when she finished and thought gladly that tomorrow she'd be out in the open air, painting. It was Saturday and turned out a glorious day, giving promise of the summer that was just round the corner. Rachel arrived over and to her delight was allowed to paint the trellis. It was a small summerhouse and Valancy had a good head for heights.

Mrs Armishaw wouldn't allow her to wear even her oldest jeans to be smeared with paint, and brought out a pair of navy-blue overalls that a youth who'd once worked on the place had left behind. It was evident he'd done a lot of painting. They were liberally bedaubed with red, blue, yellow, and now Valancy had added an incredible amount of green by sitting on a newly-painted strip. She'd found her shoulder-length red hair kept swinging across her eyes, so she'd fished out a piece of twine from the pocket, and tied it back, and the only pity was she'd not wiped her hands on the overalls first; getting paint out of hair was a hideous task. She was wearing old gymn shoes, also not hers, and very disreputable at that, and Rachel, equally shabbily clad, was behind the summerhouse having a marvellous time.

Valancy called out to her, 'I've a feeling I missed my vocation in life ... I *love* painting. And on a roof it doesn't matter if you make a mess, does it? My father's a builder and so fussy you wouldn't believe it. He'd never let me loose on any of his painting jobs. This is heaven!'

She came down two rungs of the ladder she was lying on, shifted her pail of paint to a better position on the stand Bill had rigged up for her and dabbled her brush again. At that moment a surprised voice from below her said, 'Who in the world are you? Painting that roof?'

She'd heard no footsteps, and she gave a terrific start, caught her brush on the edge of the pail, saw it rock and made a mighty but ill-judged clutch to save it. She only succeeded in knocking it clean off. She yelled: 'Look out! Look out!' and made a grab as it overturned.

She had an impression of a big fair man leaping madly out of the way, a cascade of green paint positively jetting out of the bucket, then realised she was slipping and slithered down the unpainted iron, and with a superhuman effort, managed to clutch the last rung of the short ladder that was hooked over the ridge-pole. This saved her from a bruising fall but left her ignominiously hanging from it, with her feet in their indescribable plimsolls dangling over the edge on a level with the visitor's eyes.

She turned her head, said, 'Oh, thank heaven the paint missed you ... dressed up like that ... though to be candid, you don't deserve your incredible luck, creeping up on me like that and scaring the life out of me.' Then she yelled, 'No ... don't touch me!—I'm covered in paint. I'll manage to get down myself, thanks!'

She saw a sardonic grin spread over the square-jowled face. 'Oh, will you? Well, it'll be interesting to find out just how you'll manage that.'

At that moment Rachel, scrambling madly over rose branches, arrived from the back of the summerhouse and exclaimed, 'Suffering cows and bulls! It's Godfrey himself!'

Valancy gave an agonised wriggle at this piece of information and uttered an indescribable sound. Rachel said, 'Hang on ... no, Godfrey, leave her alone. She's as tough as old boots, she won't fall. I've got a stool.'

She was back in a trice with it, plonked it on the path, and Valancy stretched her toes till she reached it and came down.

She turned to face him. She shut her eyes against the horror of this first meeting. Talk about impressing him with her efficiency! Would she ever be able to eradicate this first impression?

He looked as stunned as she felt. He said to Rachel, 'Who's this? Another of your scatty ginger cousins?'

Rachel said with dignity. 'We *aren't* ginger. We're *auburn*! And she's not a cousin, it's your new secretary. Only she isn't a he, she's a her. She left the hyphen out.'

It had to be said that Godfrey Carmichael boggled. He repeated in a sarcastic voice, 'She left the hyphen out? Of course! Now why didn't I think of that? It explains everything.'

Valancy came to life. 'I'm sure I didn't leave the hyphen out. After all, I've been putting the hyphen in ever since I could write, since I was five years old. That's twenty years. It must have been faint, that's all. Yes, faint.'

Godfrey Carmichael said, 'I feel faint myself. What's a hyphen got to do with it?'

Valancy said coldly, 'My name is Adam-Smith. My surname. Hyphenated. I signed my application V. Adam-Smith. The V stands for Valancy.

He still seemed dazed. 'Valancy? I've never heard that name before. But what a pity you hadn't put your full name. That could never be taken for a masculine one. What about references, didn't they give it? Oh, my dilly Aunt Helen!'

She found herself saying ferociously, 'She's not to be blamed for it. It's all this stupid business about not being able to advertise for a man because of discrimination. Let me tell you I'd never have answered the ad had I known you wanted a man, had I known you were a woman-hater.'

Rachel said, 'Oh, Valency, you could have used that lovely word we had in the crossword last night . . . you could have said had you known he was a misanthrope.'

It threw the other two off their argument. They said simultaneously, 'It doesn't mean woman-hater ... it means hating mankind in general.' Then they stopped and blinked at each other. Valancy had a disgruntled feeling her last statement had lost its impact.

But he made a lordly waving-away gesture. 'I know it's against the law to advertise for a man, but I thought the wording with the bit about some experience of farming life an advantage, but not essential, wouldn't have contravened any standards but to anyone with gumption it would have been obvious I wanted a man.'

Valancy's tone was tart. She had nothing to lose. It was obvious this man wouldn't retain her in his employ. 'Women can make very good farmers. My great-aunt Cecilia, for instance. She lives on a much more remote property than this, a high-country sheep station in the foothills of the Alps. She can muster as high as any of the shepherds ... even at her age ... and so can I! I spend all my holidays up there. It was she who saw the advert, and believe me, she had no doubt whatever that the position was tailor-made for me.'

Godfrey Carmichael lost the dazed look, said firmly, 'I said it was non-essential, the farming bit. But I certainly expected to come home to find my secretary in the study reducing the stack of work I left to be caught up on to manageable proportions ... not painting a summerhouse roof. You seem to have no sense of priorities.'

Valancy cast a scathing glance round the slope below them, denuded of its trees, and said, 'I know, of course, that beauty of surroundings seems to have no priority here, but in any case you're entirely wrong. Every bit of work you left is up to date, plus some you hadn't anticipated, but which I ferreted out for myself. *All* your handwritten notes of trips have been typed up and your clippings, which I found were in a very muddled state, have been filed and cross-referenced. I got all that done before I did a thing outside, except what I did in my own spare time like helping in the vegetable garden and feeding the poultry if the school bus is late home.'

Rachel felt she must put her oar in to help boost

Valancy's stock. '*And*,' she said, '. . . you ask Bill . . . he says she's nearly as good as a vet. One of the lambs dislocated its shoulder and she got it back, and Aunt Helen says she beats you hollow when it comes to worming the cats . . . you never saw anything like it . . . they just submit. Even Susie. She pops the tablets down their throats, they give one gulp and then even purr!'

Godfrey Carmichael put back his head and guffawed. Valancy felt her own mouth crumbling, and the next moment was helpless. Rachel looked offended. 'Well,' she said with dignity, 'it's . . . it's a—a qualification.'

Sobering up, he managed to say, patting Rachel's head, 'so it is. If only I'd thought of it I'd have put it in the advert. Well, in your spare time, Miss Adam-Smith, we can get you drenching sheep or treating them for foot-rot.'

Valancy found herself saying, 'I'm most relieved to find you've a sense of humour. I thought you would have, from your books.'

He held a hand up. 'Now . . . please don't tell me you adore my books. It's not necessary in a secretary. You'll probably be sick to death of them as you type on.'

She decided on frankness. 'I have got to confess I'd never even heard of you till my aunt arrived with your advert, Mr Carmichael. Now, I can't leave this job for another quarter of an hour. There's only one more strip of iron to paint, but I must clean up this horrible mess on the paving-stones, though fortunately it's water-based paint. Rachel will help. So if you go up to the house now I'll be with you in half an hour, when I've cleaned myself up.'

She looked down at her torn and paint-stained overalls, the tatty sandshoes with—oh, horrors—one big toe peeping through a hole. 'I feel far from the image of the perfect secretary. But perhaps in the circumstances that doesn't matter, Mr Carmichael.'

Rachel said anxiously, 'You're not going to carry on with this Mister and Miss business, are you? Out here at the back of beyond, it sounds stupid.'

Valancy turned swiftly upon her. 'Go and finish

tacking up the roses, then get me a bucket of water. *Right now.*'

Rachel stood not upon the order of her going.

Godfrey looked astounded. 'Well, that's something in your favour—you can manage Rachel.'

Valancy frowned. 'Can't you? I'd have thought——'

He made an impatient gesture. 'Of course I can. That is, when she doesn't beguile the heart out of me. But few other people seem able to do so. But let me regain control of the conversation. You and Rachel between you seem bid fair to create diversions. Exactly what did you mean when you said that in the circs it didn't matter you were so far from the image of the perfect secretary?'

She shrugged. 'Because I can't imagine you keeping me on.'

The penetrating grey eyes studied her intently. 'You mean because I caught you looking like this? And doing this?'

'I mean because I'm a woman. Don't worry, I won't go round complaining about discrimination; I reckon you've a right to your own preferences. The whole thing was an unfortunate mistake. This can be temporary, till you get a man.' Before he could reply she swept on, 'This may sound high-handed, but I'd prefer you not to go into the study till I can go in with you. I've several matters awaiting your attention that I'd rather you didn't touch till I can explain them. I imagine you've got a bit of jet-lag and that Mrs Armishaw will want you to have something to eat before you settle to work.'

He bent down, picked up his case, looked down on her and his lips twitched. Yet he said very coldly, 'I had an idea that the boss paid the piper and called the tune. I've gone to a great deal of trouble to arrive one day earlier than I'd said. I'll start work when *I* decide it, not you.'

Valancy stood looking after him. Then she grinned to herself, and muttered, 'That's what you think, Mr High-and-Mighty, but what you don't know is that the urgency of those proofs will demand your nose at the grindstone right away. And while I doubt if you'll find *I've* made any mistakes, *you've* certainly made a couple of bad blueys in those pages!'

CHAPTER THREE

VALANCY lost no time in finishing, cleaning up the spilt paint, giving Rachel precise instructions on how to tidy up, and said she was to go to her own home, help her mother with her chores and not to interrupt Mr Carmichael for a single instant during the day. 'I told you about those proofs. They're absolutely urgent, and this extra day is a godsend. You must wait till he sends for you.'

To her surprise Rachel said with no demur, 'I know. I've seen him in a flap before over deadlines. And the dear Carlotta was hardly the one to cope with emergencies. See you tomorrow, I hope.'

Valancy took the path to her own quarters, left the paint-saturated garments in a bucket, took a two-minute shower, slid into a grey pinafore dress with a white, blue-spotted blouse beneath it because it was demure, but which, had she but known, brought up the vivid blueness of her eyes, left off make-up, swept her hair back severely and tied it with a neat black ribbon at the nape of her neck, and put on large spectacles which she hardly ever needed save in strong sunlight. They were slightly tinted, and gave her, she knew, a faintly owlish, secretary -like look, then she walked briskly to the kitchen.

Aunt Helen didn't look as if she'd been scolded. She looked like any great-aunt would, whose favourite great-nephew has returned from overseas, faintly pink and shining-eyed. She beamed. 'Such a blessing I made that huge batch of cheese scones ... wasn't it providential, Godfrey, getting that earlier cancellation? Though mind you, Valancy, I've not told him about the proofs yet. I thought he needed fortifying before plunging into work!'

Godfrey looked aghast. 'Proofs ... that's three days' work ahead of me! I always do them twice. Hell, what a homecoming!'

Valancy said calmly, 'I've done them twice. Once more should be all they need from you. I'm experienced in proof-reading, naturally, coming from a publisher's office. And while one always picks up the odd printer's error one has missed, the second time round, the last reading, done by you, should be accomplished much more speedily, with fewer corrections to make in the margins.'

He scowled, 'Sounds good, in theory, but so often there are errors only the author can pick up, especially in fiction, where he has the deeper knowledge of his characters. Right, let's be at it.'

Aunt Helen watched with a smug expression. She'd write to dear Cecilia tomorrow and say first hurdle taken. She wouldn't mention the circumstances of their initial meeting . . . and the paint!

In view of what Godfrey Carmichael had said about only authors picking up certain errors, she wished she didn't have to point out to him the ones he'd missed himself in his actual manuscript. She mustn't sound cocky. It would only irritate him at a time when he was still sore that he'd been landed with another woman.

The atmosphere of the study calmed her a little. Her legs felt less shaky. This was her rightful sphere. She was no longer a grubby ginger urchin of the wrong sex. She was a secretary, and it would be a case of false humility if she didn't know she'd done a jolly good job for him, working all hours.

She said crisply, 'I think I should clear the decks by showing you what I could cope with, in other things, then the proofs.' She pointed to a pile of letters. 'That's non-urgent. Those are from readers none of whom seem to be expecting an immediate reply, or indeed, any. They mostly apologise for taking up your time but want to say how they enjoy your books. Three needed answers, because of questions, and Aunt Helen helped me with the information needed.'

She could have bitten out her tongue when she realised she'd used the name the older woman had asked her to use. But he made no comment. She rushed on, 'The carbons of those answers are with the letters. Upstairs I took the liberty of going through the memos you'd made for checking, for your new book—the gannet colony and the price of butter-fat at that time, which was incredibly low. For that I had to put a call through to my former office. We did a lot of factual pioneer stuff and I couldn't verify anywhere else. The trips are typed and in alphabetical order, but I also took a note of the dates you made them. I've also made out a date and season list in case you are referring to them in the future.'

'What do you mean? Date and season list?'

'Well, you'll know your farming and mountain background backwards, but as you bring in the pioneer women's work a lot, and their gardens, I've done this into Summer, Autumn, Winter and Spring, with details of what's blooming or ripening when, if you get me. I'd like later—if I'm here—to record approximate temperatures, times of sunrise, sunset and tides, too. Quicker than having to pause in a fine flow of narrative and look these things up. You might be wondering if it would really be dark still at the time when hero and heroine make their getaway ... or what-have-you ... and in New Zealand with a thousand miles between the Far North and the Deep South, the twilights and dawns differ so.'

She thought, and hoped, he looked at her with respect. 'Where did you get that idea?'

She felt more confident. 'It wasn't my own. One of our authors, a woman, got me to type up a lot of this for her, from a little notebook she'd kept for years, which was falling to bits. It was mainly Canterbury stuff, but even there, as you probably know, they lamb on the coast nearly three months earlier than just below the Alps. She allowed me to take an extra carbon of her notes. I did them at home and didn't charge her because I felt that in checking other books, it could be handy. Over there is the amount of typing I've done, that you left for your new secretary. I've corrected each day's stint as I finished it. I know it will all have to be gone over again when finished, and then, I suppose, by you finally.'

He flicked through the stack of manuscript. 'Looks okay to me . . . now the proofs.'

They crossed to the small wheeled table she had them on. He picked up the pad on which she had scrawled some queries. 'What are these two . . . ringed round in red? Looks ominous. Have they transposed pages or something?'

Valancy hesitated—and wished she'd not had to sound so irritatingly efficient about all she'd accomplished, then she took herself to task. After all, you wanted to impress him, didn't you? she told herself.

She said unhappily, 'Er—no. Not their mistake. That's very easy to do. You'd have picked it up yourself if you'd been doing them first. I mean, it's easy, I imagine, in the throes of actually producing a story not to realise. You've—you've——'

He said impatiently, 'Come on, what did I do? I don't think myself infallible. Did I give a minor character on one page blue eyes, and forty on, endowed him with brown? Though I do note all descriptions.'

She swallowed. 'You've got two full moons in the one month.'

He stared. Consternation sat heavily upon him. 'Lordy . . . how stupid! And I never picked it up.' All of a sudden, to her great relief, he burst out laughing. 'Looks as if the editors at the firm missed it too . . . which is unusual for them. But you can bet your boots dozens of readers would have noticed it. Blinking nuisance, though. If I've made too much of the second full moon, it could mean alterations that would make a shambles of several paragraphs, and that would upset any printer. I loathe trying to fit pars of the same length in, getting it down to the corresponding printers' spaces and measurements.'

Valancy took a page from the bottom of the pile. 'I did this, sir. I didn't replace that page with this idea of mine, because it's an awful cheek, a mere typist thinking she can re-write an author's work . . . we always walked warily over that, at Andersons, but I had time, you see, and though you may wish to do your own version of it, naturally, it may be near enough to give you a few short-cuts. I started with the hero saying "We may lack a moon tonight, but it has its advantages ... you can't object to my guiding you over this rough terrain." That was exactly the size of the sentence you'd started with ... in bright moonlight. And I doctored the rest of the dialogue to fit, yet be suitable for the absence of that moon. That's the bit I thought I had a nerve in doing ... but if it only gives you an idea for the size of it, it may save time. And I felt so *au fait* with your characters, I dared do it.'

He took a sharp look at her, pulled out a chair, sat down, scrutinised it thoroughly, and the page before and after, then looked up and nodded. 'I couldn't improve on that. Decidedly clever.' He stapled it to the proof sheet and made notes on the margin.

She turned the proof pages, leaning over him. 'Here you are bringing in characters from a former book. This one, Erik Rasmussen, you said had been named for his uncle, the Conrad Rasmussen of your second book. But in that book you had Conrad as not having a single living relation other than his married sister in Denmark. So her son couldn't possibly have been a Rasmussen.'

This time Godfrey Carmichael clutched his forehead and looked really rattled. 'I must be going out of my tiny mind! I did have a distracting time about then, but I feel that's unforgivable.'

His new secretary said coolly, 'I've known far worse mistakes than that, and don't they say that even Homer nodded? And that mistake could easily remain undetected. Not in the same book.'

He scowled at the page, then swung round on her. 'How come *you* twigged it? You said you'd never read a book of mine, much less heard of me!'

Valancy sat down in the basket chair beside the table and crossed one elegant leg over the other. 'I hadn't when I applied for the job. But naturally, faced with those books on your shelf, I read the lot. First I read the pile of manuscript of the current book before I went on typing it, to make sure I was familiar enough with the story to detect errors as I continued. Then—but no, I'll leave it at that.'

'You won't, you know. Finish what you were going to say.'

The blue eyes sparked. 'I didn't care for the way you told me not to tell you I adored your books, that it wasn't necessary in a secretary. So if I told you I found them compulsive reading once I started, you'd think me insincere. But I *never* toady to people.'

They measured glances. 'My tone was merely because of bitter experience,' he explained. 'My former secretary gushed over them and they just weren't her type of reading. Makes one wary.'

Her eyes were still hostile. 'Don't you ever take people as you find them? If you're going to regard all my sex as tarred with Carlotta's brush, you're going to have a miserable existence. How very *un*discriminating of you! I'd have thought an author wouldn't have been like that at all. Better watch it . . . that cynical streak might show up in your books, and thus far your women have been very likeable.

'If you're going to get all cagey about the female sex, you'll lose fifty per cent of your readers. I'm told your books are sought after by both in an unusual way. *I've* met up with some twerps of men. Indeed, it could be said that one man let me down very badly, but *I* don't lump all the male sex as the same. If I hadn't liked your books I'd have said they weren't my cup of tea, but that wouldn't have meant they weren't any good. Now what are you grinning at?'

The brown cheeks that were in such contrast to his fair, sun-bleached hair creased into lines even deeper. 'You amuse me, that's all. To hear you talk so bluntly to me, nobody would think you wanted this job despite all you'd done in my absence to convince me you're invaluable.'

She said clearly and distinctly, 'But I find I *don't* want the job. With a slant like yours on the subject of female employees, I wouldn't touch it with a bargepole. I'll see you through this transition period, that's all. You'd better re-advertise, Mr Carmichael, and to get round the no-discrimination handicap, you would be wise to state full names are required and pray to heaven no man gets turned down because he happens to have one of those names that are for either sex, like Beverley, Jocelyn, Hilary or Evelyn. There are more pitfalls than just faint hyphens and aunts who don't always wear their spectacles, believe me!'

He stood up and seized her wrist. 'You gave up a good job to take this on, didn't you? When my aunt rang me she said the applicant was still working at Andersons.'

'Yes. What——'

'Then isn't it important to try to hang on to this one?'

'Not at such a cost. I'd find it a strain working with you, Mr Carmichael. When I got such a setback on my arrival here, from both Rachel and your aunt, I made up my mind you wouldn't want to make my appointment permanent. Okay. I'm not crawling to anyone for a job, I'll find another.'

'Then what you've done over and above the call of duty wasn't a desperate attempt to convince me you were too valuable to lose?' To her annoyance he grinned again and said, 'And don't look down that very charming nose of yours in such a disdainful manner! I find it unnerving.'

'I *do* feel disdainful, and see no reason to hide my feelings. I was engaged to do a job, so I did it. I got interested enough in it to feel it must be done well. It was a challenge to have it all ready for you on your return, but I certainly don't feel obliged to work permanently for anyone as prejudiced and warped as you are. Get your advert in as soon as possible. It may take a month or two, especially with Christmas not so very far away, and the New Year summer holidays taking most of January. When the new man comes I'll bow out a day or two before his arrival.'

'Like hell you will,' said Godfrey Carmichael. 'You may not find it easy to get another job. Times aren't so good.'

'But my qualifications are,' she pointed out.

He banged with his fist on the proofs. 'I think you've just got your dander up. You're as prejudiced as I am in your own way. Do you think you can just walk back into your former job?'

He saw her instant recoil. 'No, I can't do that.' Her voice was harsh.

'Any particular reason?'

'Yes. Particular and personal. I wanted to cut away from the only job I've had since schooldays, because to remain, owing to a staff transfer from our Wellington office, would be embarrassing, or maybe even dangerous.'

The grey eyes went keen. 'The twerp who let you down?'

'Oh, *he* wasn't a twerp. Let's say the *man* who let me down. But he couldn't help it, I suppose. He found someone else and had the courage to admit it. Much better than a broken marriage. But I couldn't go on working beside him as we'd always done.'

The angular fair face softened incredibly. His voice changed. 'Haven't had much luck in the men you've worked with, have you? Don't develop a hang-up like mine. I went sour on it. I think we've cleared the decks. Perhaps we've got a chance to develop a working partnership irrespective of male or female. You know what I mean . . . as sexless as worker-bees. Just workers, producing books, not honey. Will you give it a go?'

For some reason—security, she supposed, she knew an immense relief. 'I'll give it a go,' she said.

She had to credit him with a fine power of concentration. He'd had a flight of several hours from Toronto to Los Angeles, five to Honolulu, she recalled, and about eight to Auckland where he'd arrived early this morning, then had two domestic flights within New Zealand to reach Dunedin Airport, where a friend, farming nearby on the Taieri, had garaged his car during his absence. It was surely an endurance test. Now he was tackling a job demanding a real quality of application, without much moaning.

To her tentative, 'Won't you need to catch up on some sleep first?' he had said curtly, 'I slept well on each leg of the journey. I don't believe in letting strange surroundings interfere with the rations of sleep one needs.'

She resisted the temptation to say, 'How nice to be you and able to command sleep like that,' and contented herself with a nonchalant 'Jolly good,' and said, 'then I'll go into my sitting-room and continue with this cross-referencing. That will mean I'm handy if you need to query any corrections I've made, yet not be disturbing.'

The thick brows that were only a little darker than the smooth fair hair above them came down. He said suavely, 'You won't disturb me in the least.'

Valancy got the point. Not even the fact she was a woman. He preferred a man, but she was simply a cog in the machine. Well, that suited her. She removed herself to a table near the files. She rather expected him to be a bit sticky over some of her corrections, but he wasn't; he didn't even grunt over them. Two hours of solid work passed, then Aunt Helen gently turned the door-knob and peered in. 'Dinner will be ready in ten minutes, but it can stand waiting if it's an awkward time.'

My word, Valancy thought, he had her well trained! He looked up, smiled and said, 'Thanks, but this is a good breaking-off point for me. We've worked long enough. Come on, Miss Adam-Smith.'

She rose, said, 'You can leave off the Adam if you like. We have to use it for signatures and so on, but brevity saves time: I've no objection to Smith on its own.'

He drawled, 'I've an idea I'll never be able to think of you as anything else but Adam-hyphen-Smith, I'm afraid.'

His Aunt Helen said, 'You're being very childish, Godfrey.'

He grinned, 'Nothing like an aunt for cutting one down to size!'

Valancy unbent a little and grinned back. 'Don't I know it! My Aunt Cecilia, the one I told you brought me the advert, is an expert at shrinking egos. We were never allowed to get above ourselves. Spending so many holidays up at Rimu Bush was very good for us. It was never a case of the older generation spoiling the children. Unless we were sick, then she positively coddled us.'

Godfrey sounded quite human. 'Sounds like a twin soul to Aunt Helen. It just could be that if you were brought up that way, you might suit this set-up.'

Aunt Helen had scurried away. Perhaps she was afraid something would burn. Despite this more homely touch Valancy couldn't resist it; she said, 'That decision isn't yours alone. It might not suit *me*.'

He made no reply.

She had a sense of unreality all through the meal. It was so ordinary. She might have been a welcome guest in the company of friends. Rachel had come over to help the older woman with the dinner and dished potatoes and vegetables with an air of great importance. Godfrey laid two packages beside her plate. 'Pity to wait till we've finished for you to open these. One's personal, one for your room.'

'Oh, I love things for my room. I'm doing it up like a bedsitter, or a bed-study. Can you have bed-studies, Godfrey?'

'I should think so. I like that. Does it mean you're planning to do more homework? It wouldn't hurt you.'

She gave him an impish grin. 'Always a moral . . . but yes, I think at last I've got motivated. And Valancy has suggested I get Dad to put a bolt on the inside of my door, like you have on your bedroom door, Godfrey.'

Valancy felt her colour rise and said hastily, 'I didn't suggest a bolt like his, Rachel. I suggested a bolt—full stop. *You* were the one who who said you wondered why you'd not thought of it when you saw Mr Carmichael putting his bolt on.'

Rachel, fingers busily unwrapping, said, 'Well, what's the difference? Oh, Godfrey, Godfrey, you *are* a darling!'

She brought into view some maple leaves cunningly preserved and set in what looked like alabaster but was, no doubt, some composition. It was a long panel for her bedroom wall. The small packet contained a pendant of maple leaves rimmed with gilt.

When they had finished their coffee Rachel said, 'You'll have to work on, I suppose, Godfrey?'

Unexpectedly he answered, 'No ... I'm going to rise early tomorrow to go on with it. Enough is enough. What I really need is some complete relaxation. After we've seen the news, we'll go on with the chess lessons, Rachel, we've got some leeway to make up.'

Valancy couldn't hide her surprise. He still had that drawl in his voice that made her want to take him up sharply. 'In your endeavour to impress me with your efficiency,' he told her, 'I'm finding it the easiest proofing I've ever done. A short good sleep tonight and I'll rise up like a giant refreshed and finish it tomorrow.'

She didn't reply.

It became a homely scene, Aunt Helen in her chair rocking and knitting, the huge fireplace filled with leaping flame from the quaint terra-cotta coloured logs of hundreds of years ago that were brought out from the dense bush that clothed the cliffs by the sea-shore. Valancy, reading at the other side of the hearth, found herself getting sleepy. It had been a long day with physical effort and plenty of fresh air on that roof, and also a disturbing one. She was feeling the reaction. She would find it humiliating to be the one to doze off.

She got up, went into the little sewing-room beyond the kitchen, came back with a huge darning basket swung on a wooden frame to stand beside her chair, took out wools and scissors.

She slipped a darning-egg into a huge pair of Norsewood farm socks and began weaving wool in and out of a non-existent heel. Godfrey looked up. 'Good heavens, there's no need whatever to darn my socks too ... that isn't what secretaries are for!'

She looked at him levelly. 'They aren't *your* socks. I'm not making a further bid for popularity, if that's what you mean. These are Bill's and Rod's. I was horrified when I found they were wearing two pairs of socks under their gumboots. They were most cheerful about it, said the holes rarely came in the same places, but I felt this was something I could do. I'm the most hopeless knitter, but my Aunt Cecilia saw to it that I could darn. I reckoned she used to save up all the holey socks at Rimu Hill for the holidays.'

'Crumbs,' said Rachel, 'I'm glad I haven't got an aunt like that. I loathe mending of any description.'

'I like it. I find it soothing.'

'Why are you a hopeless knitter, Valancy?' This was Aunt Helen.

'Too temperamental. The tension varies with my mood. One stretch of knitting will be so tight it doesn't give at all, the next is baggy.'

She caught a faint look of surprise on her employer's face. 'What an admission! I thought you were far too disciplined to admit to moods.' Then, 'Rachel, you're letting your attention wander. Look what you've let me do.'

Rachel was staying the night in the small room that was regarded as hers here. She went off to bed dutifully at nine. Godfrey drew up another chair, dead-centre to the fire, picked up a book, was lost in it for not more than a quarter of an hour, then suddenly it slipped against one of the arms, his head fell sideways against the high-backed wing, and the long journeying took its toll of him.

'The dear boy,' said his great-aunt fondly. Dear boy indeed! thought Valancy Adam-Smith.

She heard Godfrey moving in the study at five-thirty next morning and an unwilling admiration stirred in her. He was a demon for work! She should match him. He's said yesterday that having her at hand helped. She'd show him she didn't mind unorthodox or early and late hours. An author couldn't always work from nine till five.

She donned dun-coloured trews, with a cream polo-necked sweater, slipped her feet into lambswool slippers. The morning, though it was late spring, was decidedly nippy. No make-up ... that would look stupid this hour of the day. He might like coffee. She'd ask.

Silently, because of the slippers, she padded through

her sitting-room. Also silently, because the lock was well oiled, she turned the key, but surprisingly the door didn't open. Like a flash she realised that this too must have a bolt on the inside like his bedroom door from the upper room.

With even more care to remain silent, Valancy went back to her kitchen, made herself coffee, and, thoroughly awake now, put a match to the kitchen range, and settled at that table to write letters. A very long one to her parents, one to her sister in North Canterbury, one to Mr Anderson.

At a quarter to eight she heard a loud knock on her sitting-room door. He must suppose she was still sleeping. He looked surprised when she opened it so promptly, looked so wide awake, was fully dressed.

'Aunt Helen has breakfast ready,' he told her. 'Rod and Bill had theirs earlier. They're off today. Don't you have a sleep-in Sundays?'

'Sometimes. I woke at five, decided I'd had all the sleep I needed, so thought I'd write to the family and my former boss. Then I'd be at your elbow the rest of the day if needed.'

'I've done a couple of hours and more on the proofs. I've got three or four queries re the corrections, but they all seem to be the ones you'd doubted too, because you did those in pencil. Thanks.' He looked at her keenly. 'What did you find to write about? Aunt Helen vows you've not been off the place since you came. It might sound a dull existence for a girl your age, to your parents.'

'I'm no fledgling. I'm twenty-five, It might be dull to a teenager. Life in the country is never boring. I've found great variety here—secretarial work which I enjoy, my own quarters, a little farm work when I'm allowed, and beautiful surroundings apart from that scene of devastation in front of the house.'

Valancy took a surreptitious look to see how he'd taken that, but he merely nodded. 'Then you've been down to the sea?'

'No, merely back to the bridge and along both river banks. I've not had time for more.'

'Surely Aunt Helen didn't give you that impression?'

She said drily, 'Seeing I was expected to be a man, I felt that only a lot achieved beyond the bounds of duty would be any recommendation. Oh, I'll take my days off now, it would be daft otherwise. I'm no extremist. Just because, in the space of a very short time, my whole world turned tapsalteerie and I decided to cut and run, then found I'd been engaged under false pretences, it doesn't mean I've lost my common sense.'

Author-like he seized on a word little used. 'Tapsalteerie?' That's very much a Scots word. Was your mother Scots?'

'No, my father. At least of Scots descent. What made you think it had to be my mother?'

'Your father's name.'

She laughed mischievously and naturally. 'Both barrels of his name are Scots, Godfrey Carmichael. The Adam brothers, the famous architects and interior designers, were Scots, of course.' She waited, an expectant twinkle in her eye. They were halfway along the verandah by this time.

He rose to the bait. 'But the Smith?'

She giggled. 'Tell me, do you ever listen to that quiz programme *Ask Me Another*?'

He nodded. 'Always, if I'm home.'

'Well, perhaps you were in Canada when this came on. A contestant was asked what was the most common name in Scotland. She had three stabs. Macdonald, MacLeod, Stuart. *The answer was Smith!*'

He roared. 'One up to you, Miss Adam-Smith! I can see you're going to be an acquisition. Any more tags of information tucked away in that brain of yours?'

She said, quite seriously, 'I don't know. Have you ever thought we all have grains of knowledge buried deep that we don't know we know, and it takes a bit of mining by someone else to dig them out. Do you follow me, or do I sound woolly-headed?'

'I follow. An interesting thought. I think you come across that in whodunits—the person in danger because of what they don't know they know.'

They came into the kitchen still talking about it.

Aunt Helen felt reassured. The hostility and distrust were disappearing. She put bacon and eggs before them, and toast, and sat down with another cup of tea herself.

'Can you give me any instances, Valancy?' he continued, and her given name sounded natural on his tongue.

'Well, like just now. You recognised tapsalteerie as a Scots word. I didn't know it was because as a family we've always used it. Mother had Welsh parents and we all use the lovely word *hiraeth* for nostalgia, homesickness. It sounds more wistful than the others, I think.' She laughed at herself. 'Is that too fanciful? After all, words are only letters of the alphabet strung together. Though I can't help thinking some look more beautiful as well as sound sweeter.'

There was no hostility in the square face now. 'That's something I've always thought myself, subconsciously I suppose, but you've put it into words. Yes, words can be euphonious or harsh. So I guess it's feasible for some words to please the eye with their shape. Does this mean you wouldn't agree with Shakespeare that a rose by any other name would smell as sweet?'

Valancy swallowed a piece of egg, considered it, then said, 'I believe the author of *Anne of Green Gables* once said she was sure it wouldn't if it were called a skunk-cabbage ... hard to know, isn't it?'

He nodded, 'Yes, and we quote these things out of context. I don't suppose Shakespeare really thought that, but his character ... um ... Juliet, wasn't it?—She thought it, because she was so tired of the Capulets hating everyone called Montague and the Montagues hating the Capulets.'

Valancy nodded back. 'Stupid things, feuds.' Then she rushed on, because her relationship with this man had a smack of feuding about it, 'One of our authors said once she was afraid to express any like or dislike in her books. Just because she once had some character saying he preferred savouries to finish a meal with, instead of desserts, a woman who read her books gave everyone else pavlova and served her salmon croquettes!

And she adored pavs.' When the laughter died down, she added, 'I've read that in writing, the sense of smell, described, is the most evocative of all. That it's better to say someone paused by a lilac than by a bush. The reader gets the perfume.

'So I suppose we've associated a rose for so long with its perfume it would be hard to transfer the picture it calls up with skunk-cabbage! Because the word skunk makes most people wrinkle up their noses in disgust ... even here where we've seen them only on films. But some words are so lovely. If you say a leaf has turned reddish-brown, it's a flat description. If you say it's russet, you can see the autumn tinting the trees. If you say the artist mixed red and blue to paint a robe, you have no mental picture of it, but if you say he dabbled his brush in rich purple for the robe, you see a king in all his glory. You can even see the ermine edging without mentioning it.'

Godfrey Carmichael got up, strode to the kitchen dresser, seized his aunt's jotter-pad for grocery memos and started to scribble. 'I must get that down,' he said.

Valancy felt a glow out of all proportion spreading through her. She'd scored! Without trying. Suddenly Aunt Helen choked, spluttered, rose up, pressed a hanky to her lips and muttered, 'Excuse me,' and hurried out of the room.

Godfrey looked at her plate. 'Didn't realise she'd had more toast. She must have choked on a crumb.' He went to the door, called out, 'Aunt, are you all right?'

A muffled, 'Yes, I'll be back soon,' came to him, and some hasty throat-clearing. He wasn't to know his Great-aunt Helen had collapsed on the edge of the bath and was wiping tears of sheer mirth away. If only her old school friend Cecilia were here to see how things were going! How right they had been to bring this about. And no one need ever know about their little plot. When they met, as meet they surely must some day, what exclamations they would make. Say: 'What a coincidence ... fancy Godfrey's great-aunt being at Rangiruru with Valancy's!' Losing touch, not meeting for all those years ... not even knowing each other's

married names! Oh well, the last bit had been true . . .
till a month or two ago.

Now it looked as if Godfrey was going to stop having
such a scunner at women secretaries and in time he'd
forget Carlotta and the mischief she'd made . . . and,
which was more important, he would . . . could forget
Kathleen. If only the latter hadn't had the name of the
early Godfrey's first love. Godfrey might look upon
himself as an author who was too practical by far to be
over-impressionable, but he wasn't. That fact that that
rather sweet and gentle girl had borne that name had
got him middle stump. If this Kathleen had been of the
calibre of the pioneer girl, she'd have believed Carlotta
was lying, not Godfrey. And in the circumstances
Godfrey had no way of disproving it. That was where
men were most vulnerable. Aunt Helen fervently hoped
that Kathleen the Second would meet somebody else
during her stay in England, and return here married.

CHAPTER FOUR

FIVE hours of solid work with a quick break for a light
lunch saw the proofs finished. Godfrey had said that if
they had their usual Sunday midday dinner, they'd both
be somnolent before the task was done. Rachel had
gone off with her family to visit her grandparents and
they had a sense of isolation. The men were away and
there were only three people on the huge river delta.
The house was big and barn-like, in fact two houses in
one; outside were the wide tracts of rich river-silt land,
and there was a certain loneliness in the knowledge that
their far barrier was a wild, unpredictable sea stretching
down to the bottom of the world beyond fearsome
cliffs, and only at the westward point where the big
river became the two rivers was access to the rest of
Otago.

Godfrey, exulting in the freedom a big task
completed brings, brought his aunt in to see the finished

package of proofs ready to go airmail from Badenoch next morning. 'Let's have a cup of tea and a snack, then Valancy Adam-Smith and myself should take to the horses. We need a good gallop and so do they. Bill told me she's very much at home in the saddle but that she's not given herself much time to enjoy it. We'll make for the sea and go round a few of the sheep on the way there and back.'

Colour ran into Valancy's cheeks at the thought. She stretched her arms above her head. 'Splendid! That was close work. Living in Christchurch we were never far from the sea. That was one reason why I found your advert attractive, once I knew where it was. The sea does something for me. Especially if I'm in a restless mood. I loved my aunt's high-country run, of course, but for me there was always something missing. That glimpse of the sea when you climbed a hill. But in town I missed the horses. You can hire one, but it's not the same. Here. . . .'

'Here,' said Aunt Helen, 'you can have the best of both worlds.'

A strange feeling assailed Valancy. It made her drop her eyes. The older woman bustled out to see to her roast. Godfrey Carmichael reached out a hand and tipped up his secretary's chin. 'Got you on a sore spot, didn't it? Aunt Helen wouldn't know, of course, your reason for leaving your job. There's this guy you care for, won't risk working with. This can hardly be the world you'd label best, could it? Without him? Sorry about that. Want to talk about it?'

Suddenly the most inexplicable anger flared within her. She looked up and said fiercely, 'What's this? Looking for copy?'

He stared, then the dull red of masculine anger crept up his brown cheeks. 'Of course it isn't! I've enough imagination, thank you, for a score of books without wanting to probe any woman's feelings, *and* enough experience of my own, come to that. In some things, heartbreak and disillusionment, there's not any difference between male and female. I was let down too. I made an overture of sympathy, fellow-feeling if you like

. . . and you've slapped my face for it, symbolically. Set me back on my heels. Right, Miss Valancy Adam-Smith, back to the business footing. I must be mad! Mad to soften up like this.'

She clapped a hand over her mouth in a child's rueful gesture and said, 'I'm sorry—oh, how sorry I am! That was dreadful of me. It's just that . . . well, I'd got over what happened, had for months. But suddenly with the return of this man to the firm . . . I had to flee. It's cut me off from home too . . . for a while at least. And we've been so close-knit a family. And I was the only one left at home.'

His face, so forbidding and angry a moment ago, gentled in a most unexpected manner. 'Okay, sorry I lashed back. I'd no right. Heaven knows I ought to understand. You're still raw from the wound. But tell me, if you didn't want to leave home why didn't you just get another job in Christchurch?'

She looked away a little, then said slowly, 'Because Justin was always the boy next door. His mother was like another mother to me. When Justin was transferred to Wellington for experience there he met Greer.' She turned back and met the grey eyes steadily. 'Don't mistake me—I don't hate Greer, don't resent her. I admit I envy her. They're very happy, very suited. I wouldn't want Justin to be otherwise. But Hughsie, his mother, took a stroke, lay for some time unconscious, but is steadily fighting her way back, so she was being discharged from hospital. Greer's a nurse, and was still working, to help them buy a home later. She knew there was only one answer. Justin asked to be transferred back, Greer gave up her position and the three of them are living next door. There was also only one thing for me to do. I could so easily fade out of the picture. Only I don't feel like going home for a weekend too soon, in fact not even for Christmas.'

'What a devilish situation!' he commented. 'But your parents can come here to see you. Why not Christmas down here? It's very lovely . . . the rata is out in the bush . . . flings scarlet blossoms all over the other trees.'

She flushed with pleasure. 'That's a very generous

offer, especially seeing I flew at you a moment ago, but
the rest of the family always come home for that, from
the North Island, and Cheviot, and it means a lot to the
grandchildren. They adore Christmas at home. But
thanks. Normally I'm pretty tough. The longer I'll be
away, the easier it will be.'

'Does your father have his holidays in January?'

'Yes. All his men have three weeks then.'

'Then get your parents to come down for ten days. I
mean it.'

'That would be lovely! I had thought of asking them
to come halfway, say Oamaru. But I'm not fond of
hotel life.'

'That's settled, then.' He chuckled. 'Don't look so
surprised! I know that yesterday I seemed an ogre, but
that was only because I'd have preferred a man.'

'I wasn't looking surprised over that. Only that any
man could be so understanding.'

His snort of laughter was unamused. He shrugged.
'Let's be all novelettish and say it's because I too have
loved and lost. I'm still raw myself. That can explain
my seeming . . . what did you call me? . . . a hater of
women. I'm not, just of women secretaries in a situation
like this, where the formality of an office relationship
can so easily slide into too much familiarity. It was my
former employee, one Carlotta, who made trouble
between myself and the woman I loved. I wasn't
believed. Yet if anyone had told me that my girl had
been unfaithful to me I just wouldn't have credited it.
It's as simple as that. I vowed never to put myself in a
position like that again. But do you know what? I no
longer care a damn. My chief goal in life is what it's
been always . . . to own Inchcarmichael and bring it
back to its former grandeur, by sweat and blood and
my pen. Some day it will be mortgage-free and its
beauty restored. Listen, I sound like some pompous
landowner!' he said ruefully. 'Let's get out on the horses
and gallop on the hard sand. The wind and spray will
blow our problems away!'

After being confined to the house area so long Valancy

had a sense of adventure as they cantered along a cart track past the stables, skirted a grassy slope and rode out to the open country beyond. There was a boundary of willows in full spring green where the south stream took its way to the sea. Beyond that were the spreading coastlands and down-like countryside of what they called the mainland.

They bore round to the left, into the centre of the 'island', still following the rutted track. 'The old dray road really,' said Godfrey Carmichael, 'where my great-greats used to come to dig loads of shingle for the road they were forming out to the river-crossing and down to the beach where we still get shingle for the fowl-runs because it's impregnated with crushed shells, so we never buy grit. Occasionally for the fun of it in the school holidays we make it a dray trip to recall the old days, harness up one of the draught-horses and slip back to the leisurely days of last century. Be a bit careful now . . . the track's rough here, the rock crops through. Lots of work to be done here, when we get to the unbelievable stage of being able to spare time for something that doesn't bring in money.'

They were side by side now, on a slope of turf. Valancy glanced at him and her eyes were keen. He interpreted it. 'Sounds pinchpenny, I know, but this is a huge estate that was allowed to go back to ruinous conditions and it costs money—eats money. All we make has to be ploughed back in improvements.'

She felt rebuked. 'Sorry . . . one is so apt to judge the value of a place by its acreage and fertility.'

'Aye. It's got all the potential, but has a greedy mouth. The price of fertilisers, weed control projects by helicopter, crop spraying from the air, labour, upkeep of farm buildings . . . so the house has to wait till the new woolshed is paid for. That was top priority. Anno domini was too much for the old one—dangerous. It's going to be sheer pleasure come December when we do our first shearing. Oh, do excuse the pun!' he grinned.

Her heart lifted. Not such a curmudgeon after all. He was a dedicated man, one with a purpose, bringing back the acres his ancestors had wrested from this wilderness, then lost, into full production again. And for what? No doubt he had dreamed of bringing the woman he loved to this estate, of rearing sons to inherit. What a devilish thing life could be, putting a period to one's dearest dreams! As she herself knew—knew bitterly. No wonder he'd not wanted another woman here in the close intimacy of study work. Perhaps he hoped that some day this girl would come back to him, believe him. But she might find all doubts revived if she found yet another woman installed, another redheaded one. What bad luck! Well, perhaps she could do a short spell of work for this man, get a couple of books on their way, help him to get settled with a male secretary and depart if there was any hint of his love returning, so nothing could shadow their reunion. Valancy saw herself as a healer of breaches, and in a fine imaginative flight, prided herself she'd find great compensation in that.

They crested the hill and she reined in, a cry of delight breaking from her. Towards the north branch of the river dipped and spread the most glorious area of native bush, beech, *totara*, *rimu*, *miro*, and a hundred other trees not identifiable at this distance. It was garlanded with creepers, white-starred native clematis predominant, and dotted with the paler green of tall tree-ferns. It was cool, dewy-sweet and grotto-like. 'Look at it,' she exulted. 'New Zealand as it was before so much of this had to be felled and burned for grazing. A primeval forest in miniature. How magnificent! How wonderful for you to own an enchanted forest.'

Godfrey had brought his mare to a standstill too. He nodded. 'That's the greatest asset on Inchcarmichael.' The satisfaction in tone hit her with a horrible fear. She turned swiftly, 'Mr Carmichael . . . you *wouldn't*, would you? It would be a crime.'

The square jaw set. 'Wouldn't what?'

'Let them mill it? Oh, no . . . whatever needs the estate has, wouldn't justify that!'

Again she saw the dull red of anger in his cheeks. 'How dare you even assume I'd do such a thing! Some of the Southland beeches there are eight hundred years old. Seedlings when the Magna Carta was signed.

Saplings when Edward the First presented the first
Prince of Wales to the people at Caernarvon. What sort
of an arch-vandal do you think I am? This is part of my
heritage. At one time I thought I could never win it
back for the Carmichaels, for my sons and my sons'
sons to farm. This is the reason why I had to buy the
estate before I was in a position to do so ... the reason
why I had to raise too large a mortgage ... to save this
bush, the heart of Inchcarmichael. I just stopped the
milling contract going through.'

Valancy felt her face grow hot. She dropped her eyes
to her gelding's stubbly mane, then made herself look
up and meet that angry look. Her tone was convincing.
'I'm truly sorry. That was an extremely thoughtless and
ill-judged remark.' She paused. She dare not say: 'How
could I dream that the man who sacrificed the trees of
the homestead would feel so deeply about these native
trees?' It must have been sheer necessity that had made
him sacrifice those, to make up the deficiency between
the amount he could raise and what was needed to buy
it. It must have been the lesser of two evils.

He waited for her to say more, his flush dying down.
She said, 'It was the sudden realisation of what a
unique treasure this is, my whole heart cried out for its
preservation. You see, there was a magnificent patch of
bush we played in as children, near my aunt's estate.
Not hers, her neighbour's. It was sacrificed. And that
was unforgivable, because this man didn't need the
money to save an estate as you might have been
tempted to do. He could have set out whole hillsides in
forestry, quick-growing pines, to benefit generations to
come. Instead he lost it in death duties within a few
years, or his heirs lost it.' She looked at him quite
fearlessly. 'But I'd no right to assume you'd ever even
think of allowing a mill to come in here.'

His face cleared instantly. 'Thanks for that apology.
And I think that after all, I'm glad you feel that way.'
He laughed. 'We certainly clash, don't we? Must be too
alike. But at least you hit hard and cleanly. I like that,
I can't stand evasions or subterfuges.'

Her eyes danced. 'I must tell my former boss that.

He'd be most surprised—and pleased.'

'What can you mean? Surely he didn't want his secretary to fight him all the time?'

'Not him. But he thought in other ways I was too acquiescent, and he told me not to be in future.'

'At the risk of being told it's not my business, I find that intriguing,' said Godfrey. 'What could occasion that?'

He saw the clear colour rise. Valancy bit her lip. 'I'm speaking without thinking. He—he meant in my personal life. He thought I bent over backwards to make things easy for Justin and Greer. That wasn't nobility on my part, though. I don't want to sound all smug and forgiving, but I thought there was nothing else to do. Mrs Hughes had to be looked after. It was going to be tough enough on a newly-married couple without a former fiancée complicating things.'

His look was keen, probing. 'I won't think you smug. You've got almost a man's way of looking at things. Already I recognise that. Even though our dealings have been only in a business sense. I quite like the absence of vindictiveness. Even when we are disillusioned about people, we can still be concerned for their happiness, can't we? Oh, take no notice of me, it's the author complex. One wants to dig deeply without realising it. You'll accuse me of copyhunting if I'm not careful!'

She lifted her chin to look up at him. 'I don't think so this time.' She almost added that she felt he spoke out of his own reverse, that he would still desire the best for the woman he loved. But she mustn't. She must remember he didn't really want to be involved personally with a woman in his employ. She said, waving a hand towards the magic of unspoiled forest, 'There's something challenging and mysterious about the New Zealand bush in its density, its sense of not wanting to yield up all its secrets.'

'That's so. I promise you it will never be felled. It's to be a reserve. By the way, there's a taboo. No one is allowed to go there on their own. The undergrowth, in places, in impenetrable, and it hides unexpected gullies and underground streams, with sheer sides, disguised by spongy moss. In an area like this not far from here, long ago, in the fifties, I think, a three-year-old child was lost a day and a night. Fifty people were out all night looking for him. He was found alive by reason of sheer tiredness—he lay down in a wee clearing and slept the night through. His uncle found him at nine next morning. He sat down and wept at the sight of him just waking up. The child rubbed his eyes, sat up, and said, 'Hullo ... did Daddy get the horses yoked up all right?' An older child would have panicked. Even Rachel obeys that taboo. Now, we bear right and come to the shore.'

They went through huge grazing paddocks looking so pastoral it was hard to believe that behind them a primeval forest dreamed of a thousand years, something that made connections with the early whaling stations of this wild coast seem to have happened only yesterday.

They got their first glimpse of the sea, a glittering blue-green that dazzled their eyes from the bright yellow gorse on the headlands to where it met a lavender horizon beneath a serene sky flecked with tiny clouds.

'Before we go down to the shore,' said Godfrey, 'we'll go up that rise, to the south, the highest point on Inchcarmichael. From there you can get a far-off glimpse of the farthest point south in New Zealand. It curves back westward after this. There's Tautuku Bay with Tautuku Peninsula and Long Point where the *Manuka* was wrecked in 1927. There are still people around here who remember helping rescue the passengers from Australia who had to crawl up those cliffs. There was no loss of life. From there the view is to the South Pole.'

He said it exultantly. They dismounted, stared out to sea. The magnitude of the view stilled the words in Valancy's throat. She stood there, braced against the strong sea-wind, in bottle-green trews, with a golden cashmere top outlined against her, chin lifted to the tang of the salt air, eyes searching out headland after headland till the coastline melted into infinity, the shoulder-length copper hair blowing back from her ears. She couldn't know Godfrey's trained eyes were upon her and he was seeing her in the light of a book character ... she had something in her stance of the figurehead of a Norse ship ... he could have a modern-day heroine who was a reincarnation of a Viking forebear of long ago, from Orkney, or Shetland.

She turned, said simply, 'Unforgettable,' and put her foot into the stirrup again. Godfrey led the way down a very easy track to a more sheltered beach at the far side where rocks gave way to hard sand, that made a splendid surface for the horses. 'Well, that's it,' he said, 'you've explored the boundaries of the estate. Tomorrow we'll settle to a steady working routine. I think you'll suit me very well as a secretary.'

That was the way he wanted it. The way she wanted it. A working relationship, as sexless as worker-bees, he'd said. She'd see he got it that way.

By the time ten days or so were over she knew how ruthlessly Godfrey worked himself. She said one day, conscious he'd put in two hours before breakfast, 'Have you got some deadline?'

'Not editorially. A farm deadline. Time, tide and shearing wait for no man.'

Valancy suggested he might like to dictate to her, then leave her to do the entire lot of typing, the first rough copy, then the final one, to save him those long solitary hours when he plugged away up aloft, but he vetoed that sharply. Then he watered down his brusque recoil. 'Some can do it, but not me. The written word, not the spoken word, is my medium. To me the spoken word can be diffuse, woolly. Can you understand? But when it's formed on the typewriter in my first copy, I can blue-pencil it mercilessly, slash out the repetitive stuff, crisp up the dialogue. Besides, till you take it for the final typing, it's all mine, my own creation, to brood upon. A sort of privacy of thought.'

She nodded. 'I can understand. You don't want another person horning in on your thought processes at that juncture. It has to be all yours.'

He nodded. 'You've got the idea. He looked down on the page he'd been going over. 'Although I'm not altogether sure if that's true now.'

'What do you mean?'

He was at the long table with her, where they worked side by side occasionally checking things. It had room for many reference books. He was very close to her and his grey eyes stared down into her blue ones. 'This particular chapter has a lot of you in it.' His tone seemed meaningful, deliberate.

She kept her look purposely vague. A warning signal had sounded for her. She shrugged. 'I think you mean because I said here that you could bring in an allusion to the age of the young Queen Victoria to fix in your readers' minds, the year your MacClymonts came to South Otago. Just a little fact, not inspiration.'

He shook his head. 'I don't mean that, and I think you know it. My heroine has become more spunky ... less *acquiescent*. And the age of the Queen has nothing to do with my Catriona's sudden surge of guts. She was—in my very first draft—a gentle little thing with acorn-coloured hair and soft brown eyes, a product of her times, a mere echo of her husband with about as much animation as a straw-stuffed scarecrow! Then one night you began telling Aunt Helen about your Aunt Cecilia's forebear who followed her man to the Alps. You gave three anecdotes ... lordy, but she was a spitfire! My heroine sprang to life in these pages, not demure and complacent but full of deviltry. In fact, she developed a tongue like yours. I'll never forget how you raked me down when we first met. No hopeful employee about you there, wishing to please ... so she acquired red hair and blue eyes with tawny lashes and brows...'

His fingers came to her chin, turned it up so he could tabulate her features one by one, '... and a nose almost classical, but saved from the tedium of perfection by a funny little irregularity at the end ... a very expressive mouth, a sprinkle of freckles under your eyes, and slightly crooked teeth that for some reason soften your severest strictures. I almost turned that book in, you know, back in July, because I was bored with the first Catriona.'

Suddenly Valancy realised she was acutely conscious of his nearness, the cool feel of his fingers under her chin, the stir of his breath against her cheeks. He was close, too close to maintain this worker-bee status.

She said irritably, 'Stop dissecting me. I feel I'm under a microscope. And it would look very odd if someone came in. Oh, heavens, someone *is* coming!'

She sprang up, and the next moment Bill Watson tapped and came in, bearing mail. 'I was across the bridge and got the mail. By the look of it, we won't be getting much help come shearing. Looks to me like a lot of fan-mail and something from your publisher.' He chuckled, put it down on the table and departed.

Valancy said, 'I'll open this at my desk. You'll want to go on with what you're busy on.'

His hand came out. 'No, you won't. Sit down again, we'll go through it together.'

'Secretaries are supposed to save their bosses a lot of time opening and sorting mail. I——'

'And bosses, as I told you once, call the tune. Sit down, Miss Adam-hyphen-Smith!'

Valancy sat, sorted through with practised speed, flicking them into piles. There was a lot of farm mail. She put the publisher's letter in front of him. 'Priority . . . you'd like to open that.'

Godfrey drew out a one-page letter and uttered an exclamation that she could only take for delight or achievement. 'He's sold my book for magazine serial rights prior to publication . . . they pay on acceptance, the mail transfer is on its way to the bank. This isn't committed to anything . . . it's a bonus . . .'

He pulled her to her feet, whirled her round and round. She had to laugh. He kept hold of her hands, said exultantly, 'I'll order the bulldozers in right away.'

She tugged him to a stop. 'Bulldozers? To do what?'

'Can't you guess? To clear out those unsightly stumps. Just imagine—a clean sweep. And room to plant all the trees I want and haven't dared order. I had to keep my head above water with the estate costs and mortgage!'

She moistened her lips. 'Now I can forgive you . . . if you *had* to do it . . . yet had a plan to replant. I realise how necessary it was.'

He stared, mystified. 'Had to do it? Had to do what? And what am I being forgiven for?'

'For cutting down the trees in the first place, I felt you could have done less on the estate and kept all those oaks and chestnuts and gums. But when I realised you'd had to raise money to buy Inchcarmichael before the owner cut into the forest, I understood, a little. But if you'd already planned this . . . what are you looking like that for, Godfrey?' she asked curiously.

'Like what?'

'Explosive. Like thunder. As if you'd like to thump me.'

'I *would* like to thump you. You *couldn't* have believed *I* was the one who slaughtered those trees? Surely you've not worked here with me these weeks sharing my thoughts—on paper—in a very real way and thought *that* about me?'

She said falteringly, 'But—but those stumps look recently hacked down. They're still oozing. I thought only you could have.'

He was really scowling. 'Recent? Well, not as recent as that. Tree scars heal slowly. They stay bright a long time. It was less than two years ago. My predecessor was a shocking manager. Actually, he liked the horses too much—racing, I mean. He thought no one would ever take the place off his hands, so he tried to do something to pay his debts and timber was the only asset here by then. I heard that as soon as that was done, the mill was to go into Carmichael's Bush. I still wake up from nightmares in which I dream I'm too late to save it. How could you think that of me?'

She bit her lip in real distress. 'Godfrey, I've hurt you terribly. It's horrible to be misjudged. I'm sorry, I think it must have been because I dreaded your coming back so much. I knew you were going to be furious I wasn't a man. I pictured you a real ogre, all beetling-browed and scowling, bad-tempered and devilish to work for. I saw you as a woman-hater, a chauvinist, an arch-vandal when it came to trees. I didn't know then what odds you'd had to fight against, how you'd put all your writing money into the estate, what terrific loans you'd had to raise. But since I've come to know that, I've excused you ... felt it had been imperative, to allow you to buy it at all.

'I wanted to stay here so much, I didn't want a city job again, but I was determined not to crawl to you for my job ... I got myself into a tight, tight knot inside, determined to think the worst of you. Oh, dear,' she found she was having to blink back tears, 'I'm getting all emotional! I suppose that's why you'd have preferred a man. I'm sorry, I'll pull myself together ... give me a moment and I'll get back to the status we agreed upon ... a worker-bee state of affairs.'

The cloud of anger disappeared from his face and he gave a great bellow of laughter. His hands tightened over hers and he pulled her to him. He shook his head in mock reproof. 'Oh, Valancy Adam-Smith, you'll be the death of me! Right, I can see how it added up ... let's forget it and just rejoice in this stroke of luck. I've just got to kiss someone, and Aunt Helen isn't here ... you'll do instead!'

His very chuckle was audacious. His mouth came down on hers while she was still too surprised to step back. Valancy was aware of the most conflicting feelings. Nobody had kissed her since Justin had said goodbye to her when he left for Wellington when they were still engaged. She hadn't *wanted* anyone to kiss her. Why then was it that there was magic in this? She suddenly realised she was responding, and pushed him back and said, 'There now ... you've got your moment of wild jubilation over, Mr Carmichael! What's the name of the bulldozer firm? I'll get the number for you.'

He said solemnly, 'I've a vague idea I mightn't have kissed my aunt quite like that.'

She heaved a truly exasperated sigh. 'I had a lot to do with authors before coming down here. I found some of them very temperamental, but at least our interviews were always in the office and in the main my boss was present. And if they were told they'd suddenly gone into best-seller figures, they didn't go mad and kiss me.'

'Sounds pretty tame to me,' said Godfrey Carmichael, and reached for the phone. 'I'll do it myself. This is a bit of luck for me—the timing. I'll probably get them here before the shearers. They may have to be put up here. How would you fancy helping to cook for them? Or do you feel it's not in the contract, even if you don't object to the spot of farm-work?'

'It's entirely over to you. I'd enjoy working with Mrs Armishaw for a change.'

'Tongue like a shrew,' Godfrey remarked to the ceiling as she left the room. 'But I prefer it to cooing like a dove as the fair Carlotta used to do.'

He joined them in the kitchen in ten minutes, where he found Valancy hunting in the bookcase for something while Aunt Helen was mincing up a vast quantity of carrots for soup. He looked less elated than so short a time ago. Valancy asked, 'What's wrong?'

'Can't get them out here for three weeks . . . that'll be in the middle of shearing, blast it.'

Aunt Helen said, 'Get who?'

He looked sharply at Valancy. 'Haven't you told her? I thought that's what you rushed off to do.'

'As if I'd be so mean! I wouldn't steal your thunder on news as exciting as that. Go on, tell her.'

His eyes lit up again. 'Aunt . . . I've sold a serial! Paid on acceptance. The money's on its way; we can start on the removal of the stumps. I thought it might have to wait till the middle of next year. But I can't get the 'dozers in—not a show with either firm. And it's late enough in the year as it is for planting trees, even with our terrific rainfall. What foul luck to miss out by so little!'

Aunt Helen scooped up the orange-bright fragments of carrot, dropped them in her stock-pot, stirred, and said reflectively, 'How about using a more old-fashioned method? This man does it for love of his job and because he's attached to his old monster of an engine.'

Godfrey looked blank. 'What the——'

'You know the man who's the officer in charge of the

forest nurseries at Milton? You've got his book there. In fact Valancy's just hunting for it, that's what reminded me, though I didn't know what she wanted it for. On beautifying farm properties with trees?'

'Yes, but I've already got it worked out, from that book, what I want to plant, what'll give the best shelter, grow fastest, and so on. It's the removal I'm worried about.'

'I'm coming to that. Last week I drove down to Milton to see Kitty and he dropped in, and while we were having a cup of tea he mentioned Hoick Westerby.'

'Hoick Westerby? Hoick? What sort of a name is that?'

'If you wouldn't make so many interruptions I'd get it out. I think it's a North of England word—I'm not sure. A nickname in this case, because he hoicks stumps out of the ground like magic, like pulling teeth. Hoick means to pull out with a jerk. I looked it up in the dictionary. It could take longer than if you got bulldozers in, but quicker in the start. Just two men.'

A frustrated look passed over her nephew's face. 'But what does he do it with? Giant forceps? A sort of super-dentist?'

She cast him a withering look. 'He has a steam-engine. It's eighty-odd years old—came into New Zealand at the turn of the century. One of the machinery museums want it, but Hoick says its usefulness is not yet past, so he won't put it out to grass. He has it in Balclutha, and doesn't take it beyond a certain radius. You're just within it. He was in Owaka with it not long ago.'

'Sounds just the job,' said Godfrey, then he picked his aunt up, hugged her, dropped a kiss on her cheek, said, 'See, Valancy, good news always makes me kiss the ladies!'

Her face flamed as Aunt Helen looked from Godfrey to her and said slyly, 'What a good job your new secretary was female!'

Valancy slapped the book down on the table and said, 'What an anti-climax! I was going to surprise you by producing this book so quickly, to help you choosing your trees.'

He said, 'Never mind, it was a kindly thought. But that devastation has haunted me ever since I was able to buy this back. I had that chap out here within a month of arriving, Valancy, for his advice. I've got the plan he drew me. I'll show it to you when I get hold of this man Westerby. He may have to stay here. I expect he's got to get a good head of steam up before he starts. What fun. Much more exciting than modern front-end loaders with scoops and drags.' He smiled at her. 'Valancy, no more writing today. All hands on getting the secondary growth away from round those stumps. We're well ahead, anyway. I'll revel in enjoying the fruits of my brainwork.'

His aunt said, 'Good idea, you'll need Bill and Rod to get the ivy off from round them.'

Godfrey frowned. 'But that'll come out with the stumps.'

She shook her head. 'He was telling us the toughest job Hoick ever struck was at a country manse where a fifty-year-old macrocarpa hedge had to be pulled out. All went well till they struck a corner where ivy had grown into it. He put in a terrific effort and the big steam-engine lifted its front rollers in the air like a dog begging, and crashed down. He had to pay for repairing the bitumen on the Main South Road. You'll have to loosen the ivy first. Do you two good to be outside,' she added. 'Valancy worked far too hard to prove herself to you, and you've driven yourself to endurance levels the last eighteen months and for long enough before. Certainly you look better than you did nine months ago, but you need to.'

His tone was short. 'That wasn't overwork and you know it, Aunt Helen.'

'Sure I know it, but you've still some way to go. You did too much after it on your lone. I'd like to see you back to your old personality come February.'

'Come February? What's so important about February? What bee have you got in your bonnet now?'

She chuckled, though Valancy could have sworn it

was an effort, as if she was trying to minimise the importance to cover up a slip. 'Just an idea I had. Let it go.'

Fortunately he was so full of the idea of getting the steam-engine out he did let it go. He crossed to the kitchen phone.

He turned from it jubilant. 'He's going to run out to look at it this afternoon. Says the job could take several days and they'd be glad of quarters here. Good job I knew what weight that bridge is allowed. Look, I've got the plan up aloft. I'll get it.'

Valancy couldn't believe it when she saw not only a plan to scale, with the kinds of trees all numbered and with a key to the numbers at the foot, but an extra sketch, large, of the dream homestead garden, done by the man who'd illustrated the book on tree-planting. There was a magnificent shelter-belt of macrocarpas, gums, Douglas firs, spruce, larch, oaks, hawthorns, limes and chestnuts, all kinds of poplars, silver birch, beech.

A wide bed for a herbaceous border followed the curve of the drive and had flowers sketched in, from delphiniums and Canterbury Bells down to pansies and thrift, and in a vast lawn provision for shrubs, rose-beds, plots of annuals, and even a fernery, which Helen had insisted upon, hollowed out like a sunken garden, with rough river-stones winding in and out of it for paths.

Valancy was caught up in the enchantment of it. 'Oh, I can see it so vividly in my mind's eye that I can smell the pungency of the pines and gums, see autumn turning the poplars to living gold, hear the bees among the hollyhocks and rhododendrons ... see those ferns and mosses silver with dew. And you've got thousands of ferns in your own bush.'

Her eyes mirrored the mental pictures. He looked away, said, 'Let's hope that the trees will soften the outlines of this house. It's so uncompromisingly rectangular. The windows stare out like uncaring eyes. Oh, too fanciful, I know, but the second Carmichael married a woman who wanted a grand house, which to her meant size and solidity, not beauty of line and architecture. I don't think there's much we can do to improve it.'

Valancy said slowly, 'I know what you mean. The inside is lovely, those arches and ceilings, but the little annexe I have is far lovelier than the house. Nevertheless'—she stopped dead.

'Go on, don't be tantalising! If you've some idea, let's have it.'

She shook her head. 'It's not for me to suggest anything to do with the house. It's different with the garden, you've already planned it.'

At that moment Aunt Helen disappeared. Godfrey said, 'Why not?'

Her tone was a little reluctant. 'This is your dream for posterity, isn't it? You spoke, down at the shore, of winning it back for the Carmichaels, for your sons, and your sons' sons. That means a wife, and it would be a wife's place to suggest things to soften the outlines, not a secretary's.'

He went across to the window, drummed his fingers on the sill. Then he turned, and said, 'A figure of speech. We say those things. What about you? When you lost Justin did you automatically stop thinking you'd have children some day? Was it as final as that?'

Oddly, it didn't make her wince. She was surprised, though, to hear herself laugh. 'Evidently not, because the other day there was a little boy called Michael in a book I was reading and I found myself thinking "I'd love a wee boy called Michael" and wondered if it's ever possible to preserve that as a name and not have it shortened to Mike.'

He chuckled. 'At school I was always Mike. The kids sort of balked at shortening Godfrey. Much easier to shout "Run for it, Mike!" on the cricket field, than "Run for it, Godfrey!" Look, Miss Adam-Smith, you're sidetracking me,' he added. 'You were about to suggest house improvements.'

'Was I? I thought I'd decided against it.'

'I shall choke it out of you if you don't tell me! Don't be mean. It could have been somebody's prerogative months ago, but not now. She forfeited that when she wouldn't believe me. There ... satisfied? Would your ideas be within my financial bounds?'

'You'd better aim at another serial! Though some of this could be done reasonably. You've got some of Beverley Nichols' books on your shelves. I don't think this one is there: *Merry Hall*. It was a square Georgian house. He thought the windows looked blank. They should have had small-paned windows, not big ones. Oh, I know they've harder to clean, but they give a house such an air. He changed his, and it made all the difference. If you added shutters too it would break the lines. Have them curved at the top.

'Add an arch at one side, with creepers. Not ivy, it's too destructive, but small-leaved Virginia creeper and a wistaria, and then, on the other side, as you could afford it, a conservatory. Does that sound old-fashioned? It's been haunting me. With a slanting roof and double glass doors facing the front with a curved fanlight over them, and another fanlight, also curved, over that slab of a front entrance.'

The eyebrows shot up, the grey eyes gleamed. Godfrey seized a writing pad out of Aunt Helen's kitchen drawer, and a ballpoint, and began to rough in the outline of that house that was too tall for its width. Valancy watched fascinated as it grew beneath his fingers, the curves and trellises she'd dreamed in her own mind. In they went, the small-paned windows, the shutters, the wistaria, the conservatory, the fanlight over the door.

'I'd no idea you could sketch like that,' she said in amazement. 'If you can produce such a likeness in lightning strokes, what would you do if you spent time on it? Look, on that book you plan to write round Inchcarmichael ... the pioneer biography or saga, you ought to do tail-pieces yourself to the chapters.'

She saw the idea take hold, rivet his attention. Then he laughed. 'Valancy Adam-Smith, everything you're saying, the need to sell another serial to soften the lines of this ugly house, suggesting tail-pieces for my own family saga, is designed to keep me at my desk! First things first ... a steam-engine is about to descend upon us ... come on, girl, we've got to tackle that ivy!'

CHAPTER FIVE

REMOVING stubborn ivy from round three stumps was back-breaking work, but Rachel joined them after school, and her father carted all the debris away to the tip on the farm.

Hoick was as good as his word and had driven out to assess the job. Hoick sounded a rough bushman, so they were surprised to have him arrive in a Daimler, immaculately dressed in an outfit that suited the antiquity of his equipment, navy blue trousers and jacket, with white piping, and a peaked cap sat jauntily on his crisp grey curls, very much captain of his ship. He was as enthusiastic as they were. 'The weather forecast's good. We'll be out day after tomorrow. Should get it through in three days.'

Valancy said, 'Show him the plan, Godfrey. How about coming in to have some tea, Mr Westerby? Seeing you know the forestry adviser, you'd be interested.'

They all went up to the house and Hoick was gratified when they accepted some suggestions that hadn't occurred to them. Valancy was glad the men had gone back to their work and taken Rachel when they saw him off. Hoick said, 'I'll give you a discount on this. When I heard you'd taken it on, an author-bloke, I thought you must be mad but have a heart of gold. My grandfather remembered this when it was a showplace under the old Carmichaels. He told me when I was a nipper. If he knew, he'd like to think I had a hand in restoring it. I'm told you're doing all right with the farming too. How come?'

Godfrey grinned. 'I was a high-country shepherd with a scribbling knack. Worked for years on Dragonshill in the Mackenzie country. Know it? Beyond Lake Tekapo.'

Hoick stared. 'And I thought authors were soft people in a sedentary job! They don't come any harder than

80

Dragonshill. I went to a field day up there once, before the river was bridged. Were you up there before that?'

Godfrey nodded. 'Went up there when I was nineteen—had a hut of my own, and long nights to write in. Only farming articles then, but always with a purpose, buying this back.'

Valancy said, 'And he still does a dual job ... managing the estate, overseeing his men, working long hours at his desk.'

Hoick tipped the peaked cap at her. 'Well, my dear, with a wife like you at his side, in both capacities, he'll be able to restore Inchcarmichael to what it was, that's for sure.' The engine sprang to life and he was away before they could correct him.

Valancy felt swept by a strange feeling. She gave a weak laugh, picked up a long strand of ivy, flung it on one of the heaps and said, 'Let's hope he doesn't spread that abroad—it could be embarrassing.'

Godfrey didn't answer. When she turned he was striding to the others.

They worked on in the long twilight, had a late meal, and by the time they washed up, they had but one thought in their minds—bed. 'But no matter how late I am I always read,' said Valancy. 'I've just finished that last James Herriot book. I got so into the spirit of it I didn't know if I was in the Yorkshire Dales or the Inchcarmichael Delta. I must get myself something.'

Godfrey hesitated, then said, 'Would you—no, it would seem too much like work.'

'What would?'

'No, I was daft even to think of it. You can read it in office hours some time. Otherwise you'll find this job too demanding.'

'Please tell me,' she begged. 'I'm intrigued.'

'Just that you mentioned I might do some tail-pieces for the story of Inchcarmichael. I've got a fair bit of it roughed out. Very bitsy as it was sandwiched in between other books I was writing urgently to provide money for this. I was going to suggest you start browsing through it, but——'

She was starry-eyed. 'You give it to me right away! I can't think of a lovelier end to a very exciting and satisfying day. I must take after Dad. He's a builder, as I've probably told you. Anything to do with planning a house thrills me. I'll probably fall asleep over it, I admit, but at least I can start it. I'm like James ... licking my chops at the very thought of the chicken liver to come. Isn't that an elegant simile for a trained secretary to produce?'

The three of them laughed. 'If you're sure,' he said.

'Where is it? In the study?'

'No. On my bedside table. I was looking it over last night. I thought I'd get on to it again when I—when we—finish the current novel. Come on up. You can go through the sanctum from my bedroom into your quarters.'

Valancy caught a look of surprise on Aunt Helen's face. She came upstairs with them to her own room. Godfrey left his door open, crossed to the bedside table, from which he took a springback folder, and put it into her hands. 'I'll come through with you and put the light on for the little staircase.'

As she went through the door in his wall that led into the sanctum, her eyes were drawn to the bolts, top and bottom, that could fasten it against all intruders from the study ... or the secretary's quarters.

He caught the look, grasped her arm and said, 'You're looking at the bolts and wondering why.'

She said defensively, 'Look, it's nothing to do with me. They caught my eye, that's all. I don't have to know all the history of the house. All homes as old as this have secrets.'

'You're going to know this one, because I've nothing to hide and nothing, now, to lose.' She thought his tone was bitter.

'You don't have to, but you're a thrawn man in many ways, as my Scots grannie used to say. If you've made up your mind to tell me, I don't think I could stop you.'

His lips twitched. He was very close to her. He said, 'I run the risk of you thinking me vain, even a bit of a cad to give a woman away. It was to keep Carlotta out.'

He saw the blue eyes widen. 'But the harm had been done by then. Unknown to me she'd been dropping sly hints in a certain quarter. One day the girl I was hoping to marry drove out when I wasn't here. Carlotta saw her coming, took her up this way into the sanctum, on some pretext or other. Oh, she'd do it very cleverly. She was extremely devious, had a flair for that sort of thing. But before she'd gone down to bring her up, she'd draped some of her things over that basket chair—pantie-hose, a bra. She made a play of trying to hide them, then trotted out a feeble excuse of having brought her washing up that way, and heard someone arriving. Did it all looking guilty, I expect.

'That put the cat among the pigeons! Carlotta stuck to her story in front of me, that it was washing, I lost my block and accused Carlotta of doing it deliberately and very ungallantly said she'd already tried to get into my room but I wasn't having any. I never really credited that I wouldn't be believed, eventually. A man's so helpless in the face of an accusation like that.'

Something hot, that was resentment on his behalf, flared up inside Valancy. She could have slain not only Carlotta but this unknown girl who had had Godfrey's love yet not had trust in him.

The next moment the heat had ebbed and a strange icy hand seemed to squeeze her heart because he looked so bleak. She swallowed, 'Where is she now, this girl? Isn't it possible that as time goes on all she knows of you will add up to believing you after all? I mean, she's read your books, too, and they don't add up to someone who'd deceive. And she knew that your innate honesty wouldn't even allow you to change your book that was to be filmed, because you felt the change was too radical to be true to your characters. Oh, she's bound to realise it was a put-up job. She'll miss you, want you, come back.'

'Not now. She's in England, has been for months,' he shrugged.

'I don't know what to say, but at least I know what it's like.'

His fingers were still about her arm. She'd never seen a look like that on his square, ridgy features before—a tender look. 'You've already said the right thing. That as time goes on all she knew of me will add up to belief. That means out of the little *you* know of me, you don't believe it. It's enough. Valancy, she wouldn't even believe what Aunt Helen had to tell her.'

Valancy checked her question. She mustn't ask. He saw the look and said, 'You want to know how Aunt Helen could possibly defend me? Fair enough. Your curiosity is whetted, naturally. Three nights before this happened, Carlotta came up through the study and sanctum into my bedroom. Corny situation! I woke, snapped the light on. It's two-way, so she switched it off on that wall. I won't go into details. I jumped out of bed on the opposite side, opened the door into the passage and called out, "Aunt Helen . . . come and help, Carlotta's sleep-walking!"'

Valancy stared for a moment, then she collapsed into laughter, loud laughter. She said, 'Oh, Godfrey, please forgive me, but what an inspiration! How extremely clever. I'm proud of you!'

Godfrey didn't join in immediately, then, irresistibly, he did. 'Thanks, Valancy. That's the first time I've been able to see the funny side of this business. It puts it into a truer perspective.'

He took her through the little sanctum, put the light on above the mini-stairs and gestured her down. She said, on an impulse, 'Will you do something for me?'

'Yes, surely. What?'

'Come down to the door that leads from the study into my sitting-room and bolt that too. I can see now why you wanted a male secretary. Sorry I messed that up for you, all over that silly hyphen. But if those bolts are *always* shot at night, then when this girl returns, there'll be no chance of further mischief being made because of me.'

He came down, opened the door, put her light on, and, surprisingly, took her hand. He said, with utmost compassion, 'Your Justin must have been an utter fool to let you go for someone else,' then he bent his head, brushed his lips across the tips of her fingers in a most unexpected gesture, let her hand go, closed the door, shot home the bolt.

As she heard his steps retreating she leaned against the back of the door, and found slow tears falling down her cheeks. Why? Not because he'd mentioned Justin *but because Justin didn't matter any more.*

An hour later, as Valancy sat reading avidly, it was impossible to believe that she had been dog-tired when they'd come in. She wasn't going to sleep anyway, she was too disturbed, too aware of chaotic feelings.

Now she was one with Godfrey's history of the pioneer Carmichaels. The first pair, though they faced incredible odds, Archibald, and Effie, had known true love, an unfailing companionship, and a marriage that had lasted nearly sixty years. Their son, Godfrey, had known bitter anguish in his adulthood. His present-day descendant had a telling pen, and Valancy again felt tears running down her cheeks, but for an old sorrow and a betrayed love of nearly a century ago.

Effie and Archibald had taken a little girl into their home, Kathleen, who had been orphaned in tragic circumstances. When she was grown, Godfrey had fallen in love with her, desired nothing more than to make her his bride and keep her in this very cottage where Valancy now had her quarters.

Till someone had made mischief, had told Kathleen that the story of her adoption had been one made up to hide Godfrey's father's lapse. That Kathleen was Archibald's child, fathered on a young woman of the district who had gone away, leaving the baby in his care. That Effie had made the best of things, and brought the child up. Godfrey, said the mischief-maker, was her half-brother.

Kathleen wouldn't disillusion him about his father. No good could come of telling him. She had laid her plans, pretended she felt she'd made a mistake in betrothing herself to the man she had grown up with, that she needed to get away, to make a new life for herself. That she had mistaken affection for love. She had gone right up to Auckland, a terrific voyage by sea in those days. Valancy made a moan of protest when she discovered that Godfrey had been caught on the rebound by the mischief-maker. The worst of it was that this was fact, not fiction. Unalterable.

It was Agatha who had had the grand ideas, who had craved this four-square house, made it a place of disharmony, a house-proud, vain woman whose sole ambition, it seemed, was to create a social position in the community that she never achieved. At this stage Valancy felt quite dismayed. She didn't want the present-day Godfrey to be the descendant of a woman like that, iron-hard, shrewd, a liar.

She turned a page and was relieved. Agatha Carmichael had died at thirty-eight, unloved, unregretted. Long before that she had talked in her sleep and given herself away, had been questioned by Godfrey and admitted it.

Kathleen had never married. Just five years after Godfrey had married Agatha she had found out the truth, when she met someone who had been her parents' neighbour when they had lived on the Taieri Plain, and who had rescued their little daughter when her parents had been swept away when the Taieri River had had one of its disastrous floods. The story Kathleen had believed a fabrication had been true. The neighbour showed her the account of the baby's rescue in the *Otago Witness* of the day.

Effie Carmichael had just lost a little girl, had been distraught with grief till the orphaned baby had been brought to her.

A year after Kathleen had been told of Agatha's death, she had made up her mind to take a coastal steamer to her old home, hardly daring to hope Godfrey might have retained any of his old feeling for her. She didn't think she could tell him of his wife's treachery, but the burdensome silence hadn't been necessary ... the day before she was to take ship for Port Chalmers, Godfrey had arrived in Auckland.

Oh, what a magic pen this present-day Godfrey had, because he had caught all the singing happiness of that moment when Kathleen had opened the door of the house where she lodged in answer to a knock. Godfrey had just looked at her, smiled, caught her in his arms and said, 'She lied, heart's darling, she lied! You were no kin to me. Will you come home now?'

There hadn't been the money to build another house ... they couldn't afford a grand gesture like that. Godfrey's parents, who had disliked Agatha so much they had retired in Balclutha, came back to live in the cottage, and Kathleen had filled the big bare house with warmth and love and laughter, bright curtains and cushions, and soon, children to delight her husband's heart, and his parents' hearts.

Valancy was glad this house had known years of happiness. But she wished that—for Godfrey's sake—the cruel coincidence of history repeating itself hadn't separated him from *his* Kathleen. Would that happiness ever be restored?

Surely Kathleen would feel lonely in England, miss him horribly, see things with clarity ... come to believe that Carlotta had her own devious reasons for driving a wedge between them. She was coming back to her home in the Catlins district and she would find Inchcarmichael Homestead lovingly restored, improved beyond imagination ... as for a bride.

Godfrey himself might not know it, but she, Valancy, was sure all he was planning had Kathleen in mind. At which thought Valancy suddenly clashed the manuscript down on her bedside table, snapped off the light and pulled the bedclothes over her head. She hoped sleep came suddenly and deeply.

Hoick and his offsider, one Clint Forbes, arrived, Hoick puffing happily along on his snorting machine; Clint, who'd left long after him, driving a huge modern truck that would haul the stumps away into a quarry-hole in the centre of the Inch that needed filling. The men left their jobs and gathered to watch.

Hoick, with his cap at an even more dashing angle, leapt from his steed, came straight up to where Valancy was standing with Godfrey, doffed his cap, made a slight bow and said, 'Mistress Carmichael, you are about to see the beginning of your heart's desire come true . . . at your service!'

The men roared as Valancy coloured to the roots of her bright hair. She stammered, 'Oh, Hoick, what a delightful speech . . . but––but I'm not his wife, just his secretary, I'm afraid.'

Clint, a tall young man in his mid-twenties, gave a great guffaw and slapped his whipcord trouser leg delightedly, 'First time in my life I've ever seen Hoick at a loss for words. You'll have to think up another gracious oration, mate.' Then to them, 'He talks like this all the time . . . everything's twopence coloured to him. And he likes redheaded women.'

Godfrey chuckled. 'Hard not to like 'em. My current heroine's got red hair. I hope my readers like redheads too.'

Hoick recovered himself. 'Is she spunky with it? To match her hair, I mean. I do like my heroines spunky. If the hero is fending off fearful odds, I like the woman to snatch up a huge vase and wade in, like Boadicea or Queen Elizabeth the First.'

When they'd finally got down to the business of the day, Valancy's eyes met Godfrey's in perfect under-standing. 'You're thinking he's straight from the pages of a book, isn't he?'

He mock-groaned. 'Why is it when you meet a character like that . . . handed to you on a platter . . . they're always larger than life and would tend to be judged as overdrawn?'

'Yes, one of our authors at Andersons knew that,' said Valancy. 'He was doing a biography of his father and his father's friend came into it. Some time in the nineteen-thirties. He was told this man was in the wrong generation. The author was so indignant. He remembered him himself, as a small child. This man did say things like: "Gad, sir!" and "Hurrumph" and "Stap me." He was a survival of last century, had been in Queen Victoria's Horse Guards . . . and in actual fact some of his words and expressions were pure Regency, carried over from his own father and grandfather, I suppose. His father had hunted with the current Prince of Wales, in Derbyshire, the one who became Edward the Seventh. To hear this author talk about him gave me the feeling that the years had rolled up and that a generation or two was no time at all.'

Godfrey handed her some clippers. 'Take that lower growth off, will you? Hoick wants this higher stuff off. I'll get up on this box. It'll make it easier to get his grappling gear on if it's clear, he says.' From the box he looked down on her. 'When he said Mistress Carmichael it made me wish that form of address had never gone out. Much nicer than the ugly-sounding Mrs, don't you think?'

She bent down to snip a shoot off. 'I suppose it is. I hadn't thought of it.'

She hadn't wished *that*. The knowledge hit her with unwelcome force. She had wished it had been true. That she was Mistress Carmichael ... and that hers might be the right to choose certain trees, to ask for a sundial on the lawn-to-be, for a flagged path to wind in and out of the little copse of silver birches he was planning, to ask was it possible to set up a suitable framework among the young chestnuts for a swing for children to play.

How stupid! How crazy! Why, just six weeks ago she'd fled from Christchurch because she couldn't bear to work alongside Justin, to live next door to him and Greer.

She thought wryly, as she hacked and clipped, that all the advice columns recommended knowing a man really well before marrying him. She had known Justin from the days of her first awareness, and where had that got her? And for Godfrey whom she had known so short a time, she would have gone, trustingly, to the ends of the earth. A man whose dreams were all bound up with a girl named Kathleen, longing for her to return to say she now believed him. This was the stuff of which fantasies were made, mere gossamer and stardust. Or, more sensibly, the result of working in close contact day by day with a man who spun fictional romances out of the people who had colonised New Zealand last century, a man who was so kindred no wonder she was in this state!

In three days the homestead area at Carmichael House was transformed. It was unbelievable what a difference the removal of those ugly stumps made. Bare, yes, but no longer mutilated. Valancy said, eyes shining, 'Why, it must have looked like this when Archibald and Effie first cleared the land sloping below their cottage and began planting their first saplings, so carefully nursed on the voyage out. It must have been a great surprise to them to find how quickly trees grow here, and how magically the change of season worked its own spell on them, disregarding the calendar and turning their leaves russet and flame as the cold weather set in.'

Godfrey nodded. 'And for them, at first, it would look even worse, because theirs was the job of burning off the bush to get land for grazing and sowing. They'd look out on hideously blackened ground. What a job they'd have getting out the charred stumps! But he'd scatter grass-seed in the warm ashes and in this Catlins district, with such a rainfall, it would soon germinate. How strange, we feel we've stepped back into the past because we used a steam-engine instead of a bulldozer, but they'd have looked on *that* as a minor miracle.

'Well, I've had my dip back into the past . . . I almost feel I should put a horse and plough in to finish it, but I won't, Rod can get the tractor out—it makes short work of it. I rang the nursery at Balclutha and they've got in touch with a man who'll sow the lawns and mark out the flower-beds. Shearing's too near for us to do that. We'll be mustering next week. It's late for lawns anywhere else, but our rainfall will bring it on. Don't think it's always like this, Valancy. It's been a phenomenally dry period—heaven send it holds till we get the sheep shorn. You and Aunt Helen are going to be let off the hook as far as the cooking's concerned. With that new woolshed with all conveniences, I'm having contract shearers and they bring their own cook.'

'What a difference that serial made,' smiled Valancy. 'I'm so glad for you. It's one way of celebrating—getting stumps out and lawns in.'

Godfrey looked sideways at her. 'No, I'm planning my own celebration, thanks, a much more orthodox one. The Royal Shakespeare Company is on at Invercargill, and I'm taking a girl to see *Twelfth Night*.'

Valancy gave a vicious chop at an inoffensive foxglove close to where a stump had been. She managed to sound perfectly natural. 'Good for you! I was afraid you were going to become a recluse because you got let down by Kathleen. I almost warned you about it when you told me what Carlotta did. I may have cut and run when Justin was returning to the firm, but after he broke our engagement I didn't forswear all male company. I went out with quite a few men.'

'Good,' he grinned. 'Because you're the one I'm taking. I hope you don't mind a very late night, because it's not far off a hundred miles each way, which we think nothing of in this little old neck of the woods when we want to see something very badly. We'll go down by the solitary coast road because we'll leave early and have dinner at a hotel first, but we'll come back via the main road, make more speed. Tomorrow night's the night.'

Valancy concealed her ecstatic delight, simply said, 'I take it I don't get asked if I'd like to go.'

The grey eyes glinted. 'I knew you liked Shakespeare and particularly *Twelfth Night*. And you can hardly plead a prior engagement. Except for shopping in Badenoch, you've hardly been off the place.'

She looked impish. 'Did Aunt Helen suggest this?'

He looked squarely at her then, said, 'If you aren't careful, Miss Adam-hyphen-Smith, I'll pick you up and dump you in that stump-hole ... and it's got blackberry in it still! I don't ask girls out at my aunt's instigation. And don't dare suggest Rachel comes with us. I've got seats for her parents to take her when the show's on in Dunedin. Lordy, but I'm ready for a spot of relaxation after all these months!' he sighed.

She looked innocent. 'Didn't manage to hit any of the high spots in Canada?'

'They had the red carpet out for me, certainly, but I was still a loner, among the crowd.'

How different from going to the theatre in Christchurch, when a half-hour drive from home sufficed even for parking and all. Valancy dressed in a simple yet elegant sapphire blue velvet frock, with an edging of white nylon fur at the scooped-out neckline and elbow sleeves. She fastened a fine gold necklet with tiny sapphires set in it that her father had brought her from Singapore last year above that soft neckline, and hooked swinging earrings in to match. Rachel's mother, who had been a hairdresser, had set her hair, catching it up on top, and letting the curled-under ends fall from a blue enamelled clasp. She picked up a white camelhair coat in a loose style to wear coming home. Godfrey said it could be coolish then.

As she came into the kitchen where Godfrey was waiting, Rachel clasped her hands together and said rapturously, 'Valancy, you look simply ravishing, doesn't she, Godfrey?'

Valancy and Aunt Helen chuckled, but Godfrey, to Rachel's delight, took her seriously, said, 'Indeed I think so. That's the right word, Rachel, so full marks.'

Rachel flung her arms round Valancy, sniffed and said, 'Is that a French perfume. It really sends me!'

'Not a bit of it, my angel. It's sweet and wholesome. Yardley's Old English Lavender. Never use anything else.'

They were over the bridge and heading south before Godfrey referred to it. 'Old English Lavender—I like that. May I use it in a book some time?'

'Of course. I'm flattered. But how?'

'Hero tired of being enveloped in an aura of exotic scents with ridiculous names ... *Seduction* ... *Provocation*, and so on. All artificial. He prefers something more wholesome.'

She didn't reply, simply because she didn't know how without sounding too pleased. He said sharply, 'What's the matter? Don't girls like being called wholesome any more? Too tame? Too insipid? Because in that dress, Valancy Adam-Smith, you look exactly what Rachel said ... ravishing. Not wholesome at all. If you'd used a seductive scent, it might have been just too, too much.'

She gave a ripple of laughter. 'You absurd man! It comes of being an author, you love words so much, you can't resist them. I'm just Valancy Smith, going off as a reward for hard work, with her employer.'

She sensed the smile in his voice as he answered, 'Are you? That's not the way I'm thinking of it.' She felt her pulses stir. Steady, Valancy, don't get carried away! One hint that you were looking on him romantically, and he'd retreat into the layer-down of laws that he was at your first encounter.

He said, 'I meant to tell you. I'd asked Aunt Helen ages ago for your letter of application to see for myself why the muddle-headed old darling thought you were a man. But she vowed she couldn't find it. But a few days ago I found it pushed under some bills in a drawer in the kitchen. I meant to show it to you.'

'Why? I wrote the darned thing. Why should I want to see it? And something's just struck me. You said she *vowed* she couldn't find it, but you found it *pushed* under some bills. You said it meaningly as if you thought she didn't want you to see it. What possible reason could she have for that?'

'That's what I asked myself. She was being cagey. I could pick it. But like you, couldn't understand it. I smoothed it out and took it upstairs. The light was stronger up there. I looked to see if you'd missed the hyphen out like she said, but you hadn't. It *was* faint because it had been erased. Only the dent of it showed up—you could see the rubbing marks. What do you make of that?'

Her tone was sheer astonishment. 'I make nothing of it. You must be mistaken. Why would anyone do that?' Then she said, 'Godfrey, I don't in any way want to spoil your celebration night, but something about this makes me feel angry . . . with you. I——'

His hand came out to clasp hers as they lay in her blue velvet lap. 'Don't, Valancy. Let it go. It intrigued me, that's all.'

It seemed as if he left his hand on hers, waiting for a

return pressure of reassurance, but she didn't give it. He took it away. Presently, in a milder tone, she said, 'I've got it! I think she must have felt worse about making the mistake than I thought. She must have felt responsible for landing you with me. Perhaps she was a bit sensitive about her memory. Older folk can be. I guess she took the letter out again, found the hyphen wasn't faint, and because she thought you might be cross about it, tried to make it fainter.'

She was glad he laughed. 'I think you're dead right, Sherlock. So simple! Forgive me for making such a thing about it.'

They had been cruising on a rough road between banks of thick bush, moist and shining green so every leaf looked newly enamelled, ferns of a myriad varieties springing from mossy tree-trunks. The stars of the tree-ferns, in paler green, made it look like a carpet. They came uphill out of the stillness to a flaming sunset in the sou'west over the sea. Godfrey drew into a wider space where a tiny headland ran out. He exulted as if he'd arranged it specially.

Valancy said, 'What sheer magic! How fascinating to think that we're so far south . . . because of the bottom of the South Island bearing away to the west here, that we can see the sun rise from the sea and set over the sea. I'm twenty-five and I've never seen that before. Living on the east coast, our sun always sets behind the Alps. I've seen a sunrise over Pegasus Bay many times and a moontrack, all silver, when we've been rambling among the dunes, but never till now, this. I wish Grannie could have seen it.'

'Why particularly Grannie?'

'Because Grandad died before she did, and she always said she felt he was just beyond the sunset. She felt nearer him then. That sunrise meant another day without him, but sunset made her feel he was just there, waiting for her.' She added, a little defensively, 'But I don't mean she moped. She was such fun to be with, a real giggler.'

He chuckled. 'Oh, Valancy, you make me laugh! You fire up so quickly in defence of those you love.

Don't think you know you're doing it.' He added quickly, 'I like it. It smacks of loyalty, and to me loyalty is one of the supreme virtues. I think it's Barrie who speaks of courage as one of the lovely virtues, but people who are loyal are courageous too. It takes grit.'

She was silent. Was he thinking of his Kathleen? Who hadn't been loyal to him? Who had accepted the word of another before his? So she was surprised when he said, 'I could imagine you as keeping loyal to Justin, even when he was failing you. Did you?'

When she didn't answer instantly he said, 'Sorry, don't answer that. I'm probing, which is unforgivable. Forget it.'

Her voice was so even he was surprised. 'That wasn't why I didn't answer right away. It didn't seem like probing to me, Godfrey, more like a caring concern. I was just trying to honestly assess my feelings—my feelings at the time. I sensed a withdrawal in his letters, and it made me wonder. So it was almost a relief when his letter telling me what had happened, arrived—no, not a relief; I was horribly upset. All my future plans fell to bits in that bolt from the blue. Dad was building our house slowly in his spare time. Only the foundations were in.

'But now I come to think of it I suppose in a way I was loyal, in that I understood. Justin was always so open, you see. He couldn't have hidden this. Greer didn't know he'd written. She'd told him she wouldn't be responsible for a broken engagement. She was going to leave Wellington. He said it was beyond him to carry on as if he hadn't met her and loved her.'

She looked up, her every feature revealed by that flaming sunset striking off the sea. 'Don't condemn him, Godfrey. That would hurt me. This was something he couldn't help.'

His eyes flickered over the bright hair that swept back from a widow's peak on the creamy forehead, the eyes that were the blue of her dress, the hollow at her throat above the slender gold chain, the faint hint of cleavage, the curve of her lips over the crooked white teeth. 'Was she beautiful?' he asked almost as if the question was jerked out of him.

Her mouth crinkled at the corners. 'No, not really. That's what made him so sincere. She's a little mousey girl, most endearing—almost plain. I was all prepared for a siren-type, so it was quite a shock to me. I went up to Wellington to make quite sure it wasn't an infatuation, in case he made a mess of his life. His mother asked me to.'

Godfrey made an exclamation. His tone was harsh. 'She had no right to ask that of you! I see what your boss meant about being too acquiescent. Sorry, carry on.'

'I didn't want to,' said Valancy, 'but it was too unsatisfactory, finishing it by letter. Somehow, soon as I met Greer I knew she was right for Justin. She had something for him that I hadn't. I can't explain it— some things you just *know*. I'd always been there, from babyhood on. But for Justin some essential ingredient was missing. The only one who understood was my Great-aunt Cecilia. She muttered something about God moving in a mysterious way His wonders to perform and said I was damned lucky to have a chance to get a fresh start in life uncluttered by the old and to get at it, begin to live. And I realise she'd never wanted me to marry Justin.'

'And have you? Begun to live, I mean.'

She considered that. Then her smile flashed out, the one dimple. 'Do you know, I think I have. Having had the one job since leaving the commercial college and living in Christchurch all my life, coming here to Inchcarmichael does mean a new life.'

'Not quite what I meant. That's *where* you're living. I meant a *quality* of living. But perhaps I'm getting in too deeply. If we don't move, we'll have to rush our meal. The day will lose its light soon and farther on it's not a road to make haste on.'

She laughed mischievously, 'In the first few moments when we met, I couldn't have imagined having a conversation like this with you. I thought I was going to be thrown out on my neck!'

'For which many apologies. Mind if I ask something else?'

'I'd rather it wasn't about Justin.'

'It's not. Just that I don't remember mentioning Kathleen by name to you, but you used it the other day. Had I mentioned it?'

'I don't think so. I think you just said the girl you'd hoped to marry. But Aunt Helen did.'

'As a point of interest, in what connection?'

Valancy said, to give herself time, because this could be a touchy subject, 'I wasn't questioning her, Godfrey. Not gossiping.'

'Heavens, girl, I wouldn't think that! I've asked you far more personal things. Knowing Aunt Helen, it could have cropped up any old how.'

She was relieved. 'Well, it did. We were doing out the jam cupboard, and I said what neat writing on the labels. She said Kathleen had done them, and added that she was the girl you had nearly married.'

She certainly did not add that Aunt Helen had said, 'Throw that lot out. She overdid the sugar. It's all crystallised. Bit like her, too sugary by far.'

CHAPTER SIX

SOMETIMES they drove by wide and wild deserted shores, crossed rivers, wound round lagoons and swamps where waterbirds clustered, a lost, lonely land for the most part. There were prosperous-looking farms, sheltered from the winds of the sea by huge shelter-belts of macrocarpa, leaning away from the elements, the odd group of fishermen's huts, the small township here and there. Then suddenly they were into the large spreading city of Invercargill with its wide streets and beautiful houses scattered out on the Southland Plain.

Before they got to the main shopping avenues they stopped at a low modern tavern and entered a richly decorated lounge. She found pleasure in having so personable an escort. He took her to a secluded corner, said, 'I'll see you get something to drink in a moment, but first I want to see the manager to ask him if I can leave the car in the private park so we can take a taxi to the theatre so we don't have to walk too far. We'll come back here for supper, anyway, because with a drive as long as that ahead of us we'll need something. I won't be long.'

He was longer than he thought. Not that Valancy noticed it, for she was only just settled when she was joined by someone. She'd noticed a group of women, probably workmates, she thought, out for the evening, and saw a tall redheaded girl detach herself from them and walk towards her. She was most surprised when the girl dropped on to a chair beside the low table in front of Valancy and said, 'Hullo, Valancy Smith. Remember me?'

Valancy blinked, then realised last time she'd seen her the hair had been nut-brown, and said, 'Oh, of course— Carol Latterson! Goodness, it must be seven or eight years since we last met. Are you living in Invercargill?'

Carol nodded. 'Yes, I gradually worked my way further south trying out all sorts of new experiences. However, next month I'm going up to Auckland. Time I saw more of the sophisticated North.'

That sounded like Carol. Valancy remembered her as a discontented, ill-natured student at commercial college. Born jealous and possessive. Still, she must be polite.

Carol asked, 'Are you living here too? Married or single? I know you were keen on the boy next door.' She made it sound boring.

Valancy managed a laugh. 'Not any more. It didn't work out. But I'm a bit north of here, doing the same sort of work as at Andersons really. Only the Players weren't coming to our small town, so we came on down here.'

'Someone with you, then? I was going to ask you to join us. Don't think I saw you come in.'

'I'm with my employer. We've been flat out lately, so he thought we could take a night off.'

'Oh, lucky you. That's the sort of employer to have. Is he interesting? I mean ... well, you know. Eligible? Young?'

Valancy felt the same aversion she'd always felt for this girl. What typical questions! 'I think I could say so-so to all those queries ... but still merely my employer.'

At that moment Godfrey came through an archway. He came up behind Carol Latterson. Valancy looked up, saw his brows twitch together in a typical male gesture of annoyance and she subdued a grin. She said, over Carol's head, 'Oh, Godfrey, this is someone I was at college with, Carol Latterson.'

Carol swung round, half rose, then subsided.

Godfrey Carmichael's voice was deliberately cold. 'We've met before,' he said. 'Good evening, Carlotta ... or *is* it?'

Very plainly he considered it a good evening no longer.

Valancy had the feeling he was going to say nothing more, just stand there and look grim. She herself felt riveted to her seat and quite incapable of uttering, but she forced herself to step into the breach, swallowed, then said, 'Carlotta? *Carlotta?* But her name's Carol!'

Godfrey smiled thinly then. 'I can only suppose she thought Carlotta sounded more exotic. Her mind runs that way.'

Carol's voice held a sneer. 'Dear Godfrey—so outspoken! So incapable of hiding his feelings. I wouldn't have waited had I even dimly suspected my old chum had you for her boss ... and escort.'

His tone was cutting. 'Wouldn't you, Carlotta? I think you would. You would have contrived in some way to instil mischief into Valancy's ear. But not into her mind. Oh, no, she's a cat of a different breed from the gentle Kathleen. She's got discrimination, and spunk. She'd have turned you inside out. And if she knows you, she may easily have your measure.

'She knows all about what happened at Inchcarmichael because of you and is only indignant that Kathleen hadn't the loyalty and gumption to see through you. Now I suggest you go. You have no place in our lives, either mine or Valancy's.'

He stepped back and made a gesture of dismissal. Carol stood up, two spots of bright red humiliation on her cheekbones.

But she didn't creep away. She said, 'Your life and hers? How interesting. Linked, are they? Well, well, you didn't lose much time consoling yourself, did you?'

He was more than equal to her. 'No, I didn't. When the true gods come, the false gods go. I've been a very lucky man.'

Carol said over her shoulder, trying to look malicious rather than worsted. 'Kathleen *will* be interested. Perhaps you acted in too much haste. I suppose you know she's coming back in February?'

'So what? And don't tell me she's got the poor taste to keep in touch with you! Oh, well, they say there's one born every minute. Now, if you don't mind . . . on your way!'

Then he dropped down beside Valancy, grinned and said, 'Phew! But what satisfaction. I've been longing for a chance to do something like that for months. I must be grateful to you, Valancy. I say, are you sure you'd not rather have a brandy than that lime-and-soda I ordered for you?'

Valancy's eyes were dancing. 'Lime-and-soda will be just fine. Godfrey, please keep on talking, say anything. She's facing us across the room and I have an awful feeling I'm going to giggle my head off. I loathed that girl at college. She broke up two promising relationships I know of and goodness knows how many I don't. And not to worry, she told me that next month she's off to Auckland to live. She'll be gone long before Kathleen returns to New Zealand.'

'What's that to do with anything?' asked Godfrey Carmichael. He leaned across, his eyes full of deviltry. 'You say she's watching? Do let's give her something to see . . . and it's a good way of stopping a giggle!' He brushed his lips across hers. Valancy shook an admonitory finger at him as he straightened up, a playful gesture that only said: Not here! to any onlooker. Godfrey patted her hand, said, 'Oh, you beaut girl . . . you caught on very quickly. Oh, here are the drinks.'

That was all he said about the encounter except that when they were duly installed in the dining-room, 'Now . . . this is the season of forgetfulness. In other words, let's enjoy our dinner as we were meant to. When I take a woman out I don't want unpleasant reminders cropping up, such as Carlotta or Kathleen. I can recommend the *toheroa* soup,' he added. 'They get the *toheroas* from Oreti Beach. Dig them up themselves and always put a few in the deep freeze for V.I.P.s. Gus, the manager, told me he had some left when I rang to book.'

It gave Valancy a feeling of being very, very special, something she hadn't experienced in a very long time. They couldn't see Carlotta from their secluded table in the dining-room. No doubt Carlotta would be glad of that, afraid Godfrey would slap her down again in front of her friends.

The whole evening took on an added sparkle because of the confrontation. As far as Carlotta was concerned, she thought, it swept her under the rug. Finish. She hoped, though, that it hadn't brought things back too vividly for Godfrey, recalling how successful had been Carol's stratagem . . . something that had sent his Kathleen, perhaps desolate, to the ends of the earth.

If that was so he hid it most successfully. He was very attentive, except when the acts were on, something Valancy liked. She had never wanted to hold hands during a play or film. Between acts was the time to share appreciation.

'What a beautiful Viola,' said Godfrey, at the end of the second act, 'and she'll be even more beautiful in her woman's garb.'

Valancy turned to him, eager, sparkling, 'Oh, how lovely, you're anticipating! Oh, but I do love to see Shakespeare with someone who loves him too, and who knows the text so well. Isn't that said right at the end?'

He smiled down on her. 'Well, not the last line, but during the last act.' Then he said bluntly, 'Didn't Justin care for Shakespeare?'

'No, but he was gallant about it. He always accompanied me, but it didn't exactly add to my enjoyment.'

'Was that mean of me . . . bringing up his name?'

'Oh, it doesn't matter a bit. We must be natural about things.'

To her vast surprise she found that it truly didn't matter, not an iota. She shied away from analysing that.

'Good. Something's just occurred to me. Carlotta said Kathleen was coming back to New Zealand in February. Aunt Helen said something about being back to my old self by then. Any connection, do you think?'

'Shouldn't think so. Unless . . .'

'You've had the same thought. Aunts are shocking matchmakers! She needn't bother wasting her time. No hope of that breach ever being healed.'

Valancy put a hand on his sleeve and continued in the whisper, 'Godfrey you mean because Kathleen wouldn't believe you. Because if so, it could be just pride. You really ought to be able to forgive that. She could have been racked with jealousy.'

His face hardened. 'Who'd want a wife who wouldn't trust you? So many things can threaten a marriage. They do less harm if there's trust. My father got manoeuvred into a sticky situation once. My mother didn't hesitate for a moment. She went down to the office and made mincemeat of this woman's innuendoes. But what pleased Dad most was that not for a moment did she doubt him.'

Valancy's eyes glowed bluely with appreciation. 'Good for her! I like women to fight tooth and claw for their men!'

Godfrey forgot where he was, and gave one of his great gusts of laughter, so the people in front swung round. She choked her own mirth back and said seriously, 'But then we aren't all the same. Your mother might have been more confident about your father's love than Kathleen was about yours. Poor girl!'

He said soberly, 'She had enough time to consider,' then, indignantly, which surprised her, 'What are you trying to do, anyway? Sell me the idea of a reconciliation? In your own way you're as bad as Aunt Helen. Not that I ever thought *she* was keen on Kathleen. She was far too polite to her to be natural.' His hand came up to cover hers where it still lay on his arm. 'Blast, they're coming back just at this interesting point.'

'Heretic! You're worse than Justin!' and in that very moment Valancy knew that her own season of forgetfulness had done its trick, that she no longer cared, because Justin belonged to a past which she had no wish to revive.

The play whirled on in the true Shakespearian speed, scenes of romping and delicious foolery interspersed with moments of tenderness and longing, till with its satisfying end, Viola not only finds her lost brother, but the Duke Orsino realises where his true love lies and sees her as a woman.

Godfrey reverted to the topic while they were having supper. 'Valancy, I want you to understand one thing. I don't want Kathleen back. But by heaven, I would like an apology from her. I'd like her to admit she knows Carlotta lied, that's all.'

He chuckled then, as he handed over his cup for more coffee. 'We're supposed to be celebrating my serial and the removal of the stumps. I don't usually take a girl out and talk non-stop about her predecessor! Don't we argue splendidly? I find it very stimulating. And Kathleen didn't like Shakespeare either. I've never enjoyed any play more than tonight.'

For early summer it was very cold down there at the bottom of the world when they emerged. Valancy was glad to snuggle into her fleecy white coat, pull its high collar up round her ears. Godfrey fished in the back seat and drew out a rug in the Carmichael tartan. There were two compulsory seat-belts for passengers in the long front seat. She began fastening the one by the door around her, but his hand arrested her.

'Don't be ridiculous! You dubbed me a woman-hater at our first meeting, but it was never true. I only wanted a nice safe male secretary who wouldn't intrude personal feelings into study hours. Move into the middle seat, chump!'

She made no fuss about it. She wanted to, anyway. He buckled the belt and tucked the rug about her. She was cross with herself because she had the maddest longing to turn round and nestle into his arms. Watch it, Valancy, she warned herself. It's sheer physical chemistry. But her voice sounded quite natural and amused. 'Now I know who your secretary was, I've every sympathy with you. I can just imagine how she'd rub you up the wrong way.'

'Uh-huh, that sure describes it. But we aren't going to let thoughts of Carlotta intrude on *our* night. There's a hint of late frost, don't you think?'

She giggled. 'What a lovely safe topic—the weather! For a change of subject, you can't beat it.'

He glanced at her sideways and his look had a glint in it. 'But then the weather can often be used to advantage. Like Shakespeare used it. That frost, my girl, makes the night even more beautiful. The clear sky with only a puff or two of cloud, with such bright stars and a moon Shakespeare wouldn't have scorned to describe. He was always at it, wasn't he? Describing moonlight, I mean. "How sweet the moonlight sleeps upon this bank . . ." Tell me who said that to whom, Valancy? Don't let me down. I've come to rely on you at my desk, why not here?'

'Um . . . Lorenzo to his Jessica near the end of the *The Merchant*. The scene that starts: "The moon shines bright . . . in such a night as this . . ." It's well done, isn't it? It recalls so cleverly many other famous scenes. It was the first Shakespeare we ever did at High School. We had a marvellous teacher. She loved Shakespeare so much, did Miss Robertson, that her dark eyes used to light up like candles and we all got imbued with a love of it. She said that those lines had a magic that ought to make us look up the other references. A good many of us did.'

'I don't think I'm as good as you, memory-wise,' said Godfrey, 'but I recall one night was when "Troilus, methinks, mounted the Trojan walls, and sigh'd his soul towards the Grecian tents, where Cressid lay that night." Good picture, isn't it, of a man yearning to join his love?'

She sighed happily. This man, naturally, as an author, had a magic touch with lines he loved. He said, 'That was a very contented sigh, dear secretary.'

She said, stretching herself like a cat, 'I just thought how like my grandfather you are. He quoted and quoted. I do miss him.'

He put back his head and barked with laughter. 'Oh, Valancy, you're so unexpected! Talk about cutting a man down to size! Who wants to remind a girl of her grandfather?'

She said with spirit, 'You ought to be proud of being likened to my mother's father. He instilled all his grandchildren with a love of books, of poetry. That's why I went into the publishing world. I can't write myself, I haven't the gift, but I love working with words.'

'And you have a devastating way of using them. Tell me, what did your grandfather do for a crust?'

'He was a minister, a Methodist minister, though we're Presbyterian because of Dad. A Welsh Methodist, with all the fire and passion and poetry and song that that entails. Sometimes I can't bear to think of that melodious voice of his being stilled.'

His voice lost its teasing note. 'It isn't stilled, Valancy. I've a firm conviction that no beauty, whether of sight or sound or touch, is ever lost.'

She couldn't speak for a moment, then, 'Thank you, Godfrey. I shouldn't have said that, of course.'

He said gently, 'I think you only meant you can't bear to think you'll never hear it again on earth. But I'm sure that just as we can conjure up pictures from long ago, in our mind's eye, so we can recapture sounds loved, in our mind's ear.' Then, 'What are you doing, Valancy?'

'Scribbling that down. You could use it in a book some day, to delight readers. I can just see them, taking out their mind's eye pictures, their mind's ear sounds. I think that anything that brings back the loved past for people, who, through age or disability, are not able to visit those places now, is worth while.'

Godfrey waited till she had written it down on a blank pad from the glove compartment, writing it by feel, then he said, and the deepened timbre of his voice showed how he was moved, 'You are quite the most kindred companion I've ever known, man or woman.'

She didn't reply; she felt she didn't need to. It was quite a flawless compliment, one from mind to mind. She mustn't read anything more into it. The miles went by.

There came the time when they turned eastward, coastward. As they slid down the hill towards the bridge, she looked across the dividing waters and said, 'Gateway to the little world of Inchcarmichael.'

'Is that what it seems to you, Miss Adam-Smith? When I think of how I dreaded introducing any secretary into our lives . . . some people rub you up the wrong way, and even a man, supposing he had the qualifications, might have jibbed at the isolation. How could I have dreamed as you slid down that roof towards me, splashing paint in all directions, that here was the ideal secretary erupting into my life?'

They slid the car quietly into one of the implement sheds so there would be no banging of doors and came across to the house, on the slopes that now lay smoothed over for the lawn seed. In the moonlight the curves of the flowerbeds-to-be were plainly visible.

They halted on the ridge above the cleared land. Godfrey said, 'This time we're not recalling scenes, Valancy, we're evoking visions of the future when this will have red gums in flower, and the wind will sing in the pines and the oaks, and the aspen poplars will be perpetually aquiver. And there will be birds, and nestlings.'

He slipped his arm about her and she was content to stand there, dreaming. What matter that it was three in the morning? The world was theirs. Time was standing still.

She said dreamily, 'And at this hour, in midsummer, the dawn chorus will be starting.'

'And we'll build that fernery, and plant a new orchard over there. The old one suffered badly from frost when it lost the protection of the big trees. Some few survived.'

He'd said 'we'. How much did that mean? She must remember that the relationship he wanted from her was, as he'd said, as sexless as worker-bees. All this feeling of togetherness tonight was just a surge of emotion resulting from his dream of restoring Inchcarmichael coming faster because of his serial sale.

She turned to go inside and was caught against him. He said, 'You know the other day I said to you, re that chapter we were on, that I just wished there was some other way of describing kisses?'

She nodded, her voice seemed to have deserted her. He was smiling and he was so close his breath was warm on her cheek. He laughed teasingly, 'Don't draw away. I've got to assert myself physically after being likened to your grandfather! Did you pick the way Shakespeare described a kiss tonight? He called it "the holy close of lips," ' and at that moment he put his mouth down on hers.

The sweetness of it fired a pulse in Valancy's veins. She had never, ever, known such a response to a kiss. This was far removed from that exploring of each other's minds they had experienced together. This was sheer, physical attraction and there was a subtle magic in it she'd not known before. Perhaps because of that closeness of spirit that had preceded it. There was nothing of the worker-bee syndrome in this!

Godfrey lifted his head a little, still holding her so that she was moulded against him, her back arched a little with the intensity of his embrace. She saw his lips part in a faint smile. Then, as if reluctant to end it, he brushed his lips backwards and forwards gently across hers. He released her, steadying her.

Valancy had a moment of not knowing what to say, then gave a shaky laugh and said, 'What Shakespeare ... and the moon ... is responsible for?'

His answering chuckle held real mirth. 'Oh, Shakespeare, was it? Now, *I* thought it was me. *Us*.'

They walked up to the house, went in through the front door, shut it very quietly, hardly pausing as they said goodnight, at the foot of the stairs, he to ascend, she to go through the kitchen to her own quarters.

The good weather held, the shearers arrived and work proceeded with incredible speed, the epitome of every farmer's dream. Valancy had revelled in the rounding-up, not a hard task here as up in the high country, and mostly done on horseback. She loved Rufus, the mount they now regarded as specially hers.

'Of course he's always been a lady's mount,' said Godfrey. Then, in response to her enquiring look, he said, 'He was always ridden by one of the governesses up at Dragonshill. She left about the time I bought this place, so I brought him with me. He's a bit beneath my weight, though.'

It was heavenly after the close desk work, which was so brain-fatiguing, to be out in the yards, or in the far paddocks of Inclutha, with the tang of the moist green bush in the air, the tinge of salt in the winds that blew from east and south, being teased by the men, and the girls who worked as fleecies at the great round revolving table that was such an excellent feature of the new woolshed. Good to tumble into bed at night, dog-tired, and happy, and to sleep from that moment to cockcrow, sometimes beyond.

Never a thought of Justin or Greer disturbed her, except when ne~ mother's letters came in. Mrs Hughes was recovering well after her stroke. Valancy was glad about that. She had no regrets for that brand-new beautifully designed home in St Martins ... an architectural delight ... it would have presented no challenge as this did ... to create beauty where only ugliness had reigned, to make a living out of an estate that had been vandalised.

They settled back into the writing routine, though gradually Godfrey was able to spend more time on the farm, leaving much more responsibility to Valancy than he'd ever dreamed he could to anyone.

One night the three of them were relaxing after the

evening meal prior to washing the dishes when the phone rang in the kitchen. Godfrey answered. It sounded like a person-to-person call, which was sensible on a property this size, where you could be a couple of miles distant. Probably a bookseller.

No ... it was for her. Godfrey had a strange, wary look on his face. 'It's for Miss Adam-Smith. Justin Hughes calling you.'

She looked mystified, then alarmed. 'What can *he* have to say that Mum or Dad couldn't say? Oh, I hope nothing's wrong with them!' She held out her hand for the receiver, 'Well, I'll soon find out.'

She was glad that Justin's voice meant nothing to her. It could have done. She said quickly, 'Nothing wrong at home, is there? Are Mother and Dad okay?'

He said. 'Not at your home, Val. At ours. Mother was progressing so well, though a little vague. But suddenly she's become more aware of all this has meant. She was making splendid strides in speech, movement, everything, but now she can't be bothered. Just lies in bed worrying. She's got you on her mind.'

'Got *me* on her mind? Whatever for?'

'She's got it into her head that you're desperately unhappy, that you're eating your heart out away down there in that bleak countryside. We just can't stop her fretting about it. She's at it all the time—never hears the postman's whistle but thinks there might be a letter from you. She keeps saying she wishes she'd never recovered from the stroke because then you'd not have had to leave home. And your job. We're at our wits' end. It's pumped her blood pressure up and they're afraid of another stroke.'

Oddly Valancy seized on the one minor thing. 'It *isn't* bleak countryside! It's the most gorgeous place. It's like living on an island, river on two sides of a triangle, sea on the other. In the centre we have acres of the most unspoiled native bush, waterfalls and all. And I've got my own work to boot, *and* sheep, and a horse to ride. You know me. It's *my* kind of country.'

Godfrey hadn't heard what Justin had said, but he certainly gathered she was flying to the defence of

Inchcarmichael. Instinctively he came to stand beside her.

She said, 'Justin, can you tell Hughsie all this? Can you convince her I'm *not* eating my heart out? That I'm having the time of my life? Why hasn't Mum shown her my letters? I rave!'

She listened. 'She has? And Hughsie thinks I'm putting a brave face on it for my parents' sake. Oh dear! What on earth can we do?' Her eyes met Godfrey's over the phone.

Justin said, and now Godfrey could hear him, 'It'll take a lot to convince her. In fact only one thing will. I hate to put this to you, Valancy, but nothing short of seeing you will do. I think she imagines you a pale wraith of your former self. Is there any chance you could fly up for the weekend from Dunedin? We'll pay your fare, meet you, anything. She was crying in her sleep last night about it. It would give you time with your parents.'

She found herself saying, 'I don't really want to spend any time at all away from here. We've got a big tree-planting project needing a lot of attention and we're getting on fine with my employer's current book, but I can't really say no if Hughsie is as bad as you say. When she sees me she'll be convinced. I've put on seven pounds. Yes, I know I could stand it, but you aren't pining away if you've put on weight. I'm blooming. Nothing less like anyone suffering a broken heart could be imagined! Just a moment, I'll ask Godfrey if he can spare me.'

She put her hand over the mouthpiece. 'I don't want to go, but I must, I suppose. She's just got muddled with this stroke. It's hardly fair to Greer.'

'To hell with Greer!' retorted Godfrey. 'I've got a better idea. Why don't we go up by car? What better way of disabusing Mrs Hughes's mind that you're pining for Justin than to turn up with another swain in tow?'

Into the stunned silence that greeted this bright idea on Valancy's part came the sound of soft clapping from Aunt Helen. 'Super idea,' she mouthed.

Valancy came out of her trance. She said, 'Will do . . . offer closed with,' and turned back to the phone. 'Justin, this is Wednesday. We'll drive up on Friday. Tell Mother to prepare the spare bedroom for Godfrey, will you?' There was a suggestion of the dimple deepening, a flash of mischief in her eyes.

The next moment Godfrey had the phone off her. 'Let me speak to Justin, Valancy.' She watched him a trifle apprehensively. His eyes were positively dancing. 'That you, Justin?' he said coolly, 'Godfrey Carmichael here. This is a good idea. I'll add to what Valancy said. Would you tell her mama that my Aunt Helen will be with us? We've been thinking it's high time my people and Valancy's met, so this will be a golden opportunity. Too bad your mother started to worry like this, but I'm sure this weekend will dispel all that. You'll have her on the high road to recovery before Christmas. Did you know the Smiths are coming down here in January? M'm. Valancy flatly refused to go home for Christmas, so they're coming here for New Year. Tell Greer it'll all be plain sailing soon. You don't want to say any more, do you, Valancy? Right, we'll leave early and arrive at Smith's for dinner and come in about seven-thirty to see your mother. Good show . . . see you then.'

Valancy faced Godfrey, her knees shaking. 'I hope you realise what you've done! You've committed yourself to something you might regret. *We* know it's just a bit of mischief, but—well, all right, not exactly that, but pretence, but like in everything, you overdo it.'

The grey eyes were still dancing. 'You're not consistent. Only the other morning you told me my lovemaking was far too restrained.'

There was a distinct gasp from Aunt Helen. Valancy was cross. She actually stamped her foot. 'Godfrey! For goodness' sake! If you said that in front of anyone else it would sound terrible . . . sound torrid . . . Aunt Helen, I said it of his *hero's* lovemaking! He was being gentle and understanding when he ought to have been masterful and overbearing with the girl he loved. Godfrey said who was writing the book, him or me, and

I got mad with him and said I'd never make a criticism again, that it had been jerked out of me because I knew instinctively that it was the wrong technique.'

Aunt Helen was helpless, dabbing at her eyes. 'I can only say that if you go on like this in front of the Hughes family, you'll be so convincing you'll find yourself wed to each other before you know it.'

'We will *not*,' said Valancy quickly and hotly. 'It's all tied up with the creative temperament. It's a dangerous thing for any man. His imagination works so quickly he invents a situation before he knows it, like the other night in Invercargill.'

The older woman, eyes eager, said, 'Like what? What happened?'

Godfrey grinned. 'I didn't tell you—you froth at the mouth at the very mention of Carlotta. But Valancy's blown the gaff.'

She looked unrepentant. 'I'd no idea, Aunt Helen, when you all talked about her, that you were on about a girl I went to college with, because that one was called Carol, not Carlotta. I suppose she thought the Spanish form of her name sounded more exotic. Godfrey took me to that tavern, left me in the lounge while he went off to see about parking. Along came Carol, plonked herself down and asked where I was living.

'I was cagey, simply said I was doing the same work as at Andersons but privately. She asked who I was with that night, I said my employer, and off she went. Was he young, was he eligible? She can't evaluate people except on those terms. So I said, "Oh, so-so, but still only my employer." She kept her eyes away from Godfrey's. She resumed. 'Then Godfrey came through behind Carol, and I made the introduction, calling her by her full name. Talk about a moment! I could have gone off into a good old-fashioned swoon when he called her Carlotta.'

'And . . .?'

Valancy threw out her hands in an exasperated gesture. 'And his imagination got going. He more or less hinted that his interest was fixed on me now.' She swung round on Godfrey. 'What's so funny about that? It's as good a way of putting it as any.'

He went on chuckling in the most maddening fashion. 'Aunt Helen, temptation yawned and I went in boots and all. Told her I was glad she hadn't known who Valancy was working for, because had she known, undoubtedly she would have tried to instil poison in *her* mind though it wouldn't have worked because Valancy was a cat of a different breed from the gullible Kathleen, too much loyalty and gumption to believe such things. Then I told her to go!'

How like her great-nephew Helen Armishaw was! Her eyes too disappeared into slits of mirth, the same lines grooved down her cheeks. 'If only I could have been a fly on the wall—oh, how I wish your——' She had turned slightly towards Valancy, but came to a full stop. It was tantalising.

Godfrey looked expectant, said, 'Go on . . . you wish what?'

Aunt Helen's look was superseded by a blank, guileless expression, almost as if she wiped the other off deliberately, then, 'Oh, Adam always enjoyed situations like this . . . I just knew an overwhelming wish that he could be here.'

Her nephew looked suspicious. 'I'm pretty sure you're being evasive. Uncle Adam wouldn't have caught on for another quarter of an hour. You know, Aunt, he may have loved you deeply, but he was at times like a hen with a duckling . . . wondering how to keep you on dry land. He was always hauling you out of the deep end.'

She shrugged, said, 'But he always enjoyed a good laugh when he fully understood things. He'd have loved to see that Carlotta get her come-uppance. He could see through people. Never mind, what fun it's going to be. I'm so glad you've included me. I'll be able to see some of the old Rangi-ruru girls in Christchurch and I'll enjoy lending authenticity to the plot. Now, I must get myself a handkerchief.'

Alone Valancy said to Godfrey, 'You're a reckless man—but kind. I won't involve you too much, won't take too much of a smokescreen. We mustn't be too definite.'

Godfrey sighed. 'What's bugging you? You seem nervous. It's only fun, you know, to set Mrs Hughes' mind at rest.'

'I'll tell you what. You're a public figure whether you like it or not. You get involved with publicity. I know you dodge as much as possible, and prefer to be left in peace to write and farm, but you owe something to your publishers. One hint to the press or the T.V. that at last this wily bachelor who writes pioneer novels with a strong love interest is falling himself, and it could be very embarrassing.'

He shrugged. 'But it would certainly reassure Mrs Hughes.' Then he sensed her serious concern, came across and took her elbows, 'Valancy, you said yourself I've a vivid and fast imagination. If anything like that crops up, I'll be able to handle it. I'll rely on spur-of-the-moment inspiration. Listen, I made shameful use of you in front of Carlotta. This could be my way of paying a debt.'

'Well, if that's all it is and you don't let it get out of hand,' she said, and hoped her tone didn't sound flat.

This inexplicable man laughed again. Why? Nothing funny about that. 'I'm sure no harm will come of it. In fact some aspects of it could be most enjoyable, like this . . .'

His mouth was on hers before she could pull away. She tried not to respond . . . but didn't quite succeed.

When he released her, she schooled her voice to be steady. She said, with a well-simulated hint of amusement. 'Just as well I've had such an experience of volatile authors. All these experiences are grist to the mill, I know.'

'Rather,' he said unrepentantly. 'I look forward to a few more. It promises to be a capital weekend.'

Valancy went off to her own quarters without a backward look.

CHAPTER SEVEN

WEDNESDAY was a very different day, severely business-like in its hours and in her employer's attitude. Godfrey was out on the property with the men, attacking a vast amount of work to justify a long weekend off, Aunt Helen happily baking for Rod and Bill, and washing and ironing, and Valancy was set a tough typing job.

In the few odd moments she had, she felt she moved in an unreal world. Was it possible she was to see Justin again and to reassure Hughsie by pretending to a degree only a little short of an engagement that she'd met the love of her life in Godfrey Carmichael? Because that was how it would appear, with this big fair man, with the fertile imagination and the eagerness of a schoolboy playing a prank. How different from the woman-hating ogre of her first imaginings! In her mind, then, she had even dubbed him the Wolf of Badenoch! Though at first he'd certainly made it clear theirs was to be a business relationship only. Was this, now, the true Godfrey? The extrovert ... fun-loving, not cynical and bitter? Was this as he had been before the warped Carlotta had turned his gentle Kathleen into something hard and disbelieving?

With the first Godfrey and Kathleen, time had taken care of it, but there must have been a time when it had seemed impossible to untangle. Was there still hope that this might resolve itself? There should be more really, because in this, neither had taken the step of marrying someone else. So there was still a chance. Kathleen was coming back to New Zealand's shores, and who knew what mood she might be in? ... possibly a contrite one.

Valancy stared at the page on her typewriter and knew that she had it in her power to convince Kathleen there had been nothing in it if she told her that Carlotta had always been noted for breaking up romances. That in this case, she might realise Carlotta had acted with even more venom than usual, because she'd been the woman scorned. Valancy ought to have been exalted at the thought she could do this for Godfrey, but she wasn't. She felt bleak. She uttered an impatient exclamation and returned to her typing.

Half an hour later she made another exclamation, looking at the page she was copying from. It coincided with Godfrey coming into the study. 'What is it, Valancy? Have you lit on a mistake? Good job I came in right now, then.'

She turned round, 'No . . . just a phrase that interests me. My former boss used it once and you did, the night you sorted Carlotta out. I think it must be a quotation, though I've never come across it.'

He leaned over her, a hand on her shoulder. She pointed with her finger. 'That's it . . . "this was the season of forgetfulness, that great healer of the wounds of the spirit." Where is it from, Godfrey?'

She turned to look up to the face so near hers. She had to resist a mad impulse to touch her lips to the faint scar on his left cheek that was a memento of falling down a spur of rock among the mountains of Dragonshill. She looked back quickly at the typed page. 'Darned if I know, Valancy. It could be a quotation, if you say your boss used it too. In what context did he put it?'

She hesitated only fractionally. 'He was telling me of an experience in his own youth. Like many publishers, he was a journalist first—wrote poetry, articles, etc. And he quoted this one verse to me, that's all.' That was meant to be final, but Godfrey rarely let a matter go till he pursued it to the end.

'Don't hold out on me! You know I like to glean all sorts of bits and pieces. It could be something I could use sometime.'

'I hardly think so. It—it was so very personal. And not a verse you could acknowledge with thanks to the author, naming him, because it was something he didn't want his wife ever to read.'

The grip on her shoulder tightened as he laughed. 'Oh, Valancy, it's just as well you're saying this to me!

That sounds damning ... something a secretary can know, but not a man's wife.'

She laughed. 'M'm. No wonder we get ourselves into pickles! I'm better explain. He fell in love as a young man, had a broken engagement, took it badly, and wrote some poetry—rather agonising over it; fortunately under a pseudonym, so his wife has never seen them. He said that otherwise she'd have imagined him having an undying love for this other girl. Whereas he loved *her* so much he never failed to thank God the other was broken up. And he quoted this verse at me.'

'Go on, I want to hear it.'

'He wrote this later, when he'd proved it, but still didn't show it to Theresa, his wife, in case it set up doubts.

> *"Sweet is the season of forgetfulness,*
> *Succeeding thus the passion and the pain,*
> *The healing time, the quiet time of pausing*
> *Till, in God's wisdom, you will love again."* '

His hand left her shoulder and came to her left cheek, in a perfect gesture of understanding. He said gently, 'This would be when your own engagement was broken, of course.'

'A little later. In fact, the day I gave in my notice because Justin was coming back. He thought it was good that I was making for pastures new, just as he did when he came to New Zealand.'

He said slowly, 'There's a great deal of common sense in that.' He took his hand away and left her, but the warmth against her cheek remained.

They drove up Friday, after a substantial breakfast and with a picnic lunch packed so they needn't waste time on the way at a restaurant. Certainly what ever Godfrey did, he did well ... the big Holden station wagon was packed with big chilli-bins full of fresh farm mutton and lamb and cartons crammed with the best of Rachel's father's market produce, for both the Adam-Smith and Hughes households.

The countryside was shimmering now with the heat of

early December. Down here the hawthorns and guelder roses, or snowballs as Valancy preferred to call them, and the rhododendrons, were still in vivid colour, but the further north they went, those flowers would be past their best, because of the quicker approach of summer there, and roses and lavender and poppies would scent the air.

There was always the feeling of crossing the Border as they bridged the Waitaki River between Scottish Otago and English Canterbury. They swept through sleepy little townships, through prosperous farmlands in hill and dale, skirted the white-frilled cobalt Pacific, then, beyond Timaru settled to the monotony, yet grandeur of the Plains, bordered by the magnificent chain of the Southern Alps on the west.

As they entered the fringes of the spread-out city of Christchurch, Godfrey looked to the right, eastward, where the Cashmere Hills reared above the city, and said, 'There you are, Valancy, your hills of home.'

It was nicely said, yet in a way it was a shock, for in that moment Valancy knew they were no longer that to her ... the hills of her childhood home, yes, but now the hills of South Otago were her true home-hills. The hills that surrounded the mighty Clutha, the low rolling hills of Inchcarmichael itself ending in sheer cliffs where in the Blowholes the sea swept in to funnel up like geysers and all the force of the Pacific hurled itself against the rocks.

She was experiencing what so many daughters feel on returning to their childhood scenes after long years of marriage, realisation that the hub of the universe had shifted!

She was sitting between Godfrey and Helen. He looked at her swiftly when she didn't reply and his left hand lifted from the wheel to touch hers lying in her lap, just briefly.

'Getting to you a bit, is it? Not feeling nervous, are you, because there's no need? Leave it to me.'

There was a trace of indignation in her voice. 'I wasn't even thinking about that. It's just a nuisance. It's a busy time of year back home—I mean down south.

Godfrey, the British Pavements corner is coming up, if
you turn right there you can go through Halswell and
Spreydon to reach St Martin's. Dodges the city traffic.'

'Good for you, partner,' said Godfrey. 'That's the
spirit.'

He was commending her for not admitting to
nervousness. Well, she certainly couldn't tell him that it
no longer mattered to her. That anything that had
happened before she went to that isolated delta-land
between two rivers and the sea seemed to have
happened in another life.

Godfrey's eyes roamed over the hills above her parents'
home and he said, 'A lovely setting.'

'Yes, if you must live in the city it helps to have hills
so near. Though we lived for our holidays up at our
aunt's place in the foothills. It was practically a high-
country estate. Not like the ones you shepherded on,
Godfrey, in the Mackenzie Country, but near enough to
spell Paradise to us.'

Aunt Helen asked, 'Where exactly is this place?'

'Rimu Bush, up behind Mount Torlesse and Kowhai
Bush. All tussock and mountain streams and dry hot
weather and deep snows. My aunt, Father's aunt really,
is very vigorous. Eccentric too, in the matter of cars.
She drives an ancient Fiat, attends all the veteran and
vintage car rallies. But despite being up there she holds
the whole family together. My father adores her, says
she's got such gumption.'

'The one commodity you can't do without,' said
Aunt Helen. 'I'd love to meet her some time. Does she
take kindly to strangers? I mean, she's obviously
hospitable to her own kin. Could you wangle me an
invitation?'

'She'd love it. You'd be two of a mind, although——'
she stopped.

Godfrey took a quick look at her face and chuckled.
'Poor Valancy, she's got a feeling this mad Carmichael
family is rushing her into an embarrassing situation. It's
one thing impressing Justin and company, isn't it, and
another to have her whole darned family jumping to

conclusions. It's okay, Valancy, I won't let my impulsive aunt draw in the entire clan.'

She looked at him gratefully. 'Thanks. I don't want Aunt Helen to feel hurt, but I don't want to make too much of this. The staff at Andersons are bound to hear of it and they're in the publishing world. It's Godfrey I'm thinking of. I have to protect him.'

He slowed up for a stop sign on this country road and gave a guffaw. 'Protect *me*? Do I look in need of protection?'

'No, you don't look it. But I've an idea that . . . er . . . inwardly you're still pretty vulnerable.'

At which he laughed still more, but she was serious enough. She turned to Aunt Helen, '*You* understand, don't you? I'm grateful to Godfrey for entering into this to help relieve an intolerable situation for Justin and Greer and to ease poor Hughsie's confused mind, but he's a public figure. He may think it rather fun, at the moment, but it could be just one more complication for him eventually and create as much misunderstanding as the Carlotta skulduggery did.'

Godfrey negotiated a wide crossing at the Halswell shopping centre where the road began to run through suburban houses before he spoke. 'Misunderstanding between whom?'

'Godfrey, you must know what I mean. Carlotta said Kathleen is coming back in February. Imagine if this becomes common knowledge. It might stop any possible hope of a reconciliation dead in its tracks.'

Godfrey uttered a sound of complete scorn. Valancy said quickly, 'It had to be brought up. I feel I've been bowled along too fast.'

Aunt Helen's laughter was so mirthful it stopped their clash immediately. 'Dear Valancy, if you knew Godfrey as I do you'd not try to protect him. He needs it as little as a man in armour. He always comes out on top. Let him do what he wants to do. Now both of you stop being so absurd . . . you want to create an impression on arrival that everything in the garden is lovely, but if you arrive with thunderclouds on your brows, it won't work. Now, get all the fun you can out of the situation.'

But Valancy knew that he hadn't always come out on top, that it still rankled, Kathleen's disbelief. But the main thing now was to convince Hughsie she wasn't suffering from a broken heart.

They got a warm welcome. Valancy's father had come home early and hugged his daughter first, then reached out a hand to Godfrey and to Aunt Helen. Dilys Adam-Smith had been on the phone, so she appeared like a whirlwind a few seconds later. Godfrey gazed at her and said, 'What a very young-looking mama you've got . . . I think she rates a kiss,' and put his two hands round her mother's suddenly pink cheeks and kissed her.

A sparkle came into her eyes. 'Dear boy . . . I'm old enough to appreciate that!' Valancy knew unease. He would vanquish everyone, she knew. He was going to overplay his hand. It wasn't as if Justin and Greer were there, to be impressed by this instant rapport.

She said so when she showed him his room, but he grinned unrepentantly. 'That's a two-storey house next door, thought I'd add all the local colour I could. Greer might have been watching.'

She said scathingly, 'Theirs is the other side. A one-storey.'

He only chuckled. It was exactly as she had feared. Despite the phone call she'd put through to her mother so that the family knew it was a hoax, she could sense the weighing-up glances that flickered from her face to Godfrey's at times. Aunt Helen made it extremely natural; she chatted away, praised Valancy for the way she'd fitted into the household at Inchcarmichael.

Dilys beamed. 'I thought that advertisement sounded tailor-made for our girl . . . the work she was trained for, plus a farm setting. Helen, are you sure it won't be too much for you having us there in January?'

Godfrey said hastily, 'Dilys, don't dare put a spoke in that wheel. I'm being very crafty. When Valancy mentioned that her father was a master builder, I thought he might be able to give us a few expert ideas on the alterations. Besides, I feel so guilty about her almost complete lack of time off, this would compensate. She's so far away from you all it practically amounts to being on duty all her waking hours. She's got some pretty nifty ideas on what would soften the stark severity of the lines of Carmichael House.'

Her father raised his brows at Valancy. She said hastily, 'Well, it's not really for me to suggest improvements, but I did think small-paned Georgian windows would break the staring look. But my ideas would seem paltry to you, Dad, you're the expert.'

'I don't know. You're the only one in my family to have a flair at all for line and design. Godfrey, I'd love to give it a go. Might even be able to start something for you while I'm down there. There's plenty of timber available down South.'

Godfrey jumped up, ran up to his room and came back with a folder. 'I brought up this photo of the front of the house and also an aerial photo. Plus this sketch I did when Valancy first suggested a few things.'

Fergus Adam-Smith caught on immediately. They spread it out on the cleared table and bent over it. Godfrey put out a long arm and drew Valancy to them. He left his arm about her shoulders. Dilys looked at Helen and without a word they departed kitchenwards.

Fergus nodded. 'Lass, you've done well, you've got the right idea—the arch one side, the conservatory the other, it reduces the height, and breaks the angular look. The fan-shaped transom over the door is splendid, but I've another notion. It's over to Godfrey, of course, and would be an extension of the same idea. Know what this house wants? A return verandah. The short side on the right where you put the arch . . . it could be a continuation of arches. And bring it right along almost to the side of the conservatory. Use a trellis effect.

'You can do it in wood. In years to come if you can ever afford wrought iron, you can replace it. At each pillar you grow creepers, clematis in all colours, wistaria, perhaps honeysuckle at first because it's quick growing and if it gets too rampant later you can cut it back easily. Those steps are uncompromisingly squared off. We could curve them out. You might be able to pick up a couple of stone figures, secondhand, for the foot of them. With all the curved flowerbeds and shrubberies you're planning, this could become a very lovely house. Ever seen any pictures of early American Colonial houses? That's what I mean.' His fingers moved busily. He sketched in a couple of hollyhocks at one side, delphiniums at the other, morning glories. Godfrey was fascinated.

As the pencil stopped, he turned and caught Valancy up, hugging her. Like a stage cue the French windows on to the patio opened still wider and Justin stepped in just as Godfrey kissed the tip of Valancy's nose. Her toes were still a foot from the floor, caught up in this exuberant embrace. He swung her round and put her down, and only then seemed to become conscious of someone standing there, grinning.

No doubt it was a grin of relief. At any rate there was no tension. Justin asked, 'What's going on?'

Godfrey didn't wait for an introduction but said, 'Justin Hughes, I presume? Come and have a look here. My house is the plainest house you could possibly imagine. Valancy proposed a few ideas, but her papa has just come up with a bobby-dazzler of a notion. Look ... before ... and after!'

Valancy felt absolutely nothing at seeing Justin again. Godfrey went on explaining with that endearingly keen note in his voice. He said, straightening up, 'Fergus, any chance of starting at the left end of the verandah first, Valancy's so keen on the conservatory idea I'd like to have that finished before anything else.'

Her father's heart warmed to this man. Valancy looked as she hadn't for a long time, his own lighthearted sparkling-eyed girl again. 'Sure it can be done. I'll take a month off instead of three weeks, it's a job after my own heart. I've a young chap who'd love to assist me and have a spell on a farm at the same time. How about that?'

Valancy reflected that they were two of a kind, her father and her ... her employer. You just couldn't hold them back. Godfrey was punctilious, he asked after Justin's mother. Justin replied, 'So much better physically. In the hospital she was nervous of slipping on the polished floors. At home here, on carpet, she has a lot more confidence, and our hall is panelled halfway up and she hangs on to the ledge that runs along it. It's just been that fretting over Valancy has held her full recovery back. The doctor says it sometimes happens— some fixed idea becomes uppermost in the mind. Greer feels the whole upset possibly brought on the stroke in the first place, and she would do anything to dispel it.'

Valancy said, 'I do hope she's not developing a guilt complex. I guess her blood pressure was high long before it happened. I hope it hasn't made Greer feel unwanted.'

'It could have done, but Mother is so grateful to her for the care she's taking with her that I think Greer realises it isn't really personal. Anyway, she's pinning all her hopes on you.'

Godfrey said, 'Then let's go in and start the healing process. I take it you've prepared your mother for my arrival with Valancy? Come on, sweetheart, let's be getting at it.'

Sweetheart! The little intimate word for the one and only.

All of a sudden her sense of humour came to her aid. She giggled, picked up the photos and sketches, and said, 'If we show her these, they'll convince her. Lead on, MacHughes!'

They came, laughing together, into the big drawing-room next door, through French windows, to find Greer with Hughsie. Godfrey's arm was conspicuously around Valancy's shoulders, and she freed herself from it and, because Greer was nearest, kissed her first. 'Why, Greer, it looks as if you've done wonders for Hughsie!'

Hughsie looked up from her chair. 'Indeed she has . . . a trained nurse in my very home, how lucky can a woman get?' She added, 'But how are *you*, dear?'

Valancy laughed, spread out her hands and said, 'Like this . . . country life always suited me. Oh, Hughsie, it's all I ever dreamed life could be. Added to the farm life it's got the sea at its back door and two beautiful rivers. We even canoe down them. And as far as the eye can see, east, west, north, south, it's all ours.'

She caught Godfrey's eye. 'And this is Godfrey . . . Godfrey Carmichael, the author.'

His eyes gleamed. 'I could have thought of a better introduction than that, Mrs Hughes. I'm not just an author, I'm Valancy's Godfrey. And I'm like a cross-bred sheep . . . part author, part farmer.'

Hughsie said, 'I only started reading your books about a year ago. I got such a surprise when I came out of hospital to find Valancy had taken off away down south to be secretary to you.'

'I've got my great-aunt with me—Aunt Helen Armishaw. I'll bring her in to meet you tomorrow. Thought it might be a bit much if we all come tonight. Look, I've brought in some photos and sketches of my great barn of a place. Valancy had the ideas for softening the outlines, and Fergus has thought of even more. He's coming down in January to help us carry them out. I'd better explain that it was out of the family hands for ages, and the man I bought it back from hacked down the century-old European trees that had surrounded the house since my great-great-grandfather's day. Since Valancy came, we've had the stumps yanked out and the ground landscaped and already a good many trees—saplings—have been replaced.

'See here . . . the windows are to be small-paned with shutters, a return verandah added, and Valancy's conservatory, her pet project, is to be added here. And the steps curved.'

Betty Hughes's cheeks were pink, her eyes glowing. She reached out, took Valancy's hand, rubbed it against her cheek and said, 'I'm so pleased for you. This is so right for you. I'd no idea. I only knew you'd gone away, alone.' They could almost see her making up her mind to say no more. It had registered.

They stayed an hour, promised longer next time. Then they went out into the kitchen with Greer, leaving Justin with his mother. Greer's eyes were shining. 'I can't tell you what this means! Her worries were actually retarding her full recovery. Her doctor will be thrilled.' She stopped, looked appalled, said, 'Oh, I'm supposing Godfrey knows the whole situation. Oh, dear——'

Godfrey slipped an arm about this little brown girl, hugged her and said, 'Godfrey does ... and only thanks his lucky stars it all happened as it did, otherwise Valancy might never have answered his advert. Oh, there you are, Justin. I was just telling Greer how grateful I am that this fell out as it did, otherwise I might never have found the perfect secretary ... and my true mate ... all in one.' He peered down at Valancy. 'Oh, darling, you're blushing again! Can't take all this flattery, can you? Never mind. I still can't believe my incredible luck. I've got another aunt,' he added, 'not an old duck like Aunt Helen, this one's a thin, vinegary one. She never approved of my attempting to buy back Inchcarmichael. She even said: "Buy that and you'll probably stay unwed all your life, my boy. Who wants to live on the edge of the world between two rivers and the sea, with only a bridge for access to civilisation?" Lovely nature, that aunt!' He paused and looked at Valancy with the sort of look she wished she didn't know was simply play-acting and said, 'But Valancy sees it through rose-coloured spectacles. We went to Invercargill for *Twelfth Night* recently, but it didn't set her yearning for the high spots ... she said as we ran down to the bridge cutting, "Ah ... the gateway to my little world of Inchcarmichael." Come on, love, we've got so much to talk over with the older folk.'

Just as they reached the hedge between the two properties, Valancy got overcome with delicious laughter. Quiet laughter. Godfrey grasped her by the elbows, drew her under the thick five-foot wide arch in the dense macrocarpa hedge, a gap where Valancy had run in and out since her toddling days. He held her, laughing with her, till she subsided.

She would have moved on then, but he relinquished her elbows only to put his arms right round her. She

said, on a thread of sound, 'You don't have to keep it
up. There's no one to impress now, Godfrey.'

'I don't feel in the least *obliged* to keep it up, you
cold-blooded female! Have you any idea how you look
in that white sleeveless dress ... with your bright
coppery hair and your blue eyes? Sapphires are your
jewels all right ... I love that necklace and your little
dangly earrings. I'll buy you a ring to match for
Christmas.' He put a finger against her protesting lips.
'Just a bonus for all the extra work you've done on my
books. You look delectable. No wonder a fellow wants
to kiss you. But——' his voice deepened, 'I was so
proud of you tonight. I can guess what it cost you. And
you were so sweet with Greer. I admire your courage.
Everything in that room must have held a memory—yet
no one would have guessed.'

Her feelings were chaotic. She was moved by his
understanding; even if he was only play-acting himself;
perhaps he'd got so into the way of it he couldn't stop.
But she mustn't take him too seriously. She must
analyse it. Because he'd been through the mill himself
he was reading his own feelings into hers. Some of it,
too, could be regret that he'd given her such a hostile
reception to begin with. Part of it, she was afraid, was
that he found this situation smacked so much of the
plots and twists he liked to write about.

He gave her a shake. 'Maddening creature, you've
gone into a trance! Didn't I just say I wanted to kiss
you?'

The laughter bubbled up in her and in the starlight
her eyes danced as merrily, as provocatively, as his own.
'What's stopping you?' she asked calmly. She didn't
know what the tone of his laugh meant as his mouth
came down on hers. After a little while he lifted his
head and said, 'Want to know what *was* stopping me?'

Her eyes were still gleaming mischief. 'Yes, I do. It
upset my reckoning of you. From your books I'd taken
you for the masterful type ... in fact a little bit thrawn,
like your heroes. One hint of opposition and you'd
crash in!'

There was sheer enjoyment in his chuckle. 'Good ...

you're so businesslike and cool when you're typing my most tender scenes, I thought they hadn't stirred you at all. But I'm going to tell you why I waited.'

Her curiosity was thoroughly aroused now. 'Then tell.'

'I thought you might have taken the initiative ... I wanted very much to kiss you, and I hoped it might have been reciprocal. That you wanted it too.'

She tried to keep it light, but that was hard to do when her heart was thudding like a trip-hammer. 'My, the big words you use, boss!'

He ignored that. 'I'm waiting, Valancy.' At that moment she felt a little tremor run through him, and knew an exultancy of spirit she'd never known before. He really wants it, she thought. She put a hand on each of his upper arms, raised herself up, kissed him fairly and squarely on the lips. Godfrey drew in a deep breath, gathered her closer and closer, then turned her head into his shoulder sideways, and she felt his lips on her chin, her cheek, her ear, her eyelids ... and down the hollow of her throat. Then he rested his chin on her hair, just holding her.

Then she knew beyond shadow of doubting that the emotion she'd felt for Justin, the boy she'd grown up with, was a pale wraith beside the flesh-and-blood-and-mind longing she had for this man who held her—her boss, who through strenuous years of shepherding had burnt the midnight oil to realise a dream, the man who had been betrayed and disbelieved by the woman he'd loved. What a fool the gentle Kathleen had been!

Presently he moved. As their clasp loosened Valancy felt a terrible sense of loss, as if an indescribable strength and warmth was being taken from her. Godfrey said, 'We must go and tell them how clever we were, that marvellous actors were lost in us.'

Actors? Was it just acting?

She said, 'Yes, of course. Come on, Godfrey, what fun to tell.'

She didn't say tell them *all* about it. Not all. Not this. Something I'll always remember.

Three expectant faces lifted towards them as they came in and Valancy's father snapped off the television. Godfrey did full justice to the way they had performed. 'It must have been a darned good show,' said Fergus, chuckling. 'Thank heaven for that! We've been close neighbours since Valancy was born. It's been very painful, especially seeing Hughsie so lost in that sort of half-world of vague impressions. Nothing we could say would convince her you were all right, Valancy, and loving it down there. But this certainly has.' He stopped, looked wicked, and twenty years younger. 'But tell me, I'm dying to know, Godfrey, is the lipstick on your collar part of the local colour? I mean, was it put there purposely? Or . . .?'

Valancy felt a blush rising from her very toes, but Godfrey said calmly, 'No, sir, I never thought of it on the way there. What a pity. No, this is the result of a ten-minute delay under the arch on the way back.'

Laughter swept them all except Valancy, who pressed cool fingers to very hot cheeks. She didn't particularly relish the evident pleasure and surmise on the three faces in front of her. She sprang up and said, taking a photograph from an inconspicuous place on a bookcase, 'Aunt Helen, I've talked about my great-aunt Cecilia Thorbury a lot, the one up in the mountains. Here's a photo of her and Uncle Robert.'

Mrs Armishaw took it with a great show of interest, looked, then looked closer. 'Well, I'm blessed . . . can it be? Yes, it must be, name and all. Tell me, was she Cecilia Murray and did she go to Rangi-ruru?'

They were all delighted. 'She certainly did,' said Fergus. 'She was my aunt on my mother's side; now if she'd been Adam-Smith you'd have tumbled to it long ago. Did you know her well?'

The reminiscent grin on Helen's face gave them a glimpse of an impish schoolgirl of more than half a century ago. 'We were partners in crime for all one year,' she confessed, 'then my people moved to the North Island and we lost touch. How truly amazing! I'd love to meet her again. Valancy mentioned her several times, but I thought the Cecilia I knew had married an

Englishman and lived over there. I heard it at a reunion.'

Fergus nodded. 'That adds. Robert Thorbury came out as a farm cadet to a friend of his father's, and lost his heart to the high country. His people advanced him enough to buy Cecilia's sister out of her share of the property, so he settled there, but took her home for a honeymoon. She'll be delighted, especially as she was the one who brought Valancy the advert. I'll ring her right now. What a surprise she's going to get!'

There was a phone in the lounge. Fergus got his aunt right away. 'Aunt, you'll never believe this ... you know this job you made Valancy apply for? Well, the author's aunt is none other than a one-time schoolmate of yours! We've just discovered it. She recognised your photo. She'd thought you were living in England. Yes, she's here and dying to speak to you. Godfrey brought his aunt and Valancy here for the weekend. How about you and Robert driving down tomorrow? You could? Great! Stay the night, of course. Well, here's the lady in question ... your one-time partner in crime, she styled herself ... Mrs Armishaw, it's all yours.'

Godfrey, sitting on the arm of Valancy's chair, said in her ear, 'How odd ... Aunt Helen is the opposite of shy, but she looks for all the world as if she's nervous ...'

'Pure imagination, Godfrey. She's never in a flap. Sometimes vague, but never scuttled. Not even when she found she'd engaged the wrong person as a secretary! Knowing her woman-hating nephew would pour the vials of his wrath upon her when he returned.'

'If you allude to me just once more as a woman-hater I'll slit your beautiful throat, Valancy Adam-Smith!'

The moment Aunt Helen spoke to Cecilia she lost her nervousness, if it had been that. They oohed and aahed over the coincidence as if such things never happened, reckoned up how many years since they'd met, and finished up with eager hopes for their meeting tomorrow.

Valancy said in a whisper to Godfrey when they switched the ten o'clock news on, 'I want to see you alone before bed.'

His eyes gleamed fun. 'Ah ... an assignation! What are we about to do now? Plan an elopement? Now that would be really convincing. What a pity your grandfather isn't still alive ... very handy thing to have, a minister in the family when eloping. Did he come out from Wales, by the way, after your mother married a New Zealander?'

'Yes ... he and Grandmother both did, so I had the privilege of knowing four grandparents. Godfrey, will you be serious? I must see you alone.'

He cocked an eye at her. 'I have a feeling you're going to dress me down. Don't bother, it won't make any difference.'

He managed it neatly, said, when they'd had their last snack, 'Now, off to bed, all of you. Valancy and I will wash these up—give us a chance to plot more of our campaign.' His laughing eyes belied that. Fergus gave him a conspiratorial grin as one man to another. 'Only natural, my boy,' he said.

As her father closed the kitchen door behind him Valancy gritted her teeth. 'Godfrey, you're being so outrageously successful in this, it's going to your head! You've got my family just about believing in this darned attachment. It's humiliating!'

She plunged her hands so vigorously into the suds a tuft of them splashed up and settled on her left eyebrow. She shook her head. 'I don't want soap in my eyes.'

'Stand still.' He drew out a handkerchief and gently wiped it off, 'Oh, you nice thing. You thoroughly nice thing! But tell me, why humiliating?'

She picked up the dishmop and attacked an inoffensive cup with vigour. 'They're too keen by far. A family ought to be saying a deception like this could get us into trouble. It's stupid!'

'It's not, you know. Mrs Hughes was really distressed. Look turn round to me.'

'I can't. Not without drying my hands.'

'Well, look over your shoulder ... that's better. I like to see people's expressions when I'm talking to them. Listen, love, you're just embarrassed because everyone likes this so much. You're afraid they'll take it for real. What's the matter? Can't you stomach the thought of me as a husband if you get pushed into it?'

Valancy looked wary. 'That doesn't come into it. I—I—well, I thought you could feel . . . pursued, nudged into something. If only Dad hadn't invited Aunt Cecilia and Uncle Robert! Aunt is so black and white, organises to the nth degree. I feel terrified. She hates shilly-shallying, so she's one of those dangerous people liking everything cut and dried. A darling, but a menace.'

Godfrey said, seriously, 'I'm not worried. I hate shilly-shallying myself. As a rule I go straight to my goal, but occasionally, if it matters terribly, I hesitate.'

She looked puzzled. 'Is that relevant?'

He took the two hands she had dried as she finished, left his thumbs free and ran them gently across the insides of her wrists in a feather-like tantalising caress that set her pulses throbbing. 'Yes, it is, most relevant. But to me, not to you, so it's nothing to worry about. Leave it alone, will you? I'll tell you in its own good time.'

Wondering, Valancy let it alone. He shook his head over her. 'I think because Mrs Hughes accepted our apparent attachment so quickly you felt a little embarrassed. Was that it? As if you thought they'd exaggerated her condition and you felt you'd used me for nothing?'

She nodded. Godfrey said gravely, 'Then don't give it another thought. I proposed it. And I'm enjoying it. It only shows how convincing you were. And don't forget I'm getting free advice and labour on what to do with an ugly white elephant of a house.'

She said quickly, 'Don't call it that. Fundamentally it's got something. And the inside is so mellow. And soon——'

'Soon it will have an outward loveliness, all due to you.' Then with a quick change of theme, 'Tell me, Valancy, have you ever had a nickname, or a diminutive form of your name?'

'Oh, I have been called Val at times. Why?'

'Because I'm going to have one for you, but not to use in public. Just when we're alone. I'm going to call you Lancy. I like that—Lancy. Come on, we'll say goodnight upstairs.'

She went willingly, bemusedly. Godfrey paused at her bedroom door. The uncurtained landing window, open, was just beside it. They looked down on the sleeping garden. Their eyes were drawn to one light that showed next door, a bedroom light, that suddenly went out. 'Damn!' swore Godfrey with feeling.

Valancy was startled. 'What's that for?'

'I'm a clot, I never thought. That's rubbing it in. Sorry.'

All of a sudden she got it. 'Oh, you mean that's *their* light? Oh, Godfrey, you nice, nice man, caring like that! In case it upset me. And so unnecessarily too ... it hadn't really registered. The landing window's open and I was wondering if Mother's night-scented stock is out yet. She always grows it below here.' Instinctively they both turned to the window, pushed the casements wider, leaned on the sill, and sniffed. It came to them, delicate, hauntingly sweet.

They laughed quietly, not to disturb the others along the passage. 'I think I'll give you something to think about,' he said. 'I thought earlier I might have done it to blot all thoughts of Justin and Greer out, but now it seems I don't need to do it for that reason. Better still, because we can do it for sheer enjoyment ...' Valancy found herself clinging to him. He said softly, 'Don't spoil this moment by analysing it, just take it, like a gift from the gods.'

A sweetness pervaded her whole body, a feeling that was to go with her into the realms of sleep. What if she had a question at the back of her mind that this ... most of this ... could be because he wrote of moments like this that touched the heights between two people? That it could be all experience to be woven into some unwritten-as-yet chapter, to delight readers all over the world. It didn't matter what it was, it was sheer magic.

'Goodnight, Godfrey,' she whispered, 'and thank you,' and she was gone, closing her room door behind her.

CHAPTER EIGHT

SATURDAY was a still, hot, typical December day in New Zealand. Aunt Helen and Dilys vowed they could manage the preparations for the midday dinner they were preparing for the folk from Rimu Bush without any help and sent Godfrey and Valancy out by themselves, to be out of their way, they said.

They drove down Ferry Road, and after crossing the Heathcote River, continued round the road that skirted the hills and the estuary where the Avon joined The Heathcote just before reaching the sea. They passed Shag Rock, sticking up in the narrow waters that divided the Brighton sandspit from this highway, and Godfrey marvelled that still it hadn't been bridged. 'I believe my maternal grandfather—no, great-grand-father, who lived here all his life, agitated for it. It's bound to come some day.'

They came to Sumner, with its beautiful curving shore under the hills, that treacherous and ever-changing bay, guarded by Cave Rock that brought memories to Godfrey. 'On hot days my grandmother would take us inside the Cave at low tide, to get shade for our lunches. A fascinating place with its small exit into the sea at the other side. It used to give us a sort of fearful joy to stay with her there till the tide came swirling in. At the age of ten I wrote my first story about that, but of course I peopled Sumner with smugglers and pirates, instead of the true hazards of the early colonists attempting to cross the Bar and use Heathcote as a landing-place.'

Valancy loved hearing things like that, it built up a life image of him in her mind. It was so hard to dissociate him from Inchcarmichael as a rule. She had to keep reminding herself that it had only been a vague dream once, that not till he was quite grown-up had he ever seen the river-island of his ancestry. His parents had lived in Timaru then, and high-country shepherding had been his goal, the place where a man could have a hut of his own, solitude for writing, and little to spend his money on. A spartan, rugged, sometimes dangerous life, but it had paid dividends. Now he had made a dream come true, bought back Inchcarmichael in its glorious setting, with its endearingly ugly house ... good for him!

They went to the end of the road where it finished against great cliffs massed over with a tangle of brightly coloured geraniums and yellow and white daisies. 'Let's leave the car here and walk up Scarborough Head, Valancy,' suggested Godfrey. 'I've always loved that hill.'

She turned a glowing face to him. 'I hadn't realised you knew my birthplace so well. I like you knowing and loving the haunts of my life.'

'I loved Scarborough best of all in our August holidays, when winter was giving way reluctantly to spring. The air was sharp and the tussocks yellow-ochre, but it was sheltered here where the hills turn their backs to the bleak south. We always saw the first wattle blooming here. I remember I wrote a poem about it and, greatly daring, sent it off to the evening paper. I just about burst with pride when Granddad opened it and there, at the foot of the second page, was my poem with my own name under it. No moment has ever equalled that.'

By now they'd climbed above the houses, taken a short cut up some steps cut in the clay bank, and over a stile that led to a walking track. Just above it Godfrey paused. 'Jove, that's the very stile I sat on to compose it. Mother gave me a paper bag we'd had bananas in, to write it on, with a horrible blunt pencil stump.'

Valancy took two steps down, patted the rough, splintery wood on the top and said laughingly, 'Now that you're becoming one of New Zealand's most famous sons there ought to be a bronze plate here, "On this spot, Godfrey Shakespeare Carmichael composed his first published poem." '

He put an arm round her shoulders and said, 'Oh,

Valancy, you make everything such fun! When I think how I hated you that moment I first beheld you and thought I was stuck with another scheming female of a secretary, I feel I didn't deserve my luck. What a felicitous mistake that was!'

She disregarded that. 'Can you remember the poem, Godfrey?'

He thought, made a face, then said, 'I can only remember the last line. It began with a lark singing in a cloudless sky, and the sweep of all Pegasus Bay, a hundred miles or so of it, and the last line was: "And golden bursts of wattle on a tussock-covered hill." '

She said softly, 'I've seen those bursts of wattle. How those trees have grown! Mother loves it. She grew up in Wales, but used to holiday in London, and one of her fondest memories is of London flowersellers selling mimosa from the South of France. When Dad brought her out here, she found a tree she'd never seen before in the garden and Dad told her it was wattle. Their first spring she rushed to meet him saying, "It's not a wattle, it's a mimosa!" '

'Then when she comes down we must take her to the north branch of the river. You've not been to the wattle grove yet. A whole hillside is covered with old and young trees. Tell her next year she must come down in August. What are you looking like that for?'

She said soberly, 'Am I likely to last as long as that?'

He said shortly. 'That's absurd. We'll consider it unsaid. Must you spoil an idyllic morning?'

She was abashed, murmuring, 'Sorry.'

'Okay, forget it. Don't let what Justin did to you make you so insecure. Come on up to the top of the hill. Good job you've jeans on—I reckon we'll have to slide down, sitting.'

Valancy was wearing a loose silk shirt over them, one of her brother's, in cream, and it clung to her in the slight breeze that was springing up. He looked at her appreciatively; the outlined curves, the sea-blue eyes, and the little tendrils each side of her brow were sheer red-gold in the sun; she caught him at it and liked his male appreciation.

He said, 'Jolly good scenery wherever you look! But this view,' he waved at the huge bay, 'was, till I bought our land back, my favourite. It was here that my other grandfather told me that an even more beautiful one could be had from the cliffs of Inchcarmichael, that nothing compared with being able to look south over countless leagues of ocean to the bottom of the world. He'd been taken to visit there once. I made a vow that day that I'd bring it back into the family. Oh, here's a handy rock to sit on.' It was high enough for their legs to dangle and had a contour that made a back rest.

She felt moved. They were where his dream had first been born. Now Inchcarmichael was his, but to what purpose? He'd wanted it for his sons and daughters, and their sons and daughters, and Kathleen had come into his life, and had departed, leaving it empty.

That thought was uppermost in her mind, so it was a pity, when Kathleen's intangible presence was with her, that Godfrey spoke then. He turned to her, caught her farthest away hand in his so she had to turn to him and said, 'I told you to forget about wondering if you'd still be at Inchcarmichael in August. But I'm bringing it up again, nevertheless. I don't meant to let you go, Lancy. You're so perfect for Carmichael House. I need more than a secretary. Why don't we delight everyone and make this mock-up into reality?'

It was just as if he had stabbed her. Oh, what foolish dreams she had known last night! Dreamed that suddenly he might come to realise that he loved her as she loved him, a love that made her former attachment to Justin seem pallid and feeble. She had even wished that he, in comparison, eventually, might find her more satisfying than the gentle Kathleen.

Yes, everyone would welcome it . . . what sort of a reason was that for marrying? For giving oneself entirely to another? Godfrey needed more than a secretary . . . oh, yes, a mother for the sons he needed to inherit his river-island. Someone who'd come to love even that ugly duckling of a house . . . oh, yes, *she was so suitable*! What a reason for marriage! How cold-blooded! A fine fury rose up in her and was instantly subdued. She kept her eyes on the horizon.

How patient he was . . . he knew she was considering it . . . a man who loved her, who hungered for her, desired her, would have been more demanding, especially this man, with all the depths, passionate and idealistic, withal disciplined, whom she knew so well, because day after day, week after week, she had typed compelling words that came from his innermost being.

The amount of control she had to exercise sent an uncontrollable shiver over her. Godfrey withdrew immediately. 'All right,' he said harshly, 'you don't have to tell me. It was all eyewash last night, wasn't it, when you pretended that seeing their bedroom light go out meant nothing to you? You're shuddering at the very thought of marriage with me. You really *haven't* got Justin out of your system yet, have you? Yet I could have sworn——' He stopped.

In the very twinkling of an eye he changed to a compassionate tone. 'Oh, I'm sorry—I'm a clumsy fool! It was bound to upset you this weekend. I thought I was being so sensible, felt I could equate marriage . . . married happiness, with kindred interests. We work well together, love the same things, laugh at the same jokes, strike sparks off each other occasionally in a physical way, our people get on well together . . . like I said, I'm a fool. Forget it.'

He was surprised to see tears standing in her eyes. She turned, clutched at him. 'Godfrey, don't. Thank you for asking me.' She gave a watery smile. 'Sounds like a Victorian novel—thank you for the honour you do me, sir.' Her grip tightened. 'I don't feel a thing now for Justin, and I want you to realise that. You must. I want that very intensely for some reason. Can you understand?'

He said slowly, 'I can, when you speak like that. You sound convincing. But you shuddered at the idea . . .'

'I didn't,' she cried passionately. 'I mean, that wasn't what I shivered at. I can't explain that. It wasn't revulsion. How can you think that, when last night . . .' she stopped, confused, and the delicate colour came up in her cheeks.

In spite of himself he smiled, the lip corners quirking up. 'Well, thank heaven for that! My male ego was bruised.'

Valency bit her lip. 'If there's one thing I don't want to do it's to hurt you in any way.' She stumbled over the next words. 'I—it's *because* I responded to you like that last night, under the arch, that I'm afraid of this situation. In spite of that, Godfrey, I don't think it's enough. I—oh, perhaps it's different for men. But it's a total commitment with women, and I just can't think of making do with second-best. If I can't be sure that——'

She wanted to say 'If I can't be sure you love me as I love you, I can't risk it,' but she hadn't the courage.

His lips thinned out again. 'All right, I get it. Your love for Justin was killed stone dead when he turned from you to Greer but even so you won't settle for less than you once felt for him. All right, Valency, it was stupid of me. I thought we might have been commonsense about it, made a splendid partnership, but it's not fair to expect that from a highly-geared girl like you. It's got to be all or nothing, hasn't it? Right, mate, back to the old pretence for the weekend. Let's get as much fun out of it as possible. Are you game to slide down this hill on your bottom?'

What a very prosaic end! That showed that though he thought marrying her might have neatly tidied up his long-term plans for Inchcarmichael, it wasn't going to break his heart that she wouldn't. He'd probably find someone else.

They arrived back to find Aunt Cecilia and Uncle Robert there. They'd driven down in Robert's late-model car or they wouldn't have made it so soon. Valency saw that Godfrey knew he was being inspected by both and that he had won instant approval.

He said to Valency on the quiet. 'Think how much more she'd have approved, your aunt, had we come back engaged. The pretence turned into reality. It would have made her day. You ought to be ashamed of yourself. It was practically your duty.'

'You're impossible!' she said, but had to laugh. Yet

inwardly she sighed. If ever anything proved it hadn't gone deeply, this did. Aunt Cecilia almost flirted with him. She won his heart by knowing his characters well. She even said to Aunt Helen 'It must have been Providence that put the words in my mouth when I rang you. If I'd said "My niece" instead of "a young relation of mine" none of this would have happened and poor Hughsie would always have been convinced that Valancy was nursing a broken heart.' Oh, dear, Aunt Helen must have told of her reception. Well, they'd been bosom friends once. Aunt Cecilia went on, 'I don't like these girl-and-boy-next-door romances. Much nicer to meet someone who's a stranger and can see one as a whole personality, not just a member of a family.'

'I couldn't agree with you more, Aunt Cecilia ... I can call you that, can't I? After all, Valancy calls my aunt Aunt Helen.'

'Of course ... might as well get used to it.'

Oh, dear, Aunt Cecilia was going to try to push them over the brink of no return. After lunch, because of that, Valancy excused them from going in with Aunt Cecilia to see Hughsie. Otherwise she'd play up the situation outrageously, and Valancy didn't want to be there to see it.

Godfrey wanted to go over the plans with her father. Aunt Helen had gone with Cecilia and Robert. Valancy settled in a corner for a good yarn with her mother, the two men worked at a table and asked for advice now and then.

The phone rang, Valancy answered. Her voice warmed. 'Oh, hullo, Mr Anderson. I was going to give you a ring. I knew Justin would tell you. Oh, she's much better. Had this bee in her bonnet I was languishing, but that was dispelled when she saw me. Country life suits me. What did you say? I don't know, I'd have to ask him. We had intended going back Monday.' She put a hand over the phone, 'Godfrey, Mr Anderson, my former boss, knew you were coming. He has a friend who's a bookseller in one of the larger shops in town. They've just got a stack of your former

books in, reprints. He knows the notice is too short for
a signing session, no time to advertise, but he wonders
if you could call in on Monday and sign them so
customers can have the pleasure of a signed copy.
Could we stay till Tuesday?'

Godfrey came to the phone, he agreed, chatted away,
finished by saying, 'Sounds good to me. It'll give her
the chance of seeing everybody. I'll bring her in about
ten. I'd like to meet the staff she worked with, too. I'll
go into your friend's shop after that. We can easily
travel back on Tuesday. Valancy has worked like a
Trojan ever since she came to Inchcarmichael. See you
then.'

He grinned. 'Might as well convince everyone in one
go. The whole situation is getting hilarious. I've no
doubt the staff were rather agin Justin over it. Now
they'll think it worked out for the best. Isn't that vain
of me? As for those two aunts . . . anybody would think
they'd brought the whole thing about.' His eyes were on
Valancy as he said it.

She nodded, 'I know. Just because Aunt Cecilia
saw the advert and Aunt Helen missed the hyphen.
What a pair! Instead of being a couple of old
muddle-heads they're fancying themselves as the
instruments of Fate. As long as they don't carry it
too far. This isn't some fore-ordained conclusion with
a fairy-tale ending.'

Godfrey chuckled, 'It's because of their former
association, I suppose. When they were upstairs doing
themselves up for going next door, they were giggling
together like a pair of schoolgirls plotting some ghastly
prank.'

Valancy looked alarmed. 'I hope not! Especially if it
involves us.'

Godfrey put an arm about her on his way back to his
chair. 'Oh, not to worry, we can cope,' and he dropped
a light kiss on her head.

She said, 'For goodness' sake, you don't have to
pretend when the folk next door aren't about.'

'Perhaps not,' he said coolly, 'but very nice, just the
same.'

Her father burst out laughing. 'You can't call the tune with this one, Valancy. Let him do it his way.'

She scowled at her papa. 'I can't help it, can I? Seeing he pays the piper. I wish you'd all remember he's my boss.'

She made no impression. Her parents and Godfrey just laughed.

Hughsie was so much better on the Sunday afternoon she actually came through the arch, walking with two sticks, and sat out on the patio with them, for afternoon tea.

Greer's delight was touching to see. The two aunts looked after Hughsie while the rest of them went to the evening service. 'It will do Justin and Greer good to be off together,' Aunt Cecilia said, 'while we're here.'

Justin said quietly to Valancy, 'You know, this is astounding. I thought that Aunt Cecilia was the one person who'd never forgive me. I'm glad. She's such a good sort.' His eyes met hers smilingly. 'Of course I can realise why. She thinks Godfrey is the better man. And so he is. It's all so right for you, Valancy, isn't it, the man and the setting?'

She lifted candid eyes to him. This wasn't pretence. She said simply, 'That's the way of it, Justin.' Because it was, only he didn't know this part of it was makebelieve. She saw Godfrey watching them, and for once did the sensible thing—walked straight across to him, in the window embrasure, put her hand in his, turned so their backs were to the others and said, 'He's just told me you're the better man. I agreed.' Nothing more could be said then. They had to get ready.

Sitting in the pew they had always occupied with the Hughes family, between her father and Godfrey, with Justin and Greer at the other side of him, Valancy had the strangest feeling that she was only dreaming this.

Later that night Godfrey said to Valancy, that he was now glad for Justin and Greer's sake they'd played this charade. 'Till now it was for your sake and for Mrs Hughes, because I felt you were the one who'd had the thick end of the stick, but I can see the frightful strain they were under. They must have felt so guilty, not just in the neighbourhood and in the church, but in the office too. That's why I thought it a good idea to go into the firm tomorrow with you.' He twinkled and the grey eyes looked more blue than grey. 'Mr Anderson will be quite convinced now that it was a very short season of forgetfulness.' She blushed vividly. 'You blush so enchantingly, Valancy.'

She said, with feeling. 'It's a great drawback. I've always wished for an olive skin, that I had a poker face, that I didn't betray my feelings so quickly.'

'I don't know that you do, Lancy. I've no idea what that blush meant. Blushes can be for pleasure, warmth of feeling, or embarrassment. Even the dread of blushing can make the colour rise. And women don't have that on their own. Young boys can dread colouring up. Anyway, women who don't blush or don't cry are cold creatures.'

She blinked. 'You surprise me, Godfrey.'

His look was whimsical. 'I hope to surprise you often. Let me tell you this ... when Aunt Helen speaks of Kathleen as the gentle Kathleen, she doesn't mean it as a compliment. She only appeared gentle at first. In actual fact she's as tough as they come. I never remember her blushing or crying.'

Some innate honesty made Valancy say, 'Godfrey, when she thought Carlotta had been sharing your room she might have stemmed back the tears in front of you. She might have cried at night, alone.'

He looked at her in the most exasperated fashion. 'There are times, Miss Adam-Smith, when I could beat you! You're a contrary little devil. You always want to find excuses, to patch things up that are beyond repair. When you're on that tack, there's only one way to silence you.' He kissed her, not gently.

Valancy put nothing into that kiss. They were at the bottom of the stairs and she was acutely aware that at any moment someone could erupt from a door. The aunts did, from the kitchen. Aunt Cecilia waved a majestic hand, 'Don't let us interrupt you, we're just passing through.'

'Thanks very much,' said Godfrey just as calmly, 'but be sure to close the living-room door, won't you?'

Valancy turned and fled upstairs—and heard him follow. At her door she turned to face him. 'You devil!' she exclaimed, 'I can see wedding-bells in my aunt's eyes. And it's all your fault.'

He caught her hands. 'Why should that worry me? After all, I asked you, only this morning, if you'd marry me.'

She bit her lip, then said coolly, 'And I turned you down. Said that second-best wasn't enough for me.'

For the first time she saw him look really hard, angry. 'I know it's too soon. But you might, in fact must, consider it.'

'Must?' Now *she* was furious. (She longed to hurl hot words at him, to say: 'Why?' then add, 'No, don't tell me, I know so well why! Because you want to found a dynasty at Inchcarmichael ... and I'm the girl on the spot. And *suitable*.')

But she didn't. She might give herself away.

His fingers dug into her shoulders. He'd like to shake her, she knew. For one horrible moment she exulted in the fact that she had upset him. How dared he do this cold-blooded thing to her! As if she'd marry for less than love!

He said between his teeth, 'Yes, you must. Any man deserves an answer, an answer after careful considera-tion. Give me a date ... I like to plan my life ahead. I have for years. I've achieved one goal ... I want to know what the next goal is. So give me a date for your answer. Or are you frightened to consider it?'

'All right,' she flung at him. 'You seem to think I might turn you down flat now and live to regret it. What an extraordinary——'

'Well, I do. I think this whole false, strange weekend has been too much for you. It's coloured for you because of that fellow next door. You've said you've no feeling left for him and I could accept that, but the trouble is, he's the one you planned to live your life out with. I knew that when I saw—oh, let that pass. So I'm being fair. I'm giving you a chance when you're far enough away to look at it dispassionately, to consider my offer again ... if you're brave enough to do it.'

'Right, I'll do that. I'll consider it till March. Not a day earlier than the first of March!'

Her mind had seized on that date. Kathleen was coming back to Badenoch in February. Time enough before the first of March to meet and to know whether or not they could live without each other.

Godfrey's brows were a straight line over blazing eyes. 'That's a hell of a way off. I like things cut and dried.'

'Well, you aren't going to get them cut and dried. It doesn't seem long to me to decide something that must last a lifetime.'

Suddenly his anger evaporated. 'Right. The first day of March. The beginning of autumn.'

Valancy couldn't bear him to have the last word. She said stiffly, 'Of course, if you change your mind, let me know. And be grateful to me. You'd better give it long, long thoughts too.'

She went to open her door, but he reached out and stopped her. 'Oh, no, you don't! You're not going to upset those thoroughly nice people below by letting them have the tiniest whisker of suspicion that we've quarrelled. They've been through the hoops already, haven't they? Your people agonising over Justin jilting you; my aunt going through the same when Kathleen ditched me. Pin a smile on, hold my hand, and come downstairs.'

She pinned the smile on, slipped into the pretence, laughed and joked for what was left of the evening. She'd rather have hung on to what she thought was her righteous anger. This sort of thing was so disarming. He was so much a family man, so obsessed with the continuance of a family estate, that she believed all he proposed sprang from a desire to please the family in marriage too. Her last chaotic thought as she fell asleep was: 'And so do I, and so do I.'

There was a certain poignancy in the way the staff greeted her next morning, and a sting in it too. If only it could have been for real! Some of them had read Godfrey's books, and were delighted to meet the author in the flesh, but mostly they were glad for Valancy's sake. Godfrey played it beautifully, just conveying by the occasional intimate gesture, the casual references to their sharing of the author/farmer occupation, his use of the word 'we' frequently, that his interest in their former colleague was more than that of an employer.

She refused to go with him to the signing. 'Someone at the shop might know someone in the press, and ring him up. I've seen that happen with some of our authors. If so, I don't want to be linked with you. You know the aunts are having morning tea at Ballantyne's ... I'll join them there. Not to eat, seeing Andersons were so lavish, but just to chat. You can pick us up there. I must go. They'll be spinning out their coffee as it is.'

They had a corner table and by the look of them were still sharing reminiscences. They ordered coffee for Valancy. 'Doesn't she look lovely?' asked Aunt Helen fondly. 'I've always liked blue and white stripes and that's a darling suit. Hasn't this been a happy weekend? When is the dear boy joining us? Oh, dear, I'd better not let him hear me call him that! He's thirty-three.'

Suddenly Valancy started to giggle. The two old ladies joined in. 'What a weekend!' smiled Aunt Cecilia. 'I've not enjoyed anything so much for years, in fact, not since Rangi-ruru days. I've been heard to say modern youth is lacking in romance, but when it comes to an established author involving himself like this, there's hope for the world.'

Valancy sobered up, 'But it's because he *is* an author he thought of it. When you're used to pushing your characters round on the stage of your imagination, you can't help it spilling over into real life occasionally. I'm sure you could put it all down to that.'

Two pairs of disbelieving eyes confronted her. Then Aunt Cecilia said, 'Oh ... was that all it was?' in a mock scornful voice.

Valancy regarded them sternly. 'I think you two had better stop manipulating things too. Godfrey and I know exactly what we're doing, and it's solely for Hughsie's sake. It's over, we've almost played it out.'

But they hadn't. They'd been too engrossed to see

someone threading through the tables to them. So they didn't look up till this slim, middle-aged woman stood over them. Valancy had her back to the newcomer, but saw Aunt Cecilia register an odd look ... guilt? ... horror? Valancy turned, decided she was getting far too imaginative, because here was someone from the Rimu Bush area, a dear friend.

The dear friend pulled out the vacant chair, sat down, said, 'No, thanks, I've had my tea,' to Aunt Cecilia's quick query, 'but fancy meeting you two here in this very spot again.' She turned to Valancy. 'Hullo, I didn't expect to see you too ... on holiday, are you? Or have Andersons let you have an hour off?' Then, to Valancy's dumbfounded surprise, 'Hullo, Mrs Armishaw, you and Cecilia having a reunion *again*?' She turned to Valancy. 'I was actually present at the very moment when they met for the first time for over fifty years, two or three months ago.'

Valancy gave a weak smile, managed, 'Fancy that!' Now there was no mistaking that look on Aunt Cecilia's face for guilt. In a quick glance she found it mirrored on Aunt Helen's. She said quickly, to bridge the moment for them, 'I'm not at Andersons any more. I'm secretary to an author in the Catlins—Godfrey Carmichael ... you've probably heard of him, though I admit I hadn't till I answered his advertisement for a typist.'

Each old lady drew in a deep breath, each tried to speak, then both stopped. In pity for them, Valancy continued, 'I'm up for a weekend, so Aunt Cecilia came down too. Nice that Mrs Armishaw could come this weekend too. It's always good to meet up with old schoolfellows. Connie, how is Basil? Last time I saw you he'd broken his arm. Did it mend all right?'

Connie chatted away, asked Valancy when she was coming to Rimu Bush again. Valancy explained that she'd not be able to come for some time, her employer had a book to finish, and it was a busy time on his estate, too. Yes, it was quite true, her employer's aunt was Mrs Armishaw.

Connie West thought it was so interesting, 'I daresay

if these two hadn't met by pure chance that day here, you might not now be working for one of Basil's favourite authors. I suppose it was through them you heard about the position?'

Valancy fixed her eyes upon the pair opposite and said very deliberately, 'Yes, I think you could put it down to nothing else. Aunt Cecilia heard Godfrey needed a secretary, that he preferred someone used to country life, and she recommended me for the position. I'm no end grateful to them.' She smiled sweetly at the two poor darlings sitting miserably dumb.

Connie rose, said, 'I've got to meet Basil at twelve-thirty, so I must be on my way. It's been lovely seeing you, Valancy. And you, Mrs Armishaw. Cecilia, I'll see you back home—bye-bye.' And with a flick of her elegant skirts she was gone.

The aunts were left gazing at Valancy. For once her face gave nothing away. 'Aren't you the lucky ones! Her leaving before Godfrey arrives. Then the fat *would* have been in the fire!'

Never had she seen Great-aunt Cecilia at such a loss. Finally she swallowed and said, 'Then you aren't going to tell him?' and her voice actually croaked.

'No, nor anybody else. I realise it was all cooked up between you to get me to Inchcarmichael . . . and I can guess your real reasons, you matchmaking old horrors, but he'll never hear it from me. Which is more than either of you deserve.'

Aunt Helen breathed again. 'Valancy, you darling! I couldn't bear him to know. And it could have spoiled a lovely relationship, I mean between your family and ours. Oh, thank you!'

Valancy said sternly, 'Don't thank me, just let it be a lesson to you. My motives aren't as pure as you might think. It could be, if he ever got to know, that he might think I was in it too, and I just couldn't bear that,' and to her horror her own voice wobbled.

The two old faces looked stricken, and Aunt Helen said, 'Cecilia, we've upset her . . . oh, the dear, darling child! Surely we could convince him if ever he got to know that you know nothing about it.'

Valancy said miserably, 'I think he always thought it funny I signed it with just my initial. But he accepted that. Then one day he told me he'd found my letter shoved down under some old bills in the kitchen drawer and he thought the hyphen had been rubbed out. It wasn't just faint. I told him I thought Aunt Helen had felt so bad over the mistake, she'd rubbed it out to be convincing if he ever demanded it.'

Cecilia was recovering. 'I might as well tell all. *I* did it. When I sent you out to the car for that parcel. Thank goodness your mother didn't come this morning. We can keep this between the three of us.' Valancy leaned her elbows on the table and her chin in her hands, and looked at them. They looked steadily back. Then her mouth crumbled and she gave way to laughter. 'But because I can see the funny side of it, it doesn't mean Godfrey would. I know I'm innocent. He mightn't.'

They told her all. About Cecilia's niece being jilted, Godfrey falling for a girl who wouldn't believe him over a bit of manufactured scandal. The idea hit them simultaneously . . . *if only the pair of them could meet.* But they couldn't imagine how.

Then Aunt Helen produced an amazing belief. 'Then Providence took a hand. Godfrey asked me to advertise while he was in Canada. I rang Cecilia on toll, and she made sure she was in Christchurch when the advert appeared. It really was clever.'

'It was diabolical,' said Valancy, 'the devil had more to do with it than Providence!' and the next moment the three of them were helpless. Godfrey came in, found them, and sat down. Saved by the clock, they all thought. 'Still giggling?' he said sternly. He turned to Valancy and said, 'I reckon they've giggled more this weekend than for the last fifty years.'

'Exactly,' said Valancy. 'I've just been hearing some of their pranks, and believe me, they've shocked even me!'

CHAPTER NINE

THEY played the farce out till the very moment they left the next morning. It had a bitter-sweet quality for Valancy. She cherished most the hour they spent on the Monday night with Hughsie. It was so worth while, because Justin and Greer left them alone with her, and Godfrey was sweet with Justin's mother. He talked to her of his early struggles in being accepted for short stories and articles, written in his lonely hut on Dragonshill, his successes since. He gave her an autographed book.

Hughsie turned to Valancy. Her speech was still a little slow, but improving every day. 'And you love it down there?'

Valancy leaned forward. This wasn't acting. 'It's like something out of a Disney film. Lovely dells and glades, deep in Carmichael's Bush, and streams wander all over the place, and the contours are such that it makes for dozens of little tinkling waterfalls and cascades. You may have seen the famous Purakaunui Falls, not far away. These are like that in miniature, coming down in a series of steps.

'It's never under threat because it all belongs to Godfrey, so there's no danger of fire or depredation or milling. If he hadn't been able to buy it back when he did, that too might have gone. Every time I look at the towering *totaras* in the bush, I thank God he got it before the hands of the vandals fell on it. To picnic in a little glade and know nobody can come in without permission, so there's no need for even a litter-bin, is just heaven. Nobody on the property would drop as much as a nutshell.

Hughsie said, 'I'm so glad. It sounds ideal for you.'

'It is. It's the sort of place that takes hold of you and will never let you go. I'm unashamedly lyrical about it. The variety is amazing, even at the shore. At the south we have sheer cliffs, with the sea swirling up into the Blowholes, and then, a mile or two north of that, the most perfect bathing beach, where a stream wanders down from the bush and forms a lagoon before it enters the salt water. Rachel and I spend hours swimming there, whenever my stern taskmaster spares me from pounding the keys.' She looked saucily at Godfrey.

He grinned. 'The pair of them entice me away from my own brain-grind far too often to join them. Most of the summer the red of the *rata* vines mingles with the green of the native bush and hangs down from the banks of the lagoon, and in spring the native clematis sprinkles it with white stars. And the wading-birds are there in legions. You must come and see it for yourself some time. Fergus and Dilys could bring you. I mean it.'

Hughsie said, 'You don't know what that does for me. If people can plan for me, then I know I have a future, and modern medicine can keep blood-pressure at bay so well now. God bless you both.' Valancy went to bed with the knowledge that if Hughsie did come down the masquerade would have to continue.

But when they left next day on the six-hour plus run to Badenoch, all pretence dropped away. Perhaps Godfrey had found it exhausting. He'd certainly put everything into it. But perhaps he was playing it fair. Valancy had asked for time in which to make up her mind and she was getting it, unswayed by the intimacy their pretence had swept them into.

The tempo of life at Inchcarmichael, as everywhere in Christian countries, quickened as Christmas approached. Godfrey's parents, who had retired in Auckland, were spending Christmas with his married sister in Fiji. 'We'll spend next Christmas with you, son,' Esther Carmichael had written, 'but possibly we won't be able to restrain ourselves from a late autumn visit to you when you've done all these fascinating additions to that great stark box of a place. They sound just right. How fortunate you were in getting a secretary with the right ideas and a builder for a father. Order the creepers now as a present from us. I so like living presents.'

This meant that Christmas was celebrated with just those who lived there. Aunt Helen invited the Birchfields for dinner, and of course the two single workers, and they planned a bathing picnic at the lagoon in the afternoon with a barbecue tea to follow.

The week before Godfrey and Valancy really slogged in the study, which was bliss for the two cats, James and Susie. Godfrey laughed, 'At one time they used to fight over my chair, now Susie remains in sole possession, while James takes over yours. A boy for you, a girl for me, as the old song goes. Well, we're doing well. I always like to clear the decks before Christmas as far as desk work goes, and it's important this year, so we can leave January free for the alterations. The men can manage the farm work, in the main. In February I'd like to be able to work on the Carmichael history, getting it into shape, while you type on the current book. That, of course, depends on my getting all the revisions done. I don't like retyping started till they're all complete. Sometimes, if one changes the end, the beginning needs changing too.'

Valancy was fascinated with all this. At Andersons, of course, they'd just dealt with finished work. Just as well the work here was so demanding. Since coming home Godfrey had never held her hand, much less kissed her. Even their constant talking lacked the sparkle, the give and take of something that had held all the raillery of man-woman relationship, provocative, titillating. This was back to the sexless worker-bee syndrome with a vengeance. Was she being punished for not going along with his dreams for founding a new family strain for Inchcarmichael? She wished it didn't seem so cold-blooded, so—so Gothic!

She wished sometimes to simply yield. Every instinct urged her to accept him, every warning signal told her she might never be satisfied with less on his side than the overwhelming love she knew for him. Would she become bitter if he never loved her as much? Anyway, she was determined not to decide till he met Kathleen again.

There were a few nice moments. Godfrey's November royalties didn't reach him till the last week of December, but they were so good his spirits rose. 'Look, Valancy, translations into Italian, Japanese, and Hungarian, beside the others I've had earlier. Extra revenue for no extra writing. That's what Inchcarmichael needs!' Inchcarmichael ... always this river-island.

'Now I can bring that area between here and the bush into production for barley and oats. I can afford more aerial topdressing, more weed-spraying by helicopter. I can reduce some of the loan I raised for the woolshed.' He grinned. 'I can even raise my secretary's salary to compensate for all the extras she does, for her unpaid work in garden and in the drafting-pens. I've been wanting to for some time.'

Suddenly Valancy was enraged. She stood up, put both her hands on her desk that was in the middle of the room and glared at him. 'You'll do nothing of the sort! I've never saved so much as since being here. Any extras I do for love.' She added quickly, 'For love of Inchcarmichael. You don't have to have the blood of the Carmichaels in your veins to love a place like this, isolated from the world. Plough your translations back into the land. Transform Carmichael House into the gracious homestead it ought to have been always. Plant trees on a big scale. But don't throw it away without reason!'

She turned to rush from the room. Godfrey stood up so abruptly he caught his desk-trough with the cuff of his jacket and knocked it on to the floor. Unforgivably she laughed, 'I'll come back when I've got over being mad with you. I don't do this *just* for money any more than you do,' and before he could skirt the tumbled mass of books she was out of the door, rushed through the kitchen, mercifully empty, and though she'd have loved to fling herself on Rufus, he wasn't saddled, so she wrenched open her car door, thankful it was standing outside the shed because Rod had moved it earlier and left the keys in.

She jumped in and shot off, down the road to the bridge. Her anger lasted her till she got to Badenoch. How dared he think he could pay for all her services! It was a delightful small township, bigger than a village, but had something of village charm. Plans for it had been drawn up by an early settler from Surrey, and he'd grouped cottages round a village green that had a pond in the middle of it.

Off the main road as it was, it had never had to surrender its sleepy hollow air to motorways or through traffic. There had been a time when the old cottages had fallen into disrepair, but as prices rose, far-sighted people had restored them, some for holiday homes, some to live in. Two darling old sisters ran a library and tea-shop, that had an old-world charm. It was becoming renowned for its crumpets and bran muffins, its Devonshire cream teas. This morning a tourist bus was drawn up and when she entered, it was full of tourists en route for the Purakaunui Falls.

One table was empty. She sat down and, as she might have known, felt her anger evaporate and contrition set in. What on earth had possessed her to go off like that, half-cocked? It had been a generous, impulsive gesture on his part, wanting to share his windfall. And she'd flung it back in his face.

She knew, but he couldn't, that it was part of her chaotic feelings ... she really didn't want to take his already more than adequate salary at all. She wanted to be his wife, standing shoulder to shoulder with him in all his endeavours. To share everything, his home, his board and his bed. Oh, if only she could make up her mind to take what he was offering her! Not all men went in for impassioned declarations of undying love when they proposed marriage. No-o-o. But it was to be expected that a man like Godfrey, with his love of words, whose heroes *did* propose like that, *would*.

Miss Mabel Crumstane brought her a pot of tea, scones, jam, cream. Miss Edith paused, passing by, to say hello. Then someone appeared at her elbow, saying, 'May I join you? Because there isn't a table left.'

Valancy looked up, liked what she saw, and nodded.

'Of course. It's not often so crowded, but their fame is spreading, and no wonder.'

'Yes, aren't we lucky in a place as small as this, to have such a tea-rooms? And a jolly good pub too. I find it quite fascinating that the pub is actually in the hands of the same family as pioneered here. So many places have changed hands it's good to find that continuity.'

Valancy nodded. 'Yes, it warms the heart, doesn't it? My employer is an example of that. His estate went out of the family for years, and was practically ruined, but he was able to buy it back and is doing wonderful things to it. He's Godfrey Carmichael of Inchcarmichael, the author, and it's a river-island, on the coast.'

The woman looked startled for a moment, waited till Miss Mabel had brought her tray, busied herself pouring out and said, 'What a coincidence! I know him well. In fact I was thinking of calling on him. My husband and I have been away on a world trip, visiting our daughter in England.'

'Is she married over there?'

'No, she's not married. She's been working at the Bank of New Zealand in London recently, though she had some months in Liverpool, nursing. She's coming home next month. As a matter of fact, without seeming gossipy, but you probably know, my daughter was once engaged to Godfrey. Well, near enough. Only my silly girl believed a bit of spiteful gossip a former secretary of his made. I never believed it myself. Neither does Kathleen now.'

Valancy felt just as if a giant hand had taken her heart in a bruising grip. She forced herself to say calmly, 'Oh, yes, I knew. Then you must be Mrs Rissington.'

The woman nodded. Apart from the unwelcome news about Kathleen's soon return, Valancy felt quite drawn to this woman, because she, at least, had never believed the gossip. Mrs Rissington continued, 'I don't want to butt in, because it's a delicate sort of situation. Only Godfrey felt so terribly about Kathleen not believing him, I felt I'd like him to know she's come to the conclusion that that Carlotta lied. I suggested she wrote to him, but she didn't feel she could—said it might look as if she wanted to make it up. She wants me to tell him. Then if they meet when she comes home there'll be no awkwardness. She wanted me to tell him that now she's thought it out, she's sure Carlotta deliberately engineered it.'

Valancy moistened her dry lips and said firmly, 'She had. She's the most devious creature I've ever known. I knew her quite well. I went to college with her. She broke up several promising relationships I know of. She could attract men, but never hold them because they always finally saw through her shoddiness, her petty jealousy, her possessiveness. She isn't really called Carlotta, you know. She adopted that, I suppose, because it sounded more glamorous than Carol. I'd no idea that the Carlotta they talked of at Inchcarmichael was the one and the same as the poisonous Carol.

'I just wish your Kathleen had seen the lovely showdown Godfrey had with her, in front of me, in an Invercargill restaurant. She saw me sitting alone while he was fixing something up about the car. She had no idea who I was working for till Godfrey returned ... oh, it was most satisfying! He told her to clear out. I'm almost ashamed to say I enjoyed it. Especially when I knew here was the creature who'd ruined the romance between Godfrey and Kathleen.'

Mrs Rissington sparkled. 'I just love you for being so honest. I wish I'd been there myself. What's your name?'

Valancy added that her great-aunt and Godfrey's had been at school together but hadn't seen each other for years. 'I worked in a publisher's office and was dying to get away to the country. Otherwise I don't think Godfrey would have risked another woman secretary.' She somehow didn't want this nice woman to have an inkling of the true circumstances. Something in Valancy was forcing her to take this line. Kathleen now believed Godfrey. She, Valancy, loved him dearly, too dearly to take her own happiness at the expense of his. If there was any chance that Kathleen, contrite, might return to

him, she must foster the chance. The constriction round
her heart was still there, but this was the only way for
Valancy.

She chatted on, telling her of all Godfrey was doing
for Inchcarmichael, of the landscaping of the garden,
the replanting of the trees, the new woolshed, the
softening features to be added to the house. 'Mother
and Father will be down soon, with a young workman
of Dad's . . . a sort of working holiday.' She wanted this
woman to feel it was a family affair, the long
association of the aunts. Nothing more.

Mrs Rissington watched the delicate colour come and
go in Valancy's cheeks, observed the glow in the deep
blue eyes, the engaging sprinkle of freckles, the less-
than-classical nose, and wondered. 'I'm enjoying my tea
more than I'd hoped to. I only dropped in to postpone
the ordeal of going on and telling Godfrey this. I didn't
know how he might take it—very chicken!—Would you
do it for me? Tell him when he's quite alone. I feel you
would be the one to tell him. You're so calm, so
sensible.'

Calm! Sensible? Valancy looked away, looked back,
and said briskly, 'Yes, I'll tell him.'

'I can't thank you enough. I was terrified he'd
freeze up on me. And I'd rather not have him probe
about Kathleen, it's so hard to answer for other
people.'

Valancy knew what that meant. She didn't want him
asking did her daughter still care. She wasn't sure, that
was obvious. She hoped, on the way home, that the
felicity of the message she had to give would overlay her
own inexplicable burst of temper earlier.

He wasn't in the study as she had hoped. Aunt Helen
looked up from setting the table. 'He's in the stable
mending that leather strap for Rachel. Said he wasn't in
the mood for writing.'

Oh dear! As she got to the open half-door of the old
stable her courage suddenly failed. If he still had that
anger in him against her, he'd be in no mood to listen
about Kathleen. He might even be furious that she'd
been babbling to Kathleen's mother about his affairs.

Just as she went to withdraw her hand from the lower door, he turned.

He had a steel punch in one hand, the strap in the other, and slanting through on his fair head was a ray of sun. She saw sunbeams dancing in that beam of light. He smiled at her, the slow smile that always lifted the corners of that well-cut mouth first. 'Come in, Lancy ... got it out of your system?'

She came in, not knowing how scared she looked, how truant.

He laughed out loud then. 'You look about fifteen! It doesn't matter, you know. Anybody can lose their block unexpectedly. You're so even-tempered for a redhead, except when you fly to someone else's defence, that I've often wondered how you'll be able to put up with a temperamental chap like me, when—if—you take me.'

That brought her across the straw-covered floor to him. 'Oh, Godfrey, how sweet of you! I've no idea why I flared up like that, unless it's because you've done so much for me ... like on that weekend ... so I resented you offering me a rise. I still won't take it, of course, but it was dear of you to offer it. That's all.' She actually gulped.

'That's not all, you nit, there's this.' He drew her to him, bent his head. She instantly turned hers away to the side. He laughed, said, 'Well, I can always kiss your ear,' and proceeded to do so. Then he stopped and said, rich amusement in his voice, 'I can keep on doing it till you turn back, you know. Look, what is it?'

Valancy turned her head into his shoulder so he couldn't kiss her. 'First I'd better tell you that my burst of temper isn't all I've done this morning. There's something else. It all seemed right and proper at the time, but now it seems a nerve. I've been an interfering sort of do-gooder. I got all carried away and she was so nice and rather distressed, and so I offered and she leapt at it, but now——'

Godfrey gave her a shake. 'You've got yourself in a tizz. I'm sure there's no need. I know it's a tizz because as a rule your diction is an example of beautiful clarity.

Now it's as clear as mud. Come on ... you were supposed to laugh at that, and relax. Perhaps you'd better tell me now and laugh later, huh?'

She lifted her head and he saw tears in her eyes.

'Who leapt at what, Valancy?'

'Kathleen's mother.'

This time he did look startled. 'Kathleen's mother? What the hell's she got to do with anything? Besides, I thought she was in England.'

'She's back. There was a bus load at Miss Mabel's, so she sat at my table, and asked who I was. I told her I was your secretary. Then she said her daughter and Godfrey Carmichael had almost made a match of it but his spiteful former secretary had jinxed it ... and the silly girl had believed the scandal she created.'

'Well, you knew all that. It was no surprise to you. If you think I'll be cross because you gossiped about me, I'm not. I know how things occur. Besides, it was common knowledge. Carlotta saw to that.'

Now was the moment. She rested her chin on top of his shoulder so she didn't have to look at him, said, 'Mrs Rissington was coming out to give you a message from Kathleen.'

She felt him grow rigid. He said, 'Right. Then what's the matter with that? Except if it's to be today, we've got a busy afternoon on.'

Pride, of course. 'She isn't coming now. She was too nervous—was afraid you'd think she was interfering or that you'd freeze up.'

'She needn't have been nervous. I always liked her. She believed me—she told me and told Kathleen that.'

'Godfrey, listen. The important thing is that Kathleen herself doesn't believe what Carlotta said now. It must have taken her a long time to think it through, I admit, but she's come to that conclusion and wants you to know. She couldn't face writing to you, but now she's coming back, and wanted you to know that before she returns. So asked her mother to do it. Godfrey, what are you swearing for?'

'Never you mind. Surely a man can swear once in a blue moon without having to say why except that he's relieving his feelings. Is that really all you were het up about?'

Valancy felt and sounded indignant. 'All? Isn't it enough? You wanted very badly for her to admit it wasn't true. I even bolstered up their belief in you by telling Mrs Rissington what Carol was really like. I think when she writes and tells her daughter that, Kathleen'll feel a lot better.'

'That's nice,' said Godfrey suavely and sarcastically, 'Now, turn your face up like a good girl and let me kiss you properly.' When he released her words failed her. But not him. 'And we're not wanting visitors this afternoon. Your father rang. The young man he's bringing says he doesn't mind working during New Year holidays, so they'll be here day after tomorrow, wench!'

Valancy gasped, 'But Godfrey, it'll cost more. Isn't New Year working paid triple rates? That's throwing money away! And you need it all. The restocking of the trees cost a fortune and the farm just eats money.'

'Well, if I'm not allowed to give you a rise surely I can pay triple rates for a couple of days, especially when your papa has refused to take a penny! Besides, the farm is starting to pay for itself, so the translations can stand a verandah and conservatory.'

'I feel guilty about that conservatory. It's a frill, not a necessity.'

'Stop it this moment!' he nodded. 'You sound like Agatha, the first Godfrey's first wife. Look at the shell of that house, plain straight lines, stark and ugly ... you and I, girl, are going to make Carmichael House a thing of beauty and a joy for ever. We'll have to slog in the study this afternoon and finish everything before your people get here.'

Valancy didn't speak. She was wondering for whom, eventually, would that transformation be made?

They had two nights and a day of heavy rain after that, so the saplings were noticeably benefited by the time the three visitors arrived. She found it was wonderful to have her father and mother here, and young Dave

Sinclair, who chummed up instantly with Rod and said he hardly counted it working when he could go off to the bathing beach when he finished work, or ride, explore the bush, fish in the rivers, take Rachel's sister Cynthia to Balclutha, even to Dunedin, in the evenings.

Rachel was disgusted. 'Cynthia's been the only one who wasn't sloppy over fellows, and now look at her! She's lost her sense of humour and she's like a moonstruck calf. Thank goodness you're past that sort of thing, Valancy.'

Godfrey roared at the look on Valancy's face. Rachel, fortunately, made amends. 'Oh, I don't feel you're past falling in love—I mean it doesn't take you the same way. Cynnie wouldn't see a joke at present if it slapped her in the face. Honestly!'

Godfrey said in a would-be consoling tone, 'She means, Valancy, that you hide your unholy passion for me under a matter-of-fact exterior. Don't glare at me like that! That's carrying it too far. Don't you think so, Fergus?'

Her father burst out laughing. 'You take some awful risks, Godfrey. I can only hope you make it up to Valancy in private.'

She gave her father a look that nearly slayed him, then when Rachel and Godfrey had gone off together she said, 'Dad, you'd better forget all that nonsense we put on for Hughsie's sake. We'll only resurrect that when she comes down south. Seeing Godfrey's set on giving her a week or two here come harvest.'

Fergus looked at his girl with eyes of love. 'Lassie, it's blind you are. Can't you see Godfrey means to have you? He told me he's put it to you seriously, that for some reason you want time to think it over. I can understand it. A lesser man let you down. But I wouldna make it any longer than March if I were you. He's doing these alterations for you, no doubt about that.'

But she did have doubts. He was doing it for Inchcarmichael. Everything he did was for that, even to wanting to provide the estate with sons to follow him. If one girl wouldn't have him then another would do.

The glorious, untypical weather held, day after day. The verandah went on, brown decramastic roofing covered it, shutters in brown appeared at the upper windows and the small panes were set in only the upper halves of the sashes, because Fergus said that way you got appearance, but could still have an unimpeded view of the superb sweep of countryside from the second storey. One day a plumber's van arrived out from Badenoch.

'Is that for the spouting round the verandah?' asked Valancy,

Godfrey shook his head. 'Not entirely. I can see I won't be able to keep it secret from you. I'm extending your idea of the conservatory. Dead centre of the glass doors from the old drawing-room which I hope to furnish some day is to be a path of crazy paving leading up to a tinkling little fountain in the middle. A man who has a plant shop in Balclutha has got hold of the very thing for me. It belonged to an old homestead in Otago, destroyed by fire half a century ago. Quite Grecian, with wrought iron acanthus and grapevines round the rim of the bowl, and very safe. No floor-level pool to make it a risk to toddlers.'

She felt her colour rising. 'A delightful idea, Godfrey. It will sound so cool on hot days like this.' All day the image of the little tinkling fountain that would be safe for toddlers went with her. Mid-afternoon she went for a walk, past the saplings. Already the flowerbeds were showing promise. Her mother and Aunt Helen were on kneeling-stools planting out pansies and London Pride, pinks and petunias.

They looked after her as she disappeared into the limes of the winding drive that had been spared when the others had been sacrificed. Helen said, 'She's restless, isn't she? What is it, Dilys? Is she trying to resist falling for Godfrey?'

'I think she must be. If so she's not succeeding. I wonder why. I could swear she's not got an atom of feeling left for Justin. Perhaps being ditched by one man makes you wary of taking on another. But they're so right for each other.'

Valancy came to a bend in the drive where you could look back and see the house. From here you could see the raw unpainted newness of the additions. She screwed her eyes up so that the surroundings receded and only the softened outlines appeared in her vision. It was going to be beautiful, like Dad had said, early American Colonial, with the pillared posts of the verandah adding to that illusion. She could almost hear that little tinkling fountain . . .

She heard a car! Rachel's father's. He leaned out, said, 'I was just coming up with the mail. You'll save me time.'

She went up to the house with it and sorted it out. One of Godfrey's was a request for the source of a quotation he had used. He'd given only the name of the author.

She went out to Godfrey, busy with the plumber. He thought for a moment. 'Up in the sanctum is that small grey file . . . a seven-drawer one. The two bottom ones are bits-and-pieces for future books. I think it's the third one up that has the quotes already used. Thanks very much.'

Valancy loved the sanctum. It was so irregular in an otherwise too orthodox house. It had this splendid eyrie-like view. She could see that glorious swathe of the horizon where sea met sky. Oh, lovely, lovely island of the Carmichaels!

She found it without much difficulty. She'd post it away tomorrow, typing it out in full. Meanwhile she'd tidy this drawer. As all these had been used, Godfrey must have just stuffed scrap after scrap of paper back in. It was at the very bottom of the drawer that she found something else. What book had he used this in? It was done in letter form, but that wasn't unusual. Much of his early colonial fiction was based on old diaries and correspondence. It was in his handwriting, so perhaps he'd copied it from some library, probably from a New Zealand section of ancient papers that were allowed to be perused but not borrowed. By now she'd read all his books, but she couldn't recall a situation like this.

It was good. Every line betrayed the pain of the character who had penned these lines originally. Of course it could be a discard, a first draft. She must ask him. It could possibly be used in another book given similar circumstances.

Not till she got almost to the end of it did she realize what it was. It wasn't a love-letter written by one of his characters. When, a few lines from the bottom, the name Kathleen leaped up at her, she knew beyond shadow of doubt that Godfrey had written this to Kathleen Rissington. Had she suspected that she'd never have read beyond the first line or two.

She sat with it in her hands, and despite the fact that this was January and midsummer, the room got colder and colder.

'Dearest and Best,

It doesn't seem possible that you've gone leaving no address, that I can't reach you. I won't, I can't believe that you'll never come back. I gave it time, thought you would come to your senses. I've even tried to forget you, but I can't. In every story I read I hear your voice in the dialogue. Did I ever tell you, heart's darling, that I love your voice? It's got such a lilt in it, as if you could burst into song at any moment, anywhere. I can't post this. You've cut yourself off so completely. But only in writing this can I find any solace at all, any relief. It's just not possible to cut a person out of one's life like that, no matter what's happened. Everything reminds me of you ... the books we've read together, the waterfalls in the bush, every sunset reminds me of the ones we've watched together. You've made it so final. No address. It always comes back to that. I'll keep this, nevertheless, in case you ever come back. Then you'll know how much I still love you.

Rufus is getting too fat for want of a rider. Whenever I'm in the paddock he comes running up and nuzzles my pocket for the sugar-lumps you always gave him. He misses you too, Kathleen.

I don't see how I can bear the winter without you.

.You thought you'd like daffodils under the limes.
I've planted them. Will you ever see them? If only I
knew you'd see them some day, and read what I've
written.

Yours for ever and aye, Godfrey.'

Valancy read it twice. Oddly, what hurt most ... at
the moment, was that Kathleen had ridden Rufus too.
That was absurd. She had looked upon Rufus as *her*
horse. He still looked for sugar lumps. Godfrey had
warned her only last week not to overdo them. How
stupid to be thinking of that now!

She roused herself, put the letter in his strong black
writing back in the drawer the way she'd found it. He
must never know she'd found it. It would never do,
now, to leave this drawer so tidy. She picked up the
neat piles she'd sorted the clippings and notes into,
ruffled them up, stuffed them back. Oh, damn that
person who'd written for the quotation, damn him,
damn him!

But she was resolved in one thing. No doubt that
letter had been written in the first unbearable anguish
of her departure, and time might have softened the sense
of loss, and certainly he tried to tell himself he no
longer cared, but Kathleen *must* come to see him on her
return. The strength of the bond that had once lain
between her and Godfrey must be tested. She herself
couldn't give Godfrey his answer until they had seen
each other again.

She came down to the main study, rang Mrs
Rissington, and asked for Kathleen's address. Mrs
Rissington said, 'That's something I can't give you, I'm
afraid. She's on her way. She left earlier than she
intended, but she's not arriving till the middle of
February just the same. She's stopping off at several
places on the way, Rome, where she has a friend,
Singapore where she wants to do some shopping, and
then staying with other friends in Hong Kong. Can I
help in any way? I told her the message had been passed
on to Godfrey by his present secretary. I think it's a
load off her conscience.'

'Just tell her, when she arrives, I'd like her to come out here and tell Godfrey in person. He gave nothing away to me. That's pride, I suppose. Would you do that?'

'I will. I'll get her to let you know when she's coming out and perhaps you could see they meet in private. Thank you, dear.'

Valancy put the phone down and stared at the wall. More she couldn't do for Godfrey, but this she did know, they must be given the chance to meet again.

CHAPTER TEN

VALANCY felt as if she lived on the surface of things from then on. There was great happiness in having her parents here, in seeing the harsh lines of Carmichael House gentled more each day by curves and pillars, the fountain installed and connected up to its own water supply that came from a tiny spring. She spent hours with her mother and Aunt Helen in the garden, trundling barrowloads of sheep manure to the flowerbeds, planting out boxes of seedlings to set patches of colour where bareness still showed, planning a fernery.

This was Helen's idea, and Godfrey got Rod and Bill to dig it out so that it was sunken, and bring flat rocks from the hillsides to provide a little path to wind through it. They planted aromatic low-growing plants among the stones, and brought tiny tree-ferns from deep within Carmichael's Bush so that some day they would grow taller than the banks they had created. There wasn't the need to buy a single fern of any description; there were hundreds in that bush. 'We ought to go into business,' said Valancy gloatingly, 'and advertise "Instant ferneries supplied by Carmichael of Inchcarmichael." '

Then she put her hand to her mouth as she

remembered she might not have so much longer here
... if the old alchemy worked when Godfrey met
Kathleen again. Of one thing she was sure, he'd have to
get a male secretary then. For one thing, she herself
wouldn't be able to bear to stay.

She turned to find Godfrey had come down into the
fernery. 'Did you want me? Must I go in?'

He shook his head. 'Not to the study. Just to tell you
the smell of paint from the conservatory is all
evaporated and your papa and I have decided the other
jobs are such that we can both spare you the rest of the
day to start filling it. Rod and Bill are cutting you those
big log troughs you want for the ferns there, and they'll
bring in the native plants and so on, but we're taking
you into Balclutha right now to choose the pot-plants
and shrubs for the conservatory. The fountain is doing
its stuff cooling it down and the atmosphere is suitably
moist.'

Aunt Helen and Dilys looked at each other and said,
'We'll come too.'

Fergus chuckled, 'You haven't been asked!'

Valancy rounded on her father. 'Don't be so mean!
Look at their faces. They haven't had so much fun for
years. They're going to choose some of their own
favourites.'

'Of course,' said Godfrey. 'They're going to see a lot
of that conservatory in the years to come.'

Valancy turned swiftly away, said, 'I'd better get
some of this dirt off me. And make morning tea before
we go.'

Godfrey said, 'Fergus, you drive Dilys and Aunt
Helen in the station wagon and I'll take Valancy in the
farm truck.'

Valancy looked amazed. 'Godfrey, it isn't the Winter
Garden of the Botanical glasshouse department you're
stocking up, it's an itsy-bitsy little conservatory tacked
on to a dwelling.'

'It'll take some filling just the same. I'll leave room
for shelves of begonias and fuchsias later; I've got it all
worked out, but it looks so raw and new, all fresh paint
and glass panes, so I just can't wait till it shows

greenness through the windows. Come on!' He climbed
the steps and went ahead.

Aunt Helen said, laying down her fork, 'It's
wonderful to see him like this again, eager as a
schoolboy.' She turned to Valancy. 'You're the one who
wrought this miracle. When are you going to give him
your answer?'

Valancy said nothing for a moment. Her mother
waited, smiling. Aunt Helen didn't look abashed, as if
she'd just said something she must have been asked to
keep to herself. It was pretty clear that if Godfrey had
told Dad, Dad would have told Mother and it was
certain she and Aunt Helen would have talked it over.
So she said, slowly, 'Perhaps it isn't as ideal as it looks
on the surface. I—can't—quite—make up my mind.'

Aunt Helen said, 'Did that Justin make you so unsure
of yourself? Godfrey would never let you down like that.'

Valancy said, 'I know that.'

'Then,' said her mother, 'why——' she broke off.
'Helen, I don't think it's anything to do with Justin. Is
it, Valancy?'

Valancy's blue eyes met her mother's dark one's
candidly. 'No, it isn't. Justin ceased to matter a long
time ago. But——' her eyes held an appeal.

Both older women recognised this, though neither
could understand it. Aunt Helen, with none of her
characteristic vagueness, said, 'Dear child, we're
blundering in where angels wouldn't venture to tiptoe!
Forgive me—I'm just a foolish old woman and I'm so
impatient to see the pair of you happy and ceasing to
waste time. Only he's yours for the taking, you know.'

'I've promised to give him his answer in March. I've
got my own reasons for that. That's all, and thank you,
my darlings,' and Valancy was gone.

But was he hers for the taking? If either Helen or
Dilys had seen that impassioned, agonised letter they'd
have had doubts too.

The fernery was finished, the conservatory a bower of
greenery that added the last touch of elegance to a
house that had come into its own. Each new leaf those

saplings put forth, each blossom that bloomed in those curved flower-beds, spoke a promise of future days when once more birds would build nests and rear young, and bees would gather honey-sweetness for the hives Rachel's father tended so faithfully. Before long Miss Mabel and Miss Edith would be selling the tourists pottery jars labelled *Inchcarmichael Honey*.

Fergus and Dilys and Dave Sinclair returned to Christchurch the last week in January, and Cynthia, Rachel's sister, applied for, and obtained a position up there, to be near Dave. Rachel went back to school, Godfrey and Valancy resumed study hours, and James and Susie were thankful cats ... the hum of the typewriter lulled them, purring, to sleep.

Godfrey was pushing on with the history of Inchcarmichael, and Valancy was set some routine work that would save him much time later, typing up long lists of his characters from former books, the ones that were to have sequels.

He sighed heavily one day. 'What is it, Godfrey?' she asked. 'Something going wrong? Inspiration flagging?'

'Frustration mostly.' He put his hand on the pile of jottings on his left side. 'Some of this stuff, the diaries, the old letters, the clippings, I can't use. So much of it was never meant to be made public. Yet it's got life-blood in it, drama and self-sacrifice and a faithful picture of those days, but some have menace in them, and spite and meanness. The diaries in particular were used as wailing walls. When things were too bad to be borne, I suppose. Makes me feel as if I've been eavesdropping on conversations I wasn't meant to hear. Perhaps I've been writing fiction too long. Even though I try to be as realistic as possible, I can, to a certain extent, manipulate the characters.

'Tske Agatha, for instance. Even she isn't wholly bad, though she certainly had her moments of sheer wickedness when she parted Kathleen and Godfrey. There's a sort of household record book here, full of times of setting hens, and killing the geese and salting beans down, and curing bacon. Then two pages, facing each other, with only one entry. Look, Valancy.'

He pushed it over to her. It was written with a thick pencil that had needed sharpening. 'Hopes dashed again! If only I could give Godfrey a son for Inchcarmichael!'

Valancy knew a fierce stab of pity for Agatha, who'd cheated and lost. Who knew but what she'd paid over and over again? In unrequited love. She said so. 'It would be so terrible never to feel loved as you wanted to be loved.'

He nodded. 'I expect her conscience bothered her. It would rise up in the night and hit her. I wonder if, but for that, if, say, she'd not made mischief, but other things had parted Kathleen and Godfrey, so that he married Agatha for companionship and family life, do you think that through the years they might have reached the heights? Grown together? I mean, give me the woman's viewpoint on that?'

She felt again that constriction round her heart. This was too close to the bone. She said slowly, 'I don't know. Are you thinking of a situation like that for one of your pioneer novels?'

'Well, perhaps I am. In fact I must mean that. Don't know why I should have thought of it otherwise.'

(Valancy had an idea she knew why he'd thought of it.)

She said, 'It would be very hard in the early years to be patient. Wanting to give to the uttermost and not wanting to reveal how much one cared. I expect you would yearn for a dreamed-of day when suddenly a man would tell you that the other attachment meant nothing now ... that you were his true mate. But it would need an articulate man, wouldn't it, and not all men are.'

She wished those grey eyes would look away. She tried to make it sound just hypothetical. Perhaps she had succeeded for he nodded, kept his own tone academical. 'Thanks. I appreciate the way you assist me, Valancy. Sometimes a man can be at a loss.'

'I expect it acts that way in reverse, Godfrey. With a woman author. She might wonder how a man would feel if he was never quite sure his wife loved him as a husband ought to be loved or—or hankered after someone else.'

His answer was prompt. 'It would be hell. If you thought you never got the response you were looking for.' Then his face broke into a grin. 'Though I've an idea a man would try to force the issue, try to *make* her care. Use storm tactics.'

Valancy felt a physical tremor run over her. She strove for lightness, said, 'Ever think authors get far too analytical? Maybe life is more simple than that. That it ought to be taken at its face value, not delved into too deeply?'

'You could be right. My trouble is I'm far too intimately involved with these dead-and-gone Carmichaels. I can't re-write their history for them. Sometimes I regret I ever started it.'

She was appalled. 'Oh, Godfrey, don't give it up, please! I couldn't bear it. I've read only as far as the reconciliation of Godfrey and Kathleen. Already I'm longing to find out what they made of their lives. I've just got to where Archibald and Effie come back to my annexe. I couldn't bear it if I couldn't read on to the end, especially when it's such a happy ending. Remember, Godfrey, even if you can't see them from here, that round the end of the house, out there new trees are growing. The same kinds as the originals. It's so satisfying.'

'Is it?' asked Godfrey, his brows down. 'It's not exactly the sort of ending I had in mind. I've always been like that with writing. When I start a novel I know the beginning and I know the end ... which is the only thing that keeps me at the hard grind of all the chapters that lie between.' He stood up. 'It's no good, I can't write today. I think I'll be happier out baling that last paddock of hay. Rod said the dew would be gone by noon and they could start. I'll see what the reading is now.'

His abrupt departure seemed to make the room bleakly empty. She looked down at her desk and knew a great distaste for typing these boring lists. If the men were going to be baling hay, it might be up to her to get the big motor-mower out and do the old back and side lawns. No hurry about these lists.

The phone rang: Mrs Rissington. She spoke in a low voice, 'Miss Smith? Oh, Rhona Rissington here. Is Godfrey in the same room as you? Or anyone else?'

Valancy's heart skipped a beat. 'No, I'm alone. Godfrey's decided to help the men with their hay-baling.'

'Good. Kathleen is here. She flew in from Singapore instead of taking in Hong Kong. She wanted to speak to you but didn't want to risk getting Godfrey and having him recognise her voice. Here she is.'

The next moment Valancy was hearing the voice Godfrey had described as lilting. Not that it seemed that way now, but then it was nervous. But it was charming, low and husky. Valancy shook her thoughts free. She must concentrate.

'Mother's told me that you feel I owe it to Godfrey to tell him face to face that I no longer believe what Carlotta said had happened. I know I treated him shamefully. It must be ghastly to be innocent and not to be able to convince someone important to you that you are. And I just upped and offed. Didn't give the dust a chance to settle. I think it's very brave of you, Valancy, to do this. I'll tell Godfrey it was brave, so he doesn't go you for interfering. I knew I ought to have the courage to see him face to face and apologise, but I chickened out at the very thought. But when Mother told me what you'd said, I knew I must.

'The main reason for being so nervous was that seeing it's a whole year ago, he might have changed completely and never wanted to see me again, apology or not. Mother said you'd told him I'd changed my mind, that I know now I ought never to have believed Carlotta. Tell me, how did he take that? What was his reaction?'

In an instant Valancy's mind flew to that scene in the stable when Godfrey had sworn, then said, 'That's nice,' in a very sarcastic voice, and proceeded to kiss *her*.

She pulled herself together and said crisply, 'He was a

bit stiff about it. You know how men are. His pride was still hurt, I suppose, that it had taken you so long. But I'm sure it will be all right, face to face. But please don't feel too rebuffed, if for the first moment or two he's all starch. When will you come? I'll fix it so that he's on his own, up here in the study. Oh, and your mother will have told you that if you'd known Carlotta as I knew her, you'd never have believed it for an instant. She's a shocker. I knew her as Carol, of course—the sort of person who told so many lies she got out of the way of telling the truth.'

'Yes, Mother told me. Godfrey's been more than lucky in getting a secretary like you. Look, Valancy, I'll come out tomorrow morning about ten. If you can come out when you hear me arrive and take me to the study, if ever my shaking knees get me there, I'll be eternally grateful to you.'

When Valancy replaced the receiver, *her* knees were shaking.

She decided she wouldn't, after all, do the mowing. Gardening gave you too much time to think. Besides, when she got the two of them into the study tomorrow, she'd go out then, start up that roaring motor and mow the lawns for dear life. Meanwhile, on with this tedious task.

Lunch was on presently, much as usual, with the men talking farm activities, pleased that for once all the hay, early and late crops, had been gathered in without a drop of rain on it. 'We'll talk about this summer for years,' said Bill, with great satisfaction.

Godfrey said, 'I'm sorry I won't be with you after all. Might manage it after tea-break perhaps, but I clean forgot I had those figures to get out for Federated Farmers. Can't let them down. It shouldn't take more than a couple of hours, though. Valancy, you can continue with those lists. I wonder if in *They Came By Sailing-ship* you could trace their exact ages, and work out how old their children and grandchildren would be in World War One. And jot down all their colourings, characteristics etc. at the same time, for the sequel.'

Bill looked at Godfrey and Valancy with respect. 'I never thought there was as much in this book-writing caper till I worked here. Give me hay-baling or shearing every time! Well, come on, Rod.'

Godfrey said, 'I'll be in the farm office. If I get it all into shape, I'll type it out myself tomorrow morning. Just send my afternoon tea into me, please, Aunt Helen.'

Valancy went along to the study. There was one thing, dealing with dates and ages, you simply couldn't let your mind wander to tomorrow and all it could mean. A dull ache kept her company, but if she hadn't been busy, it would have become a stabbing pain. While Godfrey had thought of Kathleen as hard and unbelieving, there had been no chance of reconciliation, but when she came here to him, contrite and nervous and ... and sweet, because she *had* sounded sweet, anything could happen.

The afternoon wore on. She heard Godfrey go out and it sounded as if he was joining the men. So much the better. She didn't want him up here. In the intimacy of these two rooms where they had shared so many happy working hours, she might suddenly tell him Kathleen was coming tomorrow, even find herself offering to bow out if he found, after all, he still cared as he had cared when he had written that poignant, unbearably tender love-letter that had never been posted. She wrenched her mind away from it again, and waded stolidly through the shockingly low prices for sheep during the Great Depression.

Presently she heard a car arrive, voices, Rachel's and another's. Probably her mama's, come over to see Helen. Rachel came over most days after the school bus dropped her at the bridge, to feed hens, groom horses, and half a dozen other small chores which her soul delighted in, and which, in the main, were paid for.

Valancy found she'd have to go up to the sanctum to check about the change of government in 1935 when Labour came in. Godfrey had had the New Zealand Encyclopaedias up there the other day. She jotted down some notes and was almost down to the bottom stair behind the little glass-panelled door when she heard the far door open, people come in, then Rachel's voice, loud and clear.

'This room is much more efficient-looking than it used to be, don't you think? Again it's Valancy's doing. Godfrey says he still can't believe his incredible luck in getting someone trained in publishing work. He wasn't too bad—for a man—at keeping things tidy, but that was about as much as you could say. But now, all he needs to do is snap his fingers and demand a reference and Valancy has it on his desk in two shakes of a lamb's tail.'

There was a hint of laughter in the voice that answered her, no doubt occasioned by Rachel's old-fashioned precise way of speech. 'How very fortunate for Godfrey. He deserves that sort of luck, after that Carlotta as a secretary. Some people would hate the isolation here, but to get one who doesn't and who appears to be able to landscape a garden, add conservatories, to say nothing of verandahs and curved steps, makes one think he must have been born under the right stars.'

Who on earth had the child brought up? Some visitor of her mother's, probably someone who wanted to meet the author . . . and by the sound of it knew the previous set-up here. This visitor would regard her as an unlikeable paragon. Whereas it was just a child's hero-worship sort of complex. She'd stopped dead on the bottom stair. She'd a good mind to go back up till Rachel took this woman away. But these wooden stairs creaked abominably, they'd give her away. She'd have to go on in, but she would disclaim all this irritating perfection.

But Rachel was fair. 'Well, in all honesty, the landscaping was done by a Balclutha man. Godfrey sold a serial. And it was Valancy's father and a workman of his who put the verandah on . . . though the conservatory idea was Valancy's notion, Kathleen.'

That last word froze Valancy into immobility. *Kathleen.* Oh, no, no! She'd said tomorrow morning. This had to be another Kathleen. She turned that idea down immediately.

But how could she face this girl with Rachel's overdone praises still ringing in her ears? Poor Kathleen, who, unknown to Rachel, would have shaking knees. Kathleen would be sure she had taken her place . . . had a chief interest in altering the house, now Godfrey wouldn't ever have the chance to welcome back to Inchcarmichael the one he had called 'Dearest and Best', the one he said he loved 'for ever and aye'.

But what to do now? *Please God, now Rachel's seen Godfrey isn't here, let her take Kathleen down to the paddocks, the stables, wherever he is? Please?*

At that moment Rachel said, 'Oh, Aunt Helen must have found Godfrey. I can hear him coming. I'll go now. 'Bye!'

Godfrey must have passed her in the doorway. She heard him say, 'Thanks, Rachel, for doing the honours. Hello, Kathleen. When did you get back?'

There seemed to be a pause before she answered. It sounded as if there was quite a distance between them. As if Kathleen was near the window, and Godfrey no farther than a few paces from the door. *When would that space narrow?* Kathleen had yet to convince him she truly believed him.

Suddenly Valancy's knees would support her no longer. With infinite care she sat down on the bottom stair and leaned her head against the little post. She dared not mount those creaky stairs. She couldn't face going into the room, and, heaven help her and forgive her, she couldn't resist the temptation to listen-in. Only that way could she ever evaluate what Godfrey really felt about Kathleen.

His voice was anything but encouraging. Hurt pride, that was all. Kathleen said, 'I arrived two days ago. I felt I must at least come out to tell you I was absolutely wrong to believe Carlotta. In actual fact I've not believed it for a very much longer time than I even told Mother. I ought to have written long ago.'

'Yes, you ought. Not much point now. And I knew this, anyway. Valancy told me—she met your mother at Miss Mabel's. You didn't have to bother coming out here.'

Kathleen didn't speak. Valancy could only guess at her feelings.

Godfrey added, 'It has ceased to rankle. It hadn't mattered for a very long time. In fact, ever since Valancy came here. She heard the story, but even before she knew that Carlotta was actually a renowned mischief-maker she'd been to college with, accepted the fact that it was a put-up job. I can understand that in the first horrible moment of seeing Carlotta's clothing draped over my bedroom chair, you'd think what you did, but not when I gave you my word there was nothing in it.

'When Valancy first knew what had parted us, she said very comfortingly, because she's a born peace-maker, drat her, that once you thought it out, all you knew of me would convince you it wasn't true. But, to be brutally candid, all that matters to me is that Valancy herself has no doubts.'

Valancy, sitting rigidly on that bottom step, and listening with all her might and main, didn't know what to think. Was this just hurt pride lashing out? Dear God, what if it were true?

Kathleen didn't reply. Perhaps she couldn't.

Godfrey's voice came through even more clearly. 'Forgive me, Kathleen, if I appear to be taking your apology in a very churlish way, but this is so important to me that I must make it clear beyond all possible shadow of doubt ... I want no complications at this stage. The only person I need to believe me is Valancy. I've asked her to marry me, but she wouldn't give me an answer right away. She's having an inward fight with herself over it. I'm content to wait till she resolves it. She's asked me to wait till March, I don't know why. In fact, though I say I'm content, I don't know how to contain my impatience. She was let down by the man she was engaged to. I might say she behaved magnificently over it, even to sacrificing her job for the sake of the happiness of the girl he eventually married. I'm hoping that in time I can make her forget him. But if I can't, I shall never marry anyone!'

Valancy almost cried out with sheer joy. This she *had*

to believe, the ring in Godfrey's voice, the pain in it as he spoke—so erroneously—of her feeling for Justin. She clapped her hands over her mouth.

Godfrey added in an entirely different tone,' So now, Kathleen, now that you know that, I gladly accept that apology. I expect it's pride. Nobody likes to be accused of something he hasn't done. Now ... can we be normal? Just chat as old friends meeting again after a year or so with one overseas. Did you love England?'

Valancy could only guess at what the other girl must be feeling, but she couldn't subdue this tide of gladness that was sweeping over her. Then, unexpectedly, Kathleen laughed. 'Oh, Godfrey, I'm so relieved! I've more to say than that, but I was terrified you might think this meant I wanted to make up. My apology wasn't complete at all. I—I'm ashamed now when I look back and honestly analyse my feelings. I—oh, how can I make it clear? I've suffered a complete change of heart. Someone taught me to look fairly and squarely at myself, at my motives. Oh, he didn't preach at me, didn't even know about this till I told him. I didn't tell him till I'd examined my motives mercilessly. I had to tell him because he thought me so different from what I really was. He had to know how mean in nature I'd been. Oh, I'm telling this so badly. Do you remember how angry I was with you when you wouldn't allow that film to be made out of your book. Do you remember?'

'I remember. That was when the rot set in, the first doubt.'

'I don't wonder,' said Kathleen. 'I was hopelessly spoiled, Godfrey. Too much was spent on me. Oh, don't feel I'm shifting the blame for my own rotten nature. I can understand it. My parents lost their first child, then Mother had two miscarriages, so I was doted on. I didn't want to fall in love with you, Godfrey. I did, but I didn't want to make any sacrifices. I wanted you to live in the city, and just write. You had this dreadful millstone of a property hung round your neck, this overwhelming desire to bring it back into the family. You were working day and night to make it possible.

'The thought of the mortgage repayments was like a nightmare to me. The barrenness of the outside of the house and surroundings ... so different now ... and when, because of your scruples, you wouldn't allow them to change the script, and turned down that offer that would have made it possible to clear the debt, even to tear this down and build a modern house, I knew I hadn't the grit to marry you. Oh, I was wrong. Your book was the child of your brain. I know so many things I didn't know then. I couldn't face the struggle to get Inchcarmichael on its feet. I didn't want to be remembered as the girl who gave you up for that reason. I don't think I ever truly believed Carlotta's story, except right at the first. Only for a few moments. I just used it as an excuse.'

It sounded as if Godfrey took a step or two nearer her then. 'This is amazing! That's very courageous of you. It takes a lot for anyone to recognise that they've been in the wrong, much less admit it. I'm glad. Because if you give me permission to tell Valancy about it, she'll perhaps never have the slightest doubt in her mind at all, about you. Never look on you as the one I ought to have married. I'm sure there's been something there.'

Now gladness and ecstasy was sweeping over the eavesdropper at the foot of the concealed stairs. She didn't deserve this. She had listened shamelessly, avidly ... the proverbial fate of eavesdroppers hadn't overtaken her. Oh, bless him, he wasn't softening towards this Kathleen he had once called his dearest and best, his only thought was for her, Valancy.

Kathleen had more to say, though. Now there really was a lilt in her voice. 'Want to know what brought about the change, Godfrey? I'd like to tell you.'

'And I'd like to hear.' His voice now had more warmth.

'I went on nursing for a time in England, in Liverpool. A doctor there was taking a refresher course in tropical diseases. He's one of a team dealing with refugees in Thailand, near the border—quite dangerous. Against his life, his dedication, my own life seemed shoddy except for my nursing. He made me see myself as I am. Actually, I hope it's as I *was*. I feel I've changed. I'm joining him out there after this holiday with Mother and Dad.'

'Congratulations. When are you getting married?'

Her voice was a little rueful. 'He has decreed that I'm to have at least six months out there first to find out if I can really take it. That's why I'm home a bit ahead of time. I was going on to Hong Kong, but he flew down to Singapore to see me, and I felt I couldn't waste the time. I want to get this six months over as soon as possible. I know it'll be tough, but if we're married, there should be joy amidst the pain and suffering.'

Godfrey laughed, a nice laugh, full of understanding, and, Valancy thought, relief. 'You haven't any doubts about yourself have you, about being able to take it. Of course you haven't. You love him as you never loved me, don't you? A life like that takes far more facing up to than life here, mortgages and all, so good for you!'

'Thank you, Godfrey. Now I know you've really forgiven me. I know why,' a note of mischief sounded in her voice, 'because in your Valancy, just as I have in Clive, you've found your true mate.' She giggled. 'We've been so intense, so uptight about it all. You know, I always suspected you really fell for me because my name was Kathleen. You loved Inchcarmichael so much you wanted to write a fairytale ending for it. But pooh, what's in a name? I'm going. I'd have loved to have met your Valancy, Godfrey. Can I come back and meet her, say, next week? So far I've only met her as a voice on the phone. Oh, yes, she arranged for me to come, but tomorrow morning, not today. Only suddenly I couldn't stand it any longer. I want it all cleared up tonight when I write to Clive so that when I'm writing I'm not all worried about you and my apology. Can you really wait till March to be sure of her? I'll only be here another ten days. I'd love to think before I leave for Thailand that it's all right and tight. Are you sure she still hankers after this fellow?'

It was no good, it was too much for Valancy. She stood up, flung open the door, emerged, shining-eyed, 'She doesn't,' she said, loudly and clearly.

The effect on the other two was ludicrous. They simply stood and stared.

Valancy said, 'I'm that horrible creature, a shameless eavesdropper. I'd just got to the foot of the stairs, Kathleen, when Rachel brought you in and started boosting me to you. Not that I knew it was you at first. I felt too embarrassed to come in. I dare not creep up those stairs again because they creak horribly. Then Godfrey came in ... and quite frankly, I just couldn't bear to. And now I'm glad, glad, glad I didn't!'

Her shining-eyed rapture suddenly conveyed itself to Godfrey. He took two eager steps towards her, then checked and said, 'You've—you've just said you're not still hankering after Justin. Is that true?'

She gave him a saucy look. 'For an author, Godfrey, you're mighty slow on the uptake when it comes to your own affairs! I've been trying to hide my feelings for you almost as long as I've been here, but I *had* to wait till Kathleen came home, I couldn't risk it otherwise. I had to be sure you wouldn't still care when you met again. I told you that ... not about her coming home but that I couldn't, wouldn't be satisfied with second-best.'

'You absolute idiot,' he said, with the greatest affection warming his tone, 'how ambiguous do you think that sounded? Naturally I thought you couldn't— quite—forget what you once felt for Justin.'

All of a sudden they became embarrassingly aware of Kathleen's presence. They glanced helplessly towards her.

She had both hands pressed to her lips, her eyes gleaming with satisfaction. She took her fingertips away, said, 'Don't mind me, I'm delighted. This is even more than I'd hoped for ever since Mother told me she was strongly of the opinion that Valancy had fallen for you. And she only met you once, so that's pretty indicative. I adore happy endings. I thought I'd made such a mess of things, not just for me, for Godfrey. It's a horrible feeling. I'm more than sure at this moment that I ought to fade out. I'll go down and see Mrs Armishaw and Rachel. They might even give me a strong cup of coffee. My knees have only just stopped shaking.

'Poor darlings, they were so frosty to me. Though Rachel did her best to make me feel Godfrey had now found someone only a little short of an archangel, to restore the fortunes of Inchcarmichael and mend Godfrey's supposedly broken heart. Mrs Armishaw is down there now, probably hating me with all her might and main. But I'm sure, when I tell her that wedding bells are about to ring for you two, she won't be able to do enough for me. Right, I'm on my way.'

Valancy, as Kathleen passed her, put out a hand, caught hers, bent forward, and touched her lips to Kathleen's cheek. 'Thank you,' she said. 'If you hadn't come here today I might never have been sure of Godfrey.' Her eyes misted over.

Kathleen made a face. 'Don't kiss me ... kiss him,' she said. 'I think he's been waiting a long time for this moment.'

The door banged behind her. They stood stockstill till her heels stopped tapping along the verandah and they heard the kitchen door close. Then they were in each other's arms, as if they would never let go.

When, finally, Godfrey lifted his mouth from hers, he said dazedly, 'I don't believe it. I just don't believe it! To think it's Kathleen who brought this about. Just a moment, I'm not taking the risk of anyone butting in. I wouldn't put it past that Rachel.' He crossed to the door, turned the key, came back and said, 'Come on, sweetheart, up to the sanctum.'

She'd left the little glass-paned door open. He looked at the bottom step, saw below it the papers she'd been bringing down, then took her arm and urged her ahead of him.

This was the room Valancy loved best of all. Against the far wall was a chintz-petticoated old chesterfield banished long since from downstairs. There was no more comfortable seat in the whole house. She was swung off her feet and deposited upon it, cradled in arms strong, compelling. 'Oh, it's so long that we've been at cross-purposes, Valancy, that it's unbelievable that now we can kiss ... and respond ... and kiss again, without any doubts.'

She said, 'Oh, what time we've wasted! I longed to say yes that morning on Scarborough. But you were so matter-of-fact.'

'I had to be. I didn't want to scare you off. I'd lain awake for hours the night before ... longing for you, burning for you. I mean after that kiss under the arch. Remember it?'

'Remember it? What absurdity! I lay awake half the night, too, still experiencing the delight of it.' She cupped his face in her hands and kissed him as she had kissed him then.

Godfrey said, foolishly, 'I hope you mean that.'

She slipped her hands away, said, 'Would you like written proof?' He looked amazed.

'Just stay here, Godfrey, I won't be a moment.' She slipped downstairs and into her sitting-room, and came back, with a fat five-year diary in her hands, one with a lock. She looked at him, sat down again in the crook of his arm, laid her glowing cheek against his rough one fleetingly and said, 'My feelings about you were so chaotic, my darling, I had to pour them out in here. Only briefly.' She used the key, opened it. 'I'll read it to you. Listen: "Saturday. Got up early this morning and thought I'd test my feelings for G. by going round to see the house J. and I were to have lived in. Dad sold it, thank goodness. I found it didn't mean a thing to me. It *is* beautiful, I admit, on its paltry quarter-acre section ... dormer windows, diamond-paned, gracious gables, the lot. But how can it compare with Carmichael House? As C.H. will be some day! Even now, what suburban section could match a house with rivers and the sea to make its boundaries ... whose only access is by bridge? To guard its happiness like a moated grange. A house with a history, with a reserve of native bush, whose beech trees are pre-Magna Carta? There's no challenge about a house that's too perfect. Carmichael House has a whole future of change to enhance it. Not that any of that matters, against the fact that it's Godfrey's house, the one he won back from that uncaring vandaliser by sheer hard work. What a revelation this weekend has been to me!' She laughed. 'Let myself go, didn't I? I even wished I had the gift to write a poem to Inchcarmichael. Convinced, my love?' She put two hands about his face, looked into his eyes.

He convinced her, but not only in words, then, 'I'm so glad you showed me this. You see I saw you . . . hoped it was for an early morning ramble, wanted to share it with you, so I followed you. But when I saw you turn into that crescent, I knew, and I was furiously jealous. I thought you trysted with the past. I nearly let it out when I chased you upstairs that night but caught it back.' Then, 'You were such a foolish girl. Why did you think I asked you to marry me if I didn't love you? Like this?'

She sobered. 'For Inchcarmichael. To have sons to carry it on. But not since you told Kathleen you'd never marry if I wouldn't have you. So that's cleared up!'

'You chump! Besides, we might only have daughters. Valancy, if our first-born is a girl, do you imagine I'd be disappointed? That's cruel . . . when a parent resents the sex of a baby. I may hope Inchcarmichael is handed on, to a daughter or a son, but——' Suddenly her eyes were full of tears. 'To think I once dubbed you a woman-hater! This is lovely, Godfrey, sharing our dreams, like this. And to think that only an hour ago, I was filled with fear and anguish. Isn't it wonderful to be actually planning our family?'

He looked wicked. 'Sure is . . . because of all it entails . . . ah, how delightful, you're blushing! Now listen to me. What on earth possessed you to get Kathleen out here in person to tell me she no longer doubted my word? That day you told me she didn't, my reaction to that news should have convinced you once and for all. So why?'

It swept back on her again, threatening her new-won happiness. He saw the shadow darken the blue eyes almost to black. 'Come on . . . if there's even a vestige of doubt left, let's have it.'

She said, 'I think I've got to tell you, though I don't like doing it. I realise now that though at the time you meant every word of it, you don't now.'

'What on earth——' She put a hand on his mouth. 'Don't stop me, Godfrey. You know the day a reader wanted a quotation and you told me to look in that file over there? Well, it was at the bottom. Had I known it was a personal letter I'd never have read it. I thought it was one of the old pioneer letters you had copied some time. Not till I got near the bottom and read the name Kathleen. I thought then that anyone who wrote a love-letter like that, even if it was never posted, could ever love anyone else again. I didn't think I could take it. But now I can. I'll have to remember I once thought I loved Justin.'

His grey eyes were puzzled, intent. 'I haven't the foggiest idea what you're talking about. Sweetheart, I'm sure it can be explained. For one thing there have never been any private letters in that file, and for another, as far as Kathleen and I were concerned, during our fairly brief association, she was never further away than Balclutha. She was nursing there. She was home every weekend. We phoned each other in between. I've never written her a love-letter in my life. And what do you mean, it was never posted?'

He saw the deep, painful blush rise up from the low-cut neck of her pale blue blouse, and said, holding her eyes, 'Darling, you don't need to feel embarrassed with me ever again. Go on.'

There was almost a sob in her voice. 'You couldn't send this to her because she'd gone away and left you without an address.'

His fingers bit into her arms. 'Without an address? Lancy . . . you're mixed up somewhere. I didn't want or need her address, but one day I met her mother in Badenoch, and she implored me to write to Kathleen—she was sure we could make it up. I knew that was beyond possibility. I didn't want a girl who wouldn't trust my word. But she insisted on giving it to me, in case I changed my mind. I could have written her any time I wanted to, but I never did.'

She freed herself, knelt before the file, rummaged, drew it out, brought it to him. She knelt on the floor beside him, put her arm on his knee and said, 'Read it ... so you don't think I'm imagining it. If you've even forgotten it, it can't matter any longer.'

He read it swiftly, then before he even finished it, to her anger, he burst into one of his huge gusts of laughter. 'Oh, Valancy, Valancy, you'll be the death of me! But didn't you recognise it for the letter in the rough copy of the estate history? Oh, no, you'd got no further than the reconciliation of Godfrey and Kathleen ... I didn't know where to use this, so I had *that* Kathleen come across it months after they were married. It's my handwriting, yes, but the original was on such old paper and was so creased from lying at the bottom of an old cash-box, it fell to pieces. His writing was too hard to type from, so I wrote it out.'

She looked at it numbly. Why was he saying this? Was he trying to save her pain? 'But—but it talks about Rufus coming up for sugar-lumps to her. Godfrey——'

He gathered her between his knees. 'Watch it ... you'll be as unbelieving as poor Kathleen yet! Long before I bought back the estate, Dad had all the family records. I was taken with the mention, in Godfrey's diary, and in this letter, with the name of his mount, Rufus, because I was shepherding up at Dragonshill when I first came across it, and the horse they had for the governess was called Rufus. He was under my weight, but out of sheer sentiment I bought him and brought him down here. You know what I am about names, how it led me into falling for Kathleen. I never thought it would get me into trouble twice! I'll be very careful in future. Now, are you satisfied?' He didn't need to ask. She was radiant. He added, 'Kathleen doesn't ride. Doesn't even care for horses. One thing, *your* name is so unusual, it certainly didn't influence me this time.'

She said, laughing with relief, because now all pain was gone, 'Don't be too sure! I've got a second name. Know what it is?'

'Does it matter? I wouldn't care if you were called Agatha!'

'What a horrible thought! Poor Agatha. Darling, it's Catriona . . . not only the name of one of your heroines but it's the old Gaelic version for Kathleen or Katherine. What do you think about that?'

'Oh, girl, we'll call our first daughter Catriona. Oh, listen to me, we're back on to our family again and we've not even fixed the wedding date, or bought a ring. We'll make it a sapphire . . . the sapphire ring you wouldn't let me buy you for Christmas. But tell me . . . any more doubts or confessions.'

'Not a doubt. A confession. Don't groan! That morning in Ballantynes I found out it wasn't your aunt who rubbed out the hyphen. It was mine. She sent me out to the car for something, and had it sealed when I came back. She and Aunt Helen had met, a few weeks before, in that same spot, after long years, and hatched that plot. That fiendish plot. Devils! They got bowled out beautifully that morning, by a neighbour from Rimu Bush who'd been present at the first meeting. Godfrey, you don't look surprised!'

'I told you they were giggling their heads off in the bathroom that night. I eavesdropped too. I was in the shower. Those walls are very thin. I heard enough to piece it together. Aunt Helen even said, "I just hope he stays this way . . . with that unmistakable air of a man in love . . . till that disbelieving Kathleen gets back. He never looked quite like that for her." But by then I was so grateful to them I could have given them a medal for their courage and perspicacity. They said we were made for each other. I decided not to tell you in case you were mortified, whereas I could have called blessings down on their wicked old heads. Now, is that all? Because we can use the time to better advantage till we hear Kathleen's car departing. Then we'll go down and tell Aunt Helen and Rachel that we are getting married next month. Oh, yes, my darling, we are. Now we've wasted enough time.'

When they heard her go, they went through his bedroom into the upstairs hall, to stand at the window that overlooked the verandah. On the clear air they could hear the rhythmic ring of the crosscut saw cutting through great logs for the fires of Inchcarmichael for the winter; the ripple of the little stream that fed the fountain in the conservatory; the green of new lawns outlining the curving flowerbeds where already old-fashioned annuals made an Indian carpet of colour, and surely there were even more leaves on those saplings than had been there last week? Beyond all was the glimmer of the sea and that lavender horizon.

'Our little world of Inchcarmichael!' said Godfrey, tipping her face up towards his, and even the future of which they dreamed was lost in the tumultuous and tender glory of the present.

4 FREE
Harlequin Romances

Enter a uniquely exciting new world with

Harlequin American Romance™

Harlequin American Romances are the first romances to explore today's love relationships. These compelling novels reach into the hearts and minds of women across America... probing the most intimate moments of romance, love and desire.

You'll follow romantic heroines and irresistible men as they boldly face confusing choices. Career first, love later? Love without marriage? Long-distance relationships? All the experiences that make love real are captured in the tender, loving pages of **Harlequin American Romances**.

What makes American women so different when it comes to love? Find out with **Harlequin American Romance!**

Send for your introductory FREE book now!

Get this book FREE!

Mail to:

Harlequin Reader Service

In the U.S.
2504 West Southern Ave.
Tempe, AZ 85282

In Canada
P.O. Box 2800, Postal Station A
5170 Yonge St., Willowdale, Ont. M2N 5T5

YES! I want to be one of the first to discover

Harlequin American Romance. Send me FREE and without obligation *Twice in a Lifetime.* If you do not hear from me after I have examined my FREE book, please send me the 4 new **Harlequin American Romances** each month as soon as they come off the presses. I understand that I will be billed only $2.25 for each book (total $9.00). There are no shipping or handling charges. There is no minimum number of books that I have to purchase. In fact, I may cancel this arrangement at any time. *Twice in a Lifetime* is mine to keep as a FREE gift, even if I do not buy any additional books. 154 BPA NAV4

Name _____ (please print)

Address _____ Apt. no.

City _____ State/Prov. _____ Zip/Postal Code

Signature (If under 18, parent or guardian must sign.)

AMR-SUB-2